Where's Billie?

Where's Billie?

A Skeeter Hughes Mystery

Judith Yates Borger

NODIN PRESS

Acknowledgements

No book is written alone and many people own a piece in this case, sometimes unknowingly. I'd like to thank Mark Yudof, who first told me I could do this, and Vicki Olson, my first editor, cheerleader and long, long-time friend. I'm indebted to my reading group friends—Meg Graham, Susan Stark Hilt, Kristin Boldon, Gary Bush, Sujata Massey, Maureen Fischer and Stan Trollip. My children, Jennifer, Christopher and Nicholas Borger listened to my ups and downs. Nick designed this fabulous cover. Thanks, buddy. Lucy Quinlivan deserves my gratitude for more reasons than I can count here. I'm nominating Elissa Mautner Nolting for queen of commas.

In an odd way, the *St. Paul Pioneer Press* needs to be acknowledged. Had the paper paid for my car when it was firebombed while I covered a riot in North Minneapolis, I might still be working there, and not have had time to write fiction.

The biggest thanks goes to my husband, John Borger, whose unfailing support, encouragement and love is what makes all things possible.

If you see a familiar flash here, remember that I made this stuff up. But I don't work in a vacuum.

ISBN 978-1-932472-90-5
Cover design: Nicholas Yates Borger
Book design: John Toren

Library of Congress Control Number: 2009930201

Nodin Press, LLC
530 N. Third Street,
Suite 120
Minneapolis, MN
55401

for John, as always

Chapter 1

Looking back, I should never have returned that phone call.

"Hughes. I'm sending you a voice mail that's been sitting in my queue since 6:00 this morning. Listen and then we'll talk." That was Thom Savage, my editor and the next one up on the newsroom food chain.

The newsroom's first pot of coffee hadn't even finished dripping as I picked up my phone and punched in the code to get my messages. A nasal, haughty voice played back. She said her name was Cathy Berry, and she was a subscriber living in Land o' Lakes. Friday night, her daughter, Billie, left her three-to-eleven job at the SuperAmerica gas station on Hennepin Avenue in Minneapolis. She never came home.

I thought back to Friday night. It was one of those nights in mid-January we Minnesotans call "pretty cold." Cold enough to freeze your nostril hair. Cold enough to kill a teenager who may have fallen asleep in a car after smoking a joint. Or cold enough to freeze the thumb on a girl hitchhiking her way to warmer climes.

Mrs. Berry said she'd called the police six times since Saturday morning wanting them to find Billie. I listened to her message a second time, then dialed her number.

"Billie?" the woman said after picking up on the half ring.

"No, this is Skeeter Hughes returning your call to the newspaper. Are you Mrs. Berry?"

"I was hoping you were Billie," she said. "Well. The police won't listen to me. They think she ran away. But I know something terrible has happened to Billie. You need to put an article in the paper so someone will tell me where she is."

"I'm sorry Mrs. Berry, but I need some more information from you before I can put something in the paper. It's best we talk face-to-face. Could I come to your house?"

"Of course. Come. Now. " She gave me the address and hung up before I could say any more.

I trotted over to Thom's desk. "Missing girl. I want to chase this one."

"Now wait a minute, Hughes," he said. "She's only been gone forty-eight hours. Maybe the cops are right."

"It's more like fifty-six," I replied. "Those first few hours can be the most critical in a missing kid case."

"Is she a kid?" He pulled his grey-blue eyes away from his computer screen for the first time to look at me.

"I assume so, since it's her mother who called," I replied. "Usually teens are the ones who go missing like that."

"A reporter should never assume anything, except a four percent mortgage." Thom loves to repeat tired old journalism saws.

"Don't patronize me, Thom."

He let that one hang in the air without reply. "What else you working on? How's the piece on the Land o' Lakes school board coming?"

I stifled a groan. For weeks he had wanted me to write a long, boring story about plans for a new school, that I knew was never going to happen. But it was in Thom's neighborhood. There's a saying in the newsroom that a pot hole is just a pot hole until an editor loses a wheel. Then it becomes a crater.

"I'm waiting for the superintendent to call me back." A small fib.

He tucked a strand of his longish brown hair behind his right ear, a nervous habit that signals he's made a decision. "OK, head out to Land o' Lakes and talk to the mom."

Thom returned his attention to his computer screen, but kept talking to me. "Go shake some trees or something. What's important to the people of Land o' Lakes is important to you."

Land o' Lakes is my beat. That means I sit through school board meetings that last well past midnight. I interview residents when planning and zoning is considering a new K-Mart in the neighborhood. Day after every Thanksgiving I write about how many people are/aren't shopping at the mall. Neighbors complaining about too much traffic from the Taco Bell on the south end of town? You heard it from me first. I've been stuck covering this suburb for two years, and frankly, I'm getting sick of it.

A friend I knew in journalism school works at a newspaper on the West Coast, covering missing persons. I read every story she writes. Sometimes, I know, the ending to this type of story is simple. Lost people, usually young adults, turn up asleep on a park bench after closing down one too many parties. Or they float up in the Mississippi River or one of the city lakes, unidentifiable except for the plastic driver's license in a pocket. Sometimes they never show up.

I would love that job. Lately every time I see a flyer for a missing person, I can't get it out of my head that a secret is buried in that story. Truth be told, that's probably why I returned Mrs. Berry's phone call.

I'm thirty-six-years-old and I've been a reporter for the *Minneapolis Citizen* for six years. I have two beautiful daughters, Rebecca, fourteen, and Suzy, eleven. My husband, Michael Marks, is also a reporter. I should have married someone with a different profession, like an architect or a musician. But I didn't. He works for the *St. Paul Courier*, which likes to think of itself as the Minneapolis paper's archrival. That means between us we make an OK, but not great, living. We're paid about the same as teachers, but we work summers and holidays. Like cops, we have crazy hours.

I sometimes wonder if I'm doing right by my daughters. How will I know if they're troubled as they head into their teen years? What am I missing by not always being there when they get home from school? Is there delicious after-school gossip that gets lost because I don't hear it? Will they grow up to be angry women with holes in their hearts because Mom wasn't home with a hug when a teacher was mean or a boyfriend was a jerk?

Maybe it's because I have a reporter's DNA. Maybe it's because I'm a mom. Whatever the reason, it didn't seem right to me that a girl who probably worried about zits and getting her period in the middle of going to the movies with her boyfriend had evaporated into thin air. I needed to find Billie Berry, or at least figure out where she had gone.

Chapter 2

I really like my car. A lot. It's a 1995 Honda Civic del Sol, this cute little two-seater, red convertible. I bought it from my brother on a whim, which infuriated Michael. He thought it was a waste of money for a family with two young daughters. I ignored him. Wide and low to the ground, it handles like a dream on icy roads. Because it's so small, it heats up quickly in the winter. I've been known to take the top down as early as February, jack up the heater, and drive around town pretending I'm a hottie.

I drove west on Highway 212 to Land o' Lakes, a name chosen, no doubt, by a housing developer intending to make prospective buyers think of a life as rich and yummy as butter. That was before anyone knew it could clog arteries.

Until the 1960s Land o' Lakes was all farmland, so flat that you could see almost to South Dakota. There were stands of trees that had never been touched and small lakes where farmers' kids of the 1950s went fishing and played king of the raft. As farming got riskier, and the population of Minneapolis began to grow west, the land became more valuable for housing than crops. Fortunately, no one put up tract housing. Instead, there are a million cul-de-sacs all named Something Place, Something View, or Something Terrace. This is where Billie Berry grew up.

I pulled into her mother's drive and eyeballed the place. It was two stories with a red brick front and cream-colored stucco on the sides and back. The trim and the roof were black. I imagined it was built in the early 1980s to give the impression of an all-brick house without the cost.

Bay windows on either side of the front door made the house look apple-cheeked. Bright green Japanese yews with red berries squatted under the bays. Five windows stretched across the upper level of the house, while creamy sheers obscured the views into the first-floor and second-floor rooms. The front door was painted a deep Episcopalian red. A tall fence around the backyard implied a swimming pool. This time of year most pools are half-drained of water and covered with a dirty snow-laden canvas tarp. I can never understand why Minnesotans put swimming pools in their yards. The hot weather season lasts about ten weeks at best. There are fine-for-swimming lakes just about everywhere. Why would you want to fool around with chlorine levels and vacuuming when you can swim with perfectly healthy fish hassle-free?

I walked up to the door and rang the bell with one hand while reaching into my purse for my business card with the other. I heard what sounded like a poodle barking. The little rat was making enough noise to scare away a Jehovah's Witness. Anyone inside would know for sure that someone was at the door.

A minute went by. Right away I wondered what was wrong here. Why was it taking so long for Mrs. Berry to answer? If one of my daughters had been missing for two days you can bet I'd be at the door before the dog had even perked its scraggly ears. In fact, I would have been up all night, trying to decide which I should do first, wring her neck or smother her with kisses if or when she came home.

I stood on her front porch, stuck in the part of my job that I hate. Questioning victims' families is an unpleasant and dicey business. Sometimes they're relieved you asked because you give them a chance to review, out loud, the awful events that led to the worst day of their lives. Other times, people see you as an intruder who is trying to satisfy some prurient interest in their misery. Until you ask the question, there's no predicting how they'll react.

Thirty seconds later the door opened. It was only 8:30 a.m. but I could smell that Cathy Berry had laced her morning coffee with something much stronger than half-and-half.

"You're the reporter. Come in." She turned her back and headed for another room after stepping on the poodle's paw. She took no notice when it yelped.

Her living room was white. I'm talking white walls and white sofa with a matching love seat that I swear I had seen in a Roche Bobois advertisement. The brick around the fireplace was white. Even the hardwood floors were bleached white. Like bones that had lain long on the beach, the living room looked dried and hard, as though it had forgotten the warmth of flesh. It smelled like Lemon Pledge.

The stick-thin woman who greeted me was equally white, from her just-bleached platinum hair to the pearl nail polish on the toes of her bare feet. All white, except for the dark rings around her eyes, and the bruise on her forearm that bore the outline of four fingers and a thumb that had grabbed her way too hard.

"Have a seat," she said, with a wave of her coffee cup toward the white sofa. Her poodle had stopped its racket and curled into a tiny white ball of fur at her feet. She took my card, glanced at it then placed it on the glass and brass coffee table. "What do you want to know?"

I wanted to know where she got those bruises and how long it had been since she'd had a decent meal, but even reporters understand there are some questions you don't ask in the first five minutes.

"Let's talk about Billie. How old is she?" I dug my reporter's notebook and pen from my purse.

"Seventeen. I mean eighteen," she corrected herself. "Friday was her birthday. She turned eighteen. But I still think of her as seventeen."

"Tell me about Friday."

Mrs. Berry sipped her coffee, as though she were trying to wash down the bad thought with a caffeine-alcohol elixir. Her grimace made me think it didn't work.

"I wanted to throw a big party for her. Eighteen's a milestone, you know. But Billie said no."

I tapped into a rule of interviewing. Share commonality with the source, in this case motherhood. "My fourteen-year-old daughter loves birthday parties. Don't all teens like birthday parties?"

"Billie's not typical." Her voice was wistful.

"How's that?"

"For starters, she's a year older than the other juniors in her class."

"Why?"

"I held her back a year before she started kindergarten so she would be a little older than the other children," Mrs. Berry said. "I wanted her to excel among her peers."

"Has she?"

"Has she what?"

"Excelled among her peers.' "

"She's a good student. Her favorite class is pottery."

"How do you feel about that?" I asked. In some families that would be terrific. Others, not so great.

"Peter—that's her father—and I thought she should be taking more academic courses, like biology, math, English. She said there was something about working with clay that touched her. She likes the sensuousness of it slippery between her fingers. Makes her think she could actually shape something, she said. Before her pottery phase she insisted on taking acting classes in junior high school. She was quite the actress."

"How else is she atypical?"

"She tends to run with older kids and acts almost patronizing to the other students in her grade. It's particularly funny, when you think about it, because she's a tiny girl and looks much younger than she is."

"Let's get back to Friday."

"Friday. Yes. Because she wouldn't have a party, I talked her into just popcorn and a movie, with me after she got home from work at the SuperAmerica. I even bought her a present – a darling sweater from the Gap. I wanted to make peace."

"But you didn't."

"No, we didn't. We had a fight."

"What about?"

For the first time, Cathy Berry brushed a tear away from her eye.

"I was angry. I asked her four times to empty the dishwasher. She ignored me. Passive aggressive, you know? Finally, I went to her room and told her to get her butt out of bed and put the dishes away. She put on a pair of jeans, her Nikes, and that hideous red hooded sweat shirt of hers and screeched the tires as she drove away. That was the last time I saw her."

"Tell me about when you realized she was missing."

"I thought she'd be home by 11:30 at the latest."

"Wasn't that late to start a movie?"

"Yes," she replied. "I get up early in the morning. Work calls, you know? But my friends tell me teens have a different internal clock. So I said I'd try to stay awake until the end of the movie. I wanted to spend some time with her. But soon it was midnight, and no Billie."

"What did you do when she didn't come home?"

"I called the SuperAmerica just after midnight, ready to give her a piece of my mind. But the guy who answered the phone said she'd already left."

"Did that scare you?"

"Not really. I was still furious at that point. I called her cell phone but she didn't answer. Probably saw on the caller ID that it was me. So I left a message. An angry message."

"Describe Billie for me."

Mrs. Berry stared ahead, her gaze piercing the picture window that overlooked a winding road along a frozen creek. I could tell she didn't see the sunlight playing off the mounds of snow. She only saw the mental photograph of her daughter, an image Kodak could never capture. There is no clarity like a mother's sense of her daughter.

Chapter 3

"Want coffee?" She pulled herself from her reverie.

"Sure."

Every reporter knows to take coffee when it's offered, even if you gave it up for Lent or your bladder is about to burst. It's a gesture toward intimacy with your source, an early sign of friendship that hopefully will lead to sharing. I had a friend who took up smoking because his source was a chain smoker and he figured it would build a tie between them. It worked. He got the story and won a Pulitzer. Then he quit smoking. A few years later his source died from cancer.

"Need help?" I asked as I followed her into the kitchen, which gave me a view of her backside. How that woman ever bore a child, I'll never know. Her hips were too narrow to deliver a baby. Maybe she had a Caesarian. Or maybe Billie was adopted, I mused.

My disingenuous offer to help gave me a chance to peek around in her kitchen. My mother always said you can see the soul of a woman in her kitchen. Even though women spend far less time cooking these days, I think she's still right. I wondered if Cathy Berry's kitchen would have at least a dirty cereal bowl sitting on the table, with a spoon in it and a half glass of orange juice by its side. Anything to make it look like people lived there. No such luck.

The glass table was spotless, with only a vase of white silk orchids that matched the rose and cream kitchen colors perfectly. The eggplant granite countertops were gorgeous, but the kitchen was missing the stuff that makes it home. No magnetized pictures on the fridge. No flour canister. No cookie jar. No apparent bottle of bourbon, either.

She waved me off and I followed her back to the living room, where she placed a white bone china coffee cup and saucer on the cold glass coffee table in front of me. I raised the cup to my lips, praying that I wouldn't spill on the sofa, and then set it down again, the whole time careful to hold the saucer under the cup.

"I named her Willa," she said with a faint smile. "I imagined she would be lyrical, with an easy, graceful sway, like a willow tree. By the time she was two I knew no one would ever call her lyrical. Whenever her little friends could talk her into playing wedding she always wanted to be the groom. By the time she was eight she changed her name to Billie."

"Is she lesbian?"

"Of course not. She has a boyfriend. She's just a tough girl."

"What's she like emotionally?"

"Billie's a roller-coaster ride," she said. "The highs with her are full of life and screams of delight. The lows are enough to turn your stomach."

She brought her coffee cup to her lips, realized it was empty and set it down on the coffee table. I took another sip of mine before asking how Billie spent her time.

"What does she do when she isn't in school?"

"She works at the SuperAmerica three nights a week or hangs out with her boyfriend, Nate Whitehorse," Cathy said. "He's Native American."

She picked at a loose thread on the upholstery.

"After his father died, he lived with his mom. She worked two jobs. Nate was in charge of the half dozen younger kids. I think his dad was one of those drunken Indians that hang out on Franklin Avenue. That's how their culture is."

I ignored her blatantly racist remark, especially in light of her own issues with alcohol. "Did he go to school with Billie?"

"No. Nate didn't go to Land o' Lakes High. He went to one of those alternative schools for kids who don't fit in the classroom.

He took a pottery class at Land o' Lakes High. That's where he and Billie met."

"Is he still in school?"

"I don't think so," she said. "He always seems to have a lot of money. I don't know where he gets it. Peter hates him."

She started to reach for her coffee cup then pulled her hand back. Her eyes scanned the cabinet on a back wall. I wondered if she was looking for more "coffee." Then she reached for a tissue—white —to dab the tears from her eyes.

I gave her a moment to catch her breath. This was obviously difficult for her. It was tough for me, too. I often find it hard to separate myself from a person who's in pain, especially when part of my job is to capture that feeling for readers. If I were going to write a story that might help find Billie, I had to ask more questions. Lots more.

"Why did Billie work at the SuperAmerica in Uptown?" I wondered. It's at least a twenty-minute drive in good weather?

"My friends' daughters work at the malls, if they work at all. They wouldn't be caught dead employed in one of the fast-food places. Macy's is OK. They love Banana Republic. Great discounts, and a place to see and be seen."

"Billie didn't want to work there?"

"No. The goth and grunge of Uptown appealed to her much more. Just another way that girl and I are opposites."

"You and Billie quarreled about her job?"

"Fought bitterly," she said. "We probably battled two or three days over that when she first started there. Eventually I decided it wasn't worth it. She won."

"Were you worried about her working in a convenience store?" We both knew more than one clerk in a gas station has turned up dead.

"I guess so, but that didn't concern me as much as what my friends would think if they saw her working there. Of course, they seldom frequent that neighborhood."

I had to agree it was hard to imagine Land o' Lakes matrons among the purple-haired, tattooed, heavily studded crowd of Uptown Minneapolis.

"I thought she had gone home with Nate, to get back at me about the dishwasher. When she wasn't home by 1:30, I called the police."

"Did you call Nate?"

"He didn't answer."

She said the cops didn't seem to take the call seriously, but they agreed to swing by the SuperAmerica.

"This officer called about 3:00 and said he had talked to her co-worker, Joey. He told the cop he saw her get into a car with some guy and drive away. It might have been Nate. Maybe someone else. I don't know."

"How did you feel about that news?" I asked.

"That's when I knew she was truly missing. I went to bed with a sick feeling in my stomach. Do you know what it's like to lie awake all night, listening for the sound of your daughter's car?"

Then a long pause.

"Had Billie hinted recently that she might be planning to leave town?"

"What kind of hint?"

"Packing? Did stuff that was important to her start disappearing? Was she buying a new wardrobe, like for warm weather?"

"You know, she had been coming home from the Mall of America with a lot of new clothes, way more than she would be able to buy on the little she earns."

"Where do you think she got the money, if not from her job?"

"I have no idea. Would you like more coffee?"

Not really, but I wasn't going to tell her that. "Sure."

She rose from the sofa carefully. She seemed so fragile she might break. I've interviewed distressed parents in the past and they often have an aura of being caught in a bubble which is only big enough to allow them to focus on getting their child back. I wasn't sure she'd be able to answer my next set of questions, but I asked anyway.

"Can you tell me a little bit about yourself?"

"I'm a real estate agent," she said, raising her chin a bit proudly. "A good one. Made the Ten Million Dollar Club last year."

"What does Mr. Berry do?"

"He's a representative for a pharmaceutical company. We've been divorced two years."

"Was it amicable?"

"Is any divorce amicable?" she asked archly. "He has remarried."

I made a mental note to check the court files on their divorce.

"Have you talked to Mr. Berry about all this?" I asked.

Hard as it was to believe, Cathy's face turned even whiter. She tried to take another anesthetizing gulp, but it was empty, so she looked out the window again.

"Peter and I don't talk. We leave each other messages."

"On your phone or e-mail?"

"Both. Sometimes we text message."

Sounds like Michael and me, I thought.

"You haven't heard back from him?"

"There was a message on my machine this morning," she said. "He told me I was overreacting. That Billie would come home when she was ready."

"Do you think it's odd that he's not upset like you are?"

"Yes, I think it's odd," she said. "Makes me wonder."

"Wonder what?"

"I don't know what. Just wonder."

Her comment left me wondering, too. "Do you think he played a role?"

"It wouldn't surprise me."

"Why?"

"Because he and Billie have always had a special relationship. It would be like him to give her permission to disappear just to get back at me."

"I'll have to talk with him," I said.

"It's a free country."

Suddenly it dawned on me. There were no pictures, of anyone, displayed in the house. How can a mother not display images of her daughter, even if she's mad at her?

"Do you have a picture of her?"

"Yes, but it won't help you."

"Why?"

"Because she's a chameleon. She seldom looks the same two days in a row."

Mrs. Berry walked to the den. I followed her, watching as she opened the top drawer of a sleek oak desk. With long, thin fingers she drew out a five-by-seven-inch school picture and handed it to me. The girl in the photo had very long, brown hair draping her round face. No bangs, just a part on the side with her hair tucked aside with a clip. Her heavily made-up brown eyes had a certain strain about them, as though she'd seen a lot in her few years. Her skin was milky with a touch of acne on the forehead, her nose neither pug nor perky. Her jaw was set with a determination that made me think that she was rebellious by day and a teeth grinder by night.

I turned it over. On the back Mrs. Berry had crisply printed "Billie" in pencil, as though the label would help her remember it was her daughter.

"This is from seventh grade. It's the most recent we have. She doesn't like to have her picture taken."

I stared at the picture for a while, wanting to know more about her. Where are you, Billie? Have you decided you'd rather spend your junior year sipping tequila while watching the blood red sunsets off the California coast? Was home more than you could deal with? Your parents' divorce? Mom's drinking? Her bruises? Or are you dead, your body hidden so well that no one will find you?

I tucked the picture into the back of my notebook. Time to stop thinking like a mom and get back to thinking like a reporter.

"Why didn't she want her picture taken?"

"I don't know," she replied softly.

That took care of all I had to ask her, for the time being. I looked at my watch and rose from the couch. "Can you call me if you do hear from her?"

She nodded. "Will this be in the paper in the morning?"

"I'm afraid it will take a little longer. More like a week."

"A week?" she exclaimed. "That's not acceptable. You must put something in tomorrow's paper."

"That's not going to happen, Mrs. Berry," I said quietly. "I'm going to need more information. Right now all I have is an eighteen-year-old girl who didn't come home from work. My editors aren't going to see that as news."

"I can't wait that long," she replied. "I must do something now. What else can I do?"

"I read a story a while ago about a little boy who went missing. His mom went to an organization that works out of the warehouse district in downtown Minneapolis called Missing Children Minnesota. If you contacted them, I'm sure they could help you put up flyers."

While I was talking to Mrs. Berry a light rain mixed with snow had frosted my windshield. I dug in the trunk for my window scraper, then remembered that Michael had used it last to clean the windows of his Volvo. He must not have returned it to my trunk. I resorted, as most Minnesotans do, to scraping the ice away with a credit card, one of those bogus ones you get in junk-mail solicitations.

As I drove away, I looked in my rearview mirror. Cathy Berry was standing behind the clear glass storm door, the dog in one hand her coffee cup in the other, watching me.

Chapter 4

My lead foot disconnects from my brain when I think while driving. The unfortunate handicap has gotten me more than one speeding ticket. I've tried to expense them. It doesn't work. Nonetheless, the memory of the last story I read about a missing child played through my mind while I drove back to the newsroom.

He was a two-year-old boy whose father had kidnapped him the day before his mother divorced his dad. Eventually the dad and the boy were caught up in a drug bust in Texas and the boy was returned to the mom, who had put a second mortgage on their house to pay for private detectives. I learned from working on that story that missing-kid stories are never simple. Often there's some skeleton the family wants to keep in the closet. Was that the case with Billie? I didn't know, but I aimed to find out, not because I necessarily wanted to share their secrets with our readers. It's not great journalism to put that kind of stuff in the newspaper for no particular reason. But if a scandal had some bearing on Billie's disappearance, it might be important to the story.

Why didn't Mrs. Berry have a more recent picture of Billie? Even a party shot from Christmas? Kids trade photos of themselves on Facebook all the time. Most of the mothers I know have pictures of their kids somewhere, on their cell phone, or at least tucked in her purse. Why not Mrs. Berry?

I was turning that over in my mind as I pulled into my parking spot in the ramp, locked the car, and headed for the skyway that connects the ramp to the Minneapolis Grain Exchange building, where the newspaper offices are, then headed to the third-floor newsroom.

Every newsroom looks the same. Some are bigger, some are smaller. They all have paper piled everywhere and file drawers stuffed with dated dreck—in our case, county commissioner meeting minutes going back to the 1980s, lists of Winter Carnival royalty from 1962, and maps of tunnels under the Mississippi that were closed 50 years ago.

All of the reporters and most of the editors sit at desks pushed face-to-face. Some people are talking on the phone. Some are staring at computers. The desks are so close together that everyone overhears everyone's conversation. You can't make an appointment for a Pap smear without your colleagues knowing the date and time. Duct tape covers rips in the carpeting. The place smells like a soup of dry paper, stale coffee, and, well, soup.

It was ten o'clock. The editors were beginning the morning meeting, held in the middle of the newsroom. Anyone is welcome to join in and express an opinion. Most of the time, only the editors show up.

Posted on a corkboard are today's copies of our paper, the St. Paul paper, the New York Times, and USA Today, side by side. For the first meeting of the day, chairs set in the shape of a horseshoe are filled with editors who critique the papers. They talk about what we did right, what the other guys did right, and what either one of us could have done better. It's the sort of exercise that requires strong egos and thick skin.

"Can someone tell me why the September 11 Congressional hearing story went below the fold?" The wire editor, who manages national news, was irritated.

"It wasn't compelling," replied the night editor, who made the decision at midnight when the final story came across the wire. "The piece about the 11 percent rise in health-care costs in the Twin Cities hit closer to home. Besides, the photos weren't good."

"There weren't any photos with health care," commented the travel editor.

"That's true, but the hearing story was another he-said, she-said," the night editor replied. "I think it belonged inside, not on 1A. But you guys decided yesterday that it should go front, so I tried to accommodate you."

That seemed to shut everyone up.

"Let's move on," said the executive editor, who stepped from his office, where a life-size cardboard cutout of Elvis Presley wearing a feather boa around his neck graced one corner. The executive editor had recently been reassigned to Minneapolis from Memphis. "Did we do anything right in today's paper?"

"We beat the other paper and TV on the twenty-person drug bust in Apple Valley," chirped the public safety editor.

"And our art was top of the line," piped in the photo editor.

The conversation turned to white noise as I dug out my notebook and extracted the phone number Mrs. Berry had given me for Nate Whitehorse, Billie's boyfriend.

"Yo," a voice said after the phone rang half a dozen times.

"Is this Nate Whitehorse?" I asked.

"Yeah."

"My name is Skeeter Hughes and I'm a reporter with the *Citizen*. I'm working on a story about Billie Berry. She hasn't been home since Friday. I got your name and phone number from her mom. Have you seen or heard from Billie?"

"I haven't talked to her since last fall." In the background, I could hear water sloshing and what sounded like rags slapping on cars. I drew a mental picture of a muscular guy with tattoos snaking up both arms who worked in a car wash, his long, dark hair tied back in a ponytail.

"Her mom told me you were Billie's boyfriend."

"Her mom's got her head so far in the bottle she doesn't know up from down, lady."

"You and Billie are no longer together?"

"Me and Billie were a thing for a while, but that ended." I was surprised to hear a hint of sadness in his voice.

"Why did you two split?"

"We were gonna move in together so she could get away from

her fucked-up parents," he said. "Had a place all picked out. I'm makin' OK money here at the carwash, and with her money from SuperAmerica we figured we could shack up."

"So why did you two break up?"

"She backed out. Said something about some caper she wanted to work on. I didn't want nothin' to do with that kind of shit. She thought she was going to be a cop some day. Imagine that. Me sharin' a crib with a cop."

"Was she serious about that?"

"Could be. I wasn't going to stick around long enough to find out."

"Did you know anybody who might have seen her since Friday?" I asked.

"Nope," came the reply. "But a guy who works here said his girlfriend heard Billie was turning tricks and doin' meth." Again, his voice had a tinge of remorse.

In the background, I heard someone shout, "Hey, Whitehorsey—get off the phone and get your ass back to work!"

"Thanks for your time," I said. Nate had already hung up.

So much for mother-daughter confidences between Billie and Cathy. Apparently Billie hadn't told her mother about the breakup with Nate, or that they had planned to move in together. Clearly, Billie Berry was a young woman who kept secrets.

Chapter 5

I got up from my desk to get more coffee, then settled in with the day's newspaper. As I cruised through the letters to the editor, something Cathy Berry said kept nagging at me. Something about the Mall of America and a lot of money for clothes.

I fired up my computer and logged onto the search engine, looking for a story that ran in the newspaper about a year ago about pimps picking up girls at the mall. Something about fancy older guys buying them clothes. They seemed to go after the suburban-type girls too, as I recalled. Is that how Billie expanded her wardrobe?

I punched "Mall of America" and "prostitution" into the text line. Up popped the story. I love computers.

Then I remembered. Newsweek did a piece about white suburban teenage prostitution. Pimps pick up girls everywhere, of course, but the piece focused on the Mall of America. Because the mall is in our circulation area, we ran a wire story that essentially recapped what Newsweek said. A few weeks later "Oprah" devoted a whole show to teenage girls who had been lured into prostitution. One of the girls on the show said that blonds could earn $1,800 to $2,500 a day turning tricks. A fifteen-minute blow job pays $300.

I recalled watching that show with a broken heart. The girls said they had gotten into the business because a handsome man had simply paid them some attention. Soon they were trapped in a vortex of sex. The ones who spoke on the show had managed to crawl their way out of the business. Their mothers, who also appeared on "Oprah," were dumbfounded when they learned what their daughters had done.

I glanced up from my research to see Thom starting to peer around the newsroom like an eagle circling over a lake in search of a fish.

Since he first arrived in the newsroom, Thom has stood slightly apart from the others, not just because he's gay, or even because he's six feet, six inches tall, but because he wears a dark tie, a crisp white shirt, and dark dress pants every day in contrast to most of the khaki-and-denim guys in the newsroom. Thom is also smarter than the run-of-the-mill journalist. The combination seems to be working for him. He's one of the brighter lights in the eyes of the higher-ups.

"We just heard on the police radio that the guys who run the Ferris wheel at the mall are having some problem with it," he said to me. "Head out there and see what's going on. File for online if it looks like anybody's gonna get hurt."

"That sounds more like a story for someone from the public-safety team, Thom. I'm a suburban reporter. You want me to chase this because …?"

"Because we're short-handed today."

"Do you think they'll fill Laszewski's spot?"

"I doubt it. This is a dying business, Hughes. Not enough people read newspapers any more. You know that. The big guys want to keep the shareholders happy, and that means taking in a lot more money than we spend."

"And reporters are expensive, right?" I was hoping he'd counter that they're underpaid and without reporters there would be no news to put in the newspaper. He didn't.

"We're wasting time talking about this when people's lives may be literally hanging on a Ferris wheel. Go."

That meant taking a laptop computer so I could send a story to the newspaper's website, where an increasing number of our readers get news free instead of buying newspapers. I keep wondering when the brass is going to start charging for the benefit of my work. If people are willing to pay to download ring tones, surely they would pay for the latest news.

Five minutes later I pulled my favorite set of wheels out of the garage and headed south on Fourth Avenue, which leads straight into Interstate 35 W, and continued south.

Even though it's in the shape of a square, with each side clearly marked north, south, east, and west, the MOA can be the ruin of a shopper without an internal compass. The storefronts alone stretch more than four miles. The mall's public-relations folks will quote, with pride, some survey that says more people visit the Mall of America each year than Disneyland, Graceland, and the Grand Canyon combined. That statistic alone must be enough to make people in the National Park Service cry.

In the center of the mall is a seven-acre indoor amusement park, complete with its own roller coaster and Ferris wheel. This is the heart of the heartland. Shiny-faced, straightforward, good family fun. The place reeks of wholesomeness.

Security people at the mall were doing a good job diverting attention from the Ferris wheel, because shoppers seemed to be oblivious to any trouble. As I got closer, it was apparent there was a problem. A couple of young men in casual denim shirts and slacks were standing at the base of the ride, talking into walkie-talkies. Even though every car was full, the wheel was not moving.

I shuddered just looking at it. When I was a kid one of my brother's favorite tricks was to get me to go on a Ferris wheel with him, then get to the top and rock the car. To this day I remember the terror of being at the top and feeling like I was going to fall out at any moment. It was the first time in my life that I thought I was going to die. Heights have given me the creeps ever since.

With my feet planted firmly on the ground, I walked over to the men with the walkie-talkies and identified myself.

"What's going on?" I asked.

"Nothing," one said. He glanced up at the people in the cars, who were all waiting patiently for the wheel to revolve. He gave a quick look to the other guy, who stepped a few feet away and spoke into his walkie-talkie.

"We heard on the police radio that you're having a problem with the Ferris wheel," I said.

"You'll have to direct all your questions to public relations," he said. The other guy must have tipped off the front office because Melanie Fox, PR person for the mall, was already striding purposefully in my direction.

"Hello, Skeeter," she said, offering her well-manicured right hand. "It's been a while."

Melanie and I worked together at the newspaper in Rochester, Minnesota, for about three years. I was a suburban reporter and she was my editor. After her husband graduated from medical school at the Mayo Clinic, she decided to get out of newspapers and into public relations when they moved to the Twin Cities. I moved at about the same time to work for the *Citizen*.

"Yes, it has," I replied. "You're looking well."

That was an understatement. Her light brown hair had fresh highlights; her blue silk pantsuit was without a crease. I could only wonder if her feet hurt at the end of the day from walking all over the mall in those blue spiked heels. Reporters in Rochester used to call her The Fox. Apparently, the name still applied.

"So are you," she said. "What can I help you with here today?"

"I'm here to check out the problem on the Ferris wheel."

"I've talked with our maintenance people and everything is going to be fine," she said with a sincere smile. "Apparently the computer that runs the wheel had a hiccup. It should be moving again in a few minutes. Did you know the Ferris wheel was first seen at the World's Columbian Exposition of 1893 in Chicago? It was built to rival the Eiffel Tower, which was first exhibited at the 1889 World's Fair in France."

"Don't try to distract me, Melanie. How long's it been stuck?"

Then, as though her words could heal, the ride started up. The guys with the walkie-talkies looked at each other and wandered off in different directions.

"I guess there's no story here for you." Her smile glistened. Her husband must be making good money. Looked to me like Melanie, who used to smoke like a Virginia ham, had a new set of bright white teeth. "Oh, look. The riders are getting off now."

I hauled out my cell phone to call Thom to tell him the Ferris wheel had started up without mishap.

"Any more questions?" Melanie asked.

"One. Remember that story about girls getting picked up here for prostitution? That still going on?"

"Certainly not," Melanie said. "That story was way overblown. Sometimes it happens in large public places, but our security is tight. It wouldn't happen here."

Chapter 6

Figuring it was lunch time, I bought myself a sandwich and a cup of coffee, then settled at one of the tables to watch the crowd. Teenage girls ambled everywhere, most often in gaggles of three or four. In some cases, two of them were on their cell phones as they walked along. I wondered if they were talking to each other.

Given the Scandinavian heritage of the area, it's not a surprise that most of the teen shoppers were white, and most of them blond. Some were tall. Some were short. Perky little breasts pointed up under tight, scoop-neck T-shirts. Flat tummies and low-riding jeans with three-inch-wide belts made their bodies look even more curvaceous than they were, which is saying something. Tight along the hips, even tighter in the buns, their jeans looked about to fray, like the girls had been wearing them while taming wild horses. But, of course, they bought them that way.

The mall is a great place for female bonding, I learned when Rebecca was about 10-years-old. That was where she would tell me what was going on in her life. It usually cost me a bundle in purchases, and lunch, but it was money well spent.

Those times I was intent on Rebecca and didn't look at the other shoppers and mini-dramas that were going on all around me. As I watched this time, I thought of Rebecca and wondered if she behaved the same way when she was with her friends, and without me, at the mall. Probably. It's enough to give a mother hives.

Most of the girls had that pubescent glow that oozes sex. These were women in the making, soon to acquire the poise and confidence they would need to make the world a better place. In the meantime, their eyes darted around. Surreptitiously, they were checking out the other girls, who were doing the same to them, all trying desperately to appear blasé about everything and everyone around them. A few had that teenage slump, shoulders rounded as though they wished they could be part of the energy at the mall without being seen. "Ignore us," their body language said.

It's hard to imagine a more vulnerable time. The girls were old enough to be out here at the mall, open to anyone who might approach them. Not all of them were wise enough to see through a line of bull. An image of Little Red Riding Hood popped into my head.

It was biting cold outside, but the January sun was shooting a shaft of light through the skylight, making the small tree in the huge pot below think it was summer. An attractive man, who appeared to be in his early fifties, was sitting on one of the benches that circled a tree.

He caught my eye because he wasn't wearing a jacket. Maybe he left it in one of the lockers by the entrance to the mall. Maybe he was waiting for his wife to finish her shopping. But my antennae were twitching. Something was not quite right here. The reporter in me wanted to get a little closer to this guy so I could watch him without being noticed.

I guessed he was about six feet tall, maybe 160 pounds. His hair was curly blond, separated not parted, on the side. A touch of silver powdered his sideburns. He had huge, deep blue eyes meant to read a Teleprompter with great sincerity. He wore a Polo shirt in dusky blue and grey chinos. And penny loafers. Who wears penny loafers anymore? I wondered. No matter. He was gorgeous. His posture was relaxed, his right ankle on his left knee. He was leaning back on the bench, his hands in his pockets. Like the girls who passed by, he seemed to be noticing everything without appearing to see a thing. I spent forty-five minutes sipping my coffee, watching him. In that time he didn't check his watch once. If he was waiting for his wife, he must be the most patient husband on earth, I thought.

I picked up my coffee and took a seat a few feet from him on the bench but on the other side of the tree, where I could hear him. I wasn't worried about him noticing me. A nondescript mid-thirties woman was invisible on his radar screen, I decided.

After a while a girl walked by slowly, talking on her cell phone. From a few feet away I could hear her side of the conversation, which sounded like a fight with someone – her mother? She plopped down on the bench beside him and continued to shout into the phone. Something about the car and whether it had gas in it and when she was going to be home.

"Fuck you," she said, snapped her phone shut and stuffed it in her purse.

Heaving a big sigh, she sat on the bench, fuming. She was blond and looked about sixteen. She had on her tight-jeans-and-T-shirt uniform. After a few minutes, the would-be TV anchor turned to her and said in a deep, soothing voice, "Tough day?"

"Yeah," she replied, almost on the verge of tears. "My mother is such a bitch. She doesn't understand. All I want is some new clothes. There's nothing in my closet. I haven't had anything new in six weeks."

"You don't need any clothes to be beautiful," he cooed.

She did a little toss of her long blond hair and smiled.

"You're really lovely just as you are," he continued. "I understand how you feel, though. Parents can be so difficult. I know. My daughter tells me that all the time."

I couldn't believe what I was overhearing. The guy was smooth as chocolate mousse. I held my breath as he went on.

"In fact, you remind me of my daughter. She's blond like you. She's grown and left the house now. Lives on the West Coast. She's hoping to break into the movies. She's been out there about six months. I really miss her. I used to buy her clothes all the time. "

The girl seemed to be getting over her fit of pique. She listened to the mystery man with a look of longing on her face. I watched her closely as she shifted slightly on the bench. Twirling her hair with her right forefinger, she segued from sullen teen to sultry vamp.

My God, she's going to take the bait, I thought. That darling girl was about to fall for the line from the Big Bad Wolf. I wanted to grab her and tell her to run away, fast. Don't you see he's a creep?

She didn't respond directly, just pulled out her phone and appeared to be playing a game. He just sat there saying nothing, for a long time.

"Would you let me buy you some clothes?" he asked after about 20 minutes had passed. "You'd be doing me a favor. I've got a couple hundred dollars here and no one to spend it on. It could be like when I used to take my daughter shopping. What harm could there be? I'm thinking you're about a size four, right? That's the size my daughter wears."

"I really wear an eight," said the girl, casting her eyes down sheepishly.

"No matter," he said. "C'mon, let's take a few minutes. It would help ease the loneliness. Please. It would make both of us happy. What harm could that be?"

"I suppose it would be OK." She spoke haltingly.

They rose from the bench and rode up the escalator, hung a sharp right, and headed into Abercrombie & Fitch.

I ditched my empty cup and followed them. They were so wrapped up in each other they didn't even notice me. I gave them a few minutes to get ahead before I entered the store. Background music throbbed. Posted at the back of the store was the top half of a twice-the-size-of-life black-and-white photo of a bare-chested couple. It appeared they were standing in a field and she was playing the violin, with her eyes closed. He was slightly behind her with his arms around her, gazing at her breasts.

Real, live young men in their late teens were standing around in the front of the store, ostensibly as sales clerks. Judging from the looks of them—tight T-shirts over bulging biceps and even tighter jeans over butts begging to be pinched—what they did best was look cute.

Oh, yeah. And Abercrombie was selling clothes there too.

I headed for a rack of cargo pants, pretending to be looking for something for my daughter. From that vantage point, I could see

Mr. B. B. Wolf sitting on one of the brown leather chairs in front of the cash registers. He leafed through the latest Abercrombie catalog, which was titled the "Sex Ed textbook."

Little Red Riding Hood came bouncing out of the dressing room, in a pair of pants that appeared to be identical to the ones she had been wearing before, but in mud brown. The T-shirt said "Slim Pickin's." Wolf looked up from the catalog and gave her what could be considered a paternal smile. With his forefinger he motioned her to turn around. As she did, another girl in the store who was shopping alone glanced at her longingly out of the corner of her eye. Ah, to have such a nice father, her look seemed to be saying.

He said something softly and she skipped back into the dressing room, returning in the same pants, a size smaller. This time he flashed her a big smile full of straight, white teeth, as she skipped back to the dressing room.

Moments later, she was back with him in front of the cash registers—stonewashed bell-bottom jeans slightly frayed at the bottom, the salmon-colored "Slim Pickin's" T-shirt, and a grey cotton cardigan thrown casually over her arm. He paid for them with cash, and they walked out of the store and headed for the escalator.

I followed as far as the railing outside the store and watched as they took the escalator to the floor below. He said something to her, and then gave her a gentle hug. She gave him a peck on the cheek and they parted company, heading in opposite directions. I tried to follow her but there was a line getting on the escalator and by the time I got to the lower level she had disappeared into the crowd. I spent an hour checking the other stores that sold teen clothes. Didn't find her. There was nothing more I could do but head back to the newsroom.

I was back at my desk going over my notes from my interview when Thom plopped down in the chair at the side of my desk.

"Forget about whatever happened to what's-her-name. Murphy left a message on my voicemail and I bumped it over to yours. He says a councilman told him the school board has finally got the votes together to get rid of some principal in Land o' Lakes. He didn't know which one. They're not saying why, but the last time they dumped a guy he had his own monogrammed chair at the blackjack table."

"But I'm just getting going on the Billie Berry story."

"I told you. Forget about her for now," Thom said. "The school board meets tomorrow night. Find out who's getting dumped and why. I want it for tomorrow's paper."

This job can give you whiplash. The guy who usually throws the switch is Thom. When he sees a bright, shiny object in his periphery he's got to chase it. When kids behave that way it's called attention deficit disorder. When an editor does it, it's called competitive journalism. I must admit, though, that he's probably got the toughest job in the newsroom. There are about six layers of editors above him and as many reporters below him. Worst of all, he's got to put up with irritants like me.

"Remember what happened last time I tried to get an advance on a firing?" I reminded him. "I got zilch."

"Use your wiles this time," he snapped.

Shaking my head, I put my notes on the Billie story to one side. As desks go, mine is neater than most. I have a framed photo of Michael and the girls to the right of my computer so I can look at them whenever I feel lonesome, which is about twice a day. I dialed Michael's cell phone. Got his voice mail.

"I love you. Call me," was the message I left.

I grabbed my coffee mug that has a picture of the girls when they were babies printed on the side and headed for the bathroom, where I dumped the sludge left from yesterday. I filled it with the stuff that had been sitting in the pot for too long and added some of that white powder cream stuff that's cement for your arteries.

After firing up my computer, I punched in my password—PeterPickle, after a before-I-was-married boyfriend—and logged on. I called up my Microsoft Outlook list of contacts and tapped in "sch brd mbrs." In the list were the names, phone numbers, and e-mail addresses of all nine of them. I called each one, working my way through office assistants, public relations people, and answering machines. Four called me back before my 5:00 p.m. deadline. Only one was willing to tell me the board would be taking up a personnel matter. With only the barest of information—no reason for the planned beheading, no name for the intended beheaded—I filed my story, then waited around about half an hour for Thom to read it and get back to me with questions.

I hadn't heard from Mrs. Berry and decided I'd call her about Billie in the morning. It was time to drag my tired body home and get some quality time with my own girls. By 5:45 Thom still hadn't gotten to my story, so I slipped him a note saying he could call me on my cell phone if he wanted to know anything more.

Had I known I was in for an explosive evening, I'd have taken one of the newspaper's cars home.

Chapter 7

With Rickie Lee Jones playing on my CD, I headed south on 35W, carefully skirting a three-car pileup caused, no doubt, by black ice—the slick stuff that forms on roads when exhaust freezes. I pulled the del Sol into the garage, plugged in the head-bolt heater to keep the engine warm enough to start in the morning, and trudged into my 1915 Craftsman-style duplex. Snow crunched under every step. As I tripped through our mudroom, where two-foot-tall stacks of newspapers waiting for recycling intermingled with snow boots, down jackets, ice skates, hats, mittens and scarves strewn about the hardwood floor, I thought about Cathy Berry's pristine kitchen. No one would confuse hers with ours.

After being an employed mom for thirteen years, I haven't gotten over missing the girls when I'm at work and missing work when I'm at home. I enjoy my job, most days. I love the intellectual challenge. I love the mix of people, the funny quirks of life that I get to see firsthand, the sense that I'm a part of the fabric of my community. And, of course, two incomes are better than one.

We bought our duplex from an elderly couple. They had lived here forty years and the place needed serious updating. We figured we'd live on the first floor and rent out the second. We keep meaning to upgrade the kitchen, but there's never enough money or time.

Rebecca was stirring a pot of spaghetti, barely keeping the long bell-shaped sleeves of her favorite aqua sweater out of the sauce.

Suzy was watching some obnoxious cable show on the TV on the kitchen counter.

I see my daughters now on the cusp of pubescence, and I realize how fragile and strong they are, both at the same time. I try to look past Rebecca's purple hair and studded tongue, and thank God that she is in my kitchen and not standing on the highway with her thumb in the air. I watch Suzy's enthrallment with trash TV and remember that by age seven she had started reading with a vengeance, and hasn't stopped. Once she was so involved in a book that she didn't want to go out to dinner with us.

"I'm afraid something will happen in the book while I'm at dinner and not reading," she said, a tale that is now part of family lore.

I turn a deaf ear each time Rebecca uses "fuckin' " as the universal adjective for anything that is more than the norm. A couple of years ago she started to show signs of trouble. Sometimes she didn't come home from school when we expected and didn't have a good explanation for where she was. There were times when she would shut herself in her room for entire evenings. It felt like she was slipping away and I didn't like it. One day I read about a mother-daughter karate class offered at the YWCA. Hoping it would improve our relationship, I asked her if she wanted to take the class with me.

We went twice a week to the dojo, where we would neatly line our shoes outside the door and begin class by bowing to Sensei, our hands folded as though in prayer. Barefoot and dressed in white duck pants and jacket, called a gi, we learned a series of catas, sort of exercises that take enormous concentration. We kicked and punched at each other for hours. Although I got busy at work and couldn't continue after a while, Rebecca eventually earned a black belt.

I thought about Cathy Berry. Did the loss of Billie drive her to drink? Or did the drink drive Billie away? And what of Peter? Where was he in this story? Why wasn't he looking for her more actively? And where did Cathy get those bruises on her arm?

"How was your day, Rebecca?" I asked as the smell of garlic toast wafted through the kitchen where we sat at the round oak pedestal table.

"Fine."

"Come on, tell me more than 'fine.' Tell me the best thing, or the worst thing, that happened at school today."

"I know something." Suzy's yellow tennis shoes matched perfectly with her yellow sweat shirt. "I got ten out of ten right on my math quiz today."

"Good job," I said. "And you, Rebecca?"

"I got my paper on Clara Barton back."

"Was that the best thing or the worst thing?"

She flashed the first smile I had seen since I got home.

"Got a B plus."

"Good for you. Did Dad call?"

"No," both girls answered.

I went into our bedroom to change out of my "uniform"— black slacks, a white cotton blouse and a black cotton sweater—and into jeans and a sweatshirt. A minute later I heard Michael walk in the door, say hi to the girls and head for our bedroom. I gave him a quick kiss and lingered in the bedroom while he changed from his "uniform"—khaki Dockers, a denim shirt and a ragged navy tie. I married Michael for a lot a reasons, and his body is certainly among them. At 36, he's still long and lean, partly because he picked parents with skinny DNA, and partly because he makes a point to bicycle 10 to 20 miles every day. He's got a great butt.

I sat on our unmade queen-sized bed while he undressed silently. I looked around. We have two bedside tables. Mine was piled high with books I hope to read and copies of *People* magazine and *Entertainment Weekly*. A leaning tower of business nonfiction and biking magazines was about to fall from his table.

"Why didn't you return my calls today, Michael?"

"Busy day." He pulled on jeans and a sweatshirt. I followed him to the kitchen.

"How busy?"

"Another good reporter is leaving the paper to go into public relations," he said as we took our usual spots around the scarred wooden table. "Third one this month."

"Are they going to replace him?" Suzy wanted to know.

"Doubt it," Michael replied. "But if they do it will be with somebody much younger, and cheaper. The shareholders are running the newspaper business these days and they're not happy."

The silence around the table was broken by the twitter of my cell phone.

"Hughes," Thom said in a low, controlled voice. "A meth lab blew up. Looks like somebody may have been hurt. Get out there. We need you to file by 10:30."

"Gotta go," I said, leaving the rest of my dinner on my plate.

The girls looked at me with resignation. Was that anger I read in Michael's eyes?

Chapter 8

It's amazing how fast my heart starts pumping when there's news to be had. I hear "fire" and my fingers start to twitch, my adrenalin kicks in, and my heart starts to pump. It's my cocaine.

I gave the girls each a quick kiss, told them to be in bed by ten, grabbed the keys to the del Sol, and headed to the garage. Soccer balls and shin pads rattled around in the trunk of the car from last week when Rebecca played at the indoor sports center in Blaine, a northern suburb. Damn, I thought. I told her to get them out of there.

Here in the northland, where the sun sets about 4:30 in January, it's pitch dark by supper time and eight o'clock may as well be midnight. It's that dark. But my eyes adjusted quickly in the moonlight. Driving through my neighborhood, I admired snow stuck like marshmallow on the sides of trees that faced into the wind. Many houses were strung with Christmas lights. Arborvitae were covered with what looked like bright frosted strawberries and limes.

Soon I could smell smoke and see flames shooting into the air a few blocks ahead. I figured I was getting close when my cell phone rang.

"Are you there yet?" Thom asked.

"No, but I can see fire from here."

"We sent out two photogs. Apparently there were some people in the crowd watching the fire who don't want any publicity. Somebody hit Growler with a brick. Eggert's taking him to the hospital.

We're counting on you to get this one."

Foolishly, I kept driving.

The newspaper had been running articles about meth—meth-amphetamine—labs lately. It's a highly addictive, nasty drug that can turn nice folks into self-absorbed, paranoid monsters and a problem that's been growing in the Midwest. People who run meth labs don't like a lot of press around, shining lights on their business. Sometimes a meth lab can operate for years without neighbors knowing it.

With only an hour until deadline I knew I had to work fast once I got to the site. I would grab a cop for a couple of quick quotes. When did it blow? Anyone inside? Anyone hurt? Estimate of damage? Threat to nearby homes? Any idea how long the lab had been in operation?

I spotted a convenience store shop next door to the burning building, pulled into its lot under the brightest light I could find, and parked up close to the shop. I took my cell phone, a notepad, and a pencil out of my purse. In Minnesota we always take a pencil for outside work in January. Pens freeze, but carbon writes, even in the cold.

I stuffed my purse behind the driver's seat and locked the car doors, then grabbed my Sorel boots and my red goose-down jacket. I never wear it in the car because it's too hot, but it's warm enough for a night like this. For Christmas, my girls had "SOC-CER MOM" embroidered on the back of it in big, black letters. My hair was pulled back in a scrawny ponytail held on the sides with mismatched hairclips I found in the car ashtray. My face hadn't seen makeup since 7:30 that morning.

This was a particularly volatile part of town where guns, drugs and stray dogs are in good supply. Broken glass and yellow caution tape that littered the street made it appear the cops and firefighters had been there earlier.

I pulled out my cell phone and called Thom.

"The cops are gone," I told him.

"Yeah, we just heard on the scanner. Somebody loosed a pit bull on them. When they shot the dog, the bullet hit the sidewalk and ricocheted and got a kid in the arm. The crowd got pissed off, so the cops pulled out."

"I'm here without any protection."

"Are there any other reporters around?"

"No," I replied.

"Good," he said. "This one will be ours alone."

If I live to write it, I thought closing my phone.

Knots of people, mostly in their late teens and early twenties, stood around. Tension sparked in the icy night. Young men breathed in small, quick puffs like agitated stallions. More than one pair of eyes darted through the scene watching to see who was watching.

"She's a reporter," I heard one man hiss to another.

I spied a man in front of a convenience store holding a cordless phone to his ear with one hand while waving the other hand in the air. Smoke from his mouth punctuated his angry words as his breath met the frigid air. He was about forty years old, halfway to bald, and dark-skinned.

"Excuse me. I'm Skeeter Hughes from the *Citizen*," I said, waving my press badge in his direction. "Do you know what's going on here?"

"I was locking up when I heard a big bang from over there," he said.

"What caused the bang?"

"Don't know. I saw people running from the house. I think they cook meth in there."

"Have you called the cops?"

"Yes. About four fire trucks and five police cars came right away. The TV trucks came about ten minutes after that."

"Where are they now?"

"More people came out of the house and threw bricks and chunks of ice at the cops. It was crazy. When that started, the cops and TV guys left. Fire truck's gone, too. The fire's out, I guess."

I looked at the TV van parked across the street. Its antenna was flopping on its side like a broken wing on a duck.

"What happened to it?"

"They broke the antenna," he said. "Then a girl ran out of the house with these guys chasing her."

"Did she get away from them?"

"They knocked her down on the ground and started to kick her. She was rolled up in a ball with her arms over her head when I came out. The guys saw that I had a wrench in my hand and left."

"Where is she now?"

"I dragged her into the store and called 911, again. It's been twenty minutes."

It was obvious that I was not going to have time to sit down and write anything, so I hauled out my cell phone to call the newsroom and dictate what I saw.

"I don't like the feel of the crowd," I told Thom. "I'm not getting any closer to these guys."

"We're counting on you, Hughes. Get the story."

As I spoke with Thom, a small station wagon parked under a big oak about fifty feet away caught my eye. The tree was in front of a house, which appeared vacant. Someone was running away from the car. I looked a little more closely, then realized a fire had started to kindle in the back. The crowd was beginning to notice it too. People gathered around, stamping their feet against the cold while watching as the fire in the station wagon grew. They moved a little closer to the vehicle, warming their hands.

A moment later, kaboom! The car exploded, scattering the crowd and quickly turning the oak branches into flames fingering the winter night sky. It was terrifying and awesomely beautiful at the same time. Sirens began to wail.

"Cops must be coming back." The words had just left my mouth when we heard zing . . . zing, zing, zing!

Just above my head the sign on the store splintered from the gunshots and rained glass down on us. I couldn't see where the shots came from, but it was close and the acrid smell of gunpowder hung in the air. One more shot blazed through the shoulder of my jacket, scattering goose down everywhere.

My heart jumped into my throat and suddenly I could hear my pulse in my ears. The store owner and I scurried into the shop.

"Are you all right?" I asked him.

"OK. How about you?"

"Terrified and my jacket is ripped. Otherwise OK, I guess."

I pulled out my cell phone. "A bullet just missed me," I told Thom.

"Then I guess you better get out of there," Thom said. "Sounds like you're OK. We're almost to deadline anyway."

I told him there was a girl bleeding in the store. She was sitting on the floor holding a blood-soaked paper towel to her head. She was a plump stub of a girl with short dyed-blond hair sticking out in spikes all around her head. Her mascara was smeared, making her look like a raccoon. I noticed her belly-button stud, shaped like a shamrock, peeking out from under her blood-smeared T-shirt. She looked about sixteen going on forty. Her eyes didn't seem to be focusing.

"Where am I?" she asked.

"We're safe in a store. Looks like a meth lab blew up across the street. You ran out of the building and some guys were chasing you."

"How did I get here?"

"They knocked you down and kicked you around a bit, then split. This guy pulled you in and called 911."

"Who are you?"

"My name is Skeeter Hughes and I'm a reporter for the *Citizen*. Who are you?"

"Oh my God, you're a reporter." Suddenly her eyes focused.

I popped into mom mode, where I can read a kid's body language. It's far more telling than words. My practiced eye told me she knew exactly where she was and who she was. And she didn't want anyone else to know.

"Ahhhh, I'm confused," she said. "Are the police coming?"

"I certainly hope so."

With that, a dozen police cars roared up the street like the cavalry with blue and white lights twirling. The cars screeched to a stop and cops in full riot gear jumped out. One cop had a rifle and another tugged at a German shepherd on a leash. People who had been watching the station wagon burn scattered. A cop ran to the store, yanked open the door, looked at me, and said, "Who are you?"

"People keep asking me that. I'm Skeeter Hughes with the *Citizen*. This is Mohamed. He owns the place and saved this girl. She's been beat up and she needs medical attention."

"What happened?" He eyed the glass splinters in my hair and the hole in my jacket. "Somebody sent a message," I said.

"OK, we're going to get you out of here."

The firefighters were laying down hoses and spraying water, which froze on the oak in a surreal pattern, as more trucks arrived. The cops were directing the crowd away from the charred station wagon. Everyone's attention was fixed on the fire as the cop motioned Mohamed, the girl, and me toward the black and white.

The girl limped along slowly, trying to give the impression that she was still dazed. Mohamed and I, who were walking toward the police car, climbed in the back, but the girl hesitated. Apparently the cop bought her act because he took her right elbow to help her in.

Big mistake.

All in one motion, she jammed him in the gut with her right elbow, slammed the car door shut with her left hand, then, using the door handle to balance herself, she kicked him in the balls, leaving him bent over in pain while she bolted into the night. She moved so fast that Mohamed and I could only watch in stunned silence. Amid the other chaos, none of the other cops noticed. By the time the poor officer could get his breath back, she was gone.

I watched him curse a blue streak for a few minutes, and then my gaze shifted to my car, which was parked unprotected next to Mohamed's store.

I knocked on the window. "Officer, I'm really sorry about what happened to you, but that's my car over there."

"So?" he said, his voice high and angry.

"I just watched a station wagon get fire bombed. My del Sol is next."

"Why do you think that?"

"People saw me get out of it, with my reporter's notebook and cell phone. I'm one of those jackals from the media. Drug dealers don't want publicity. They've already shot at me."

"What do you want me to do about your car?"

"Can I drive it away?"

"No," he said. "It's not safe to leave alone tonight. You'll have to pick it up in the morning."

I called Thom and filled him in, including the gunshots and my fears about my car, while another cop drove Mohamed and me home.

"Do you need anything more from me tonight?" I asked.

"No, that'll do it," Thom replied. "Show up for work tomorrow. We need you back on the missing-girl story."

Thanks for your overwhelming concern there, Boss.

Chapter 9

Michael apparently had gotten the girls off to school before I woke in the morning, then left for work. I couldn't tell him about my harrowing night, or ask him for a ride to pick up my car. Instead, I persuaded another reporter to give me a lift.

We took the same route I had taken the night before. Hulking buildings that had been nothing more than outlines in the dark stood in stark relief against the white snow. As we got closer to the convenience store, the smell of burning rubber mixed with a hint of snow in the air. My palms started to sweat into my woolen mittens as dread covered me like a wet blanket. The brick wall next to where I had parked the car was scorched. Apparently the fire department had hauled away the carcass of my del Sol because all that remained was a pile of burned metal.

Mohamed, who had seen the remains of the car before it was towed, said it looked like someone had thrown a concrete block through the windshield, breaking off the steering column. Some incendiary device was apparently heaved through the hole in the windshield, because the inside of the car was ashes. That meant my purse, which contained $200, all my credit cards, and the newspaper's charger for my cell phone, was ash, too. Even the girls' soccer equipment was gone.

My new friend from last night was out there with a broom and a dustpan, sweeping up the burned rusty remains.

"That was my car," I said, pointing to the pile of debris.

He brushed away the metal scraps to find the "H" hood ornament, wiped it off on the side of his pants, and handed it to me.

"I'm really sorry," he said, his brows knitted with concern.

I stood there and stared, hood ornament in hand and cried. This had been more than just a car to me. I had wanted a sexy red convertible since I was old enough to drive. I even told Michael to bury me in it when the time came. Now, all I had left of my dream machine was a memento.

It was almost 11:00 before I dragged my tail into the newsroom. I ran into Thom as I got off the elevator.

"What happened there, Hughes?" Thom asked, pointing to the hole ripped in the shoulder of my red down jacket.

"I was dodging bullets last night, remember?" I said. "One almost got me."

Thom stepped over to his desk, opened his top drawer, and pulled out a roll of duct tape.

"Here," he said.

"What am I supposed to do with that?"

"Tape the hole," he said in all seriousness.

Yet another reminder that his degree is in journalism, not management. Crisis or otherwise.

"Nice job on the meth lab story last night. Sorry 'bout your car. We're looking into how we can pay for it."

"What do you mean, 'looking into how we can pay for it'?" I asked. "You're going to pay for it. . . . Right?"

"We've never had a reporter's car destroyed before," he replied. "I don't know what the policy is. I'm checking."

Replacing my car was the newspaper's responsibility, so I gave the matter no more thought as I poured my coffee and asked, "What do you want me to do now?"

"One of the police reporters can take the meth lab story from here," he said. "You may as well get back to the Billie Berry thing. Has her mom heard from her yet? And what exactly is the story with the family? When someone turns up missing, there's often some funny stuff going on. Is there any funny stuff going on in the Berry household?"

I had no idea. It wasn't like I'd had the time to check. I picked up the phone and hit the speed-dial button to retrieve messages. Cathy Berry's voice came through loud and clear.

"Skeeter," she said, "I thought you'd be back out to talk about Billie. Can you come this afternoon? I've got more I want to say about her."

I dialed her number. She picked up on the first ring.

"Billie?" she shouted into the phone.

"No, Mrs. Berry. It's Skeeter. I got your message. I can be out there this afternoon. Will you be around?"

"Of course, I'll be around. I'm waiting for Billie to call and tell me she's fine, that she ran off and got married to that deadbeat boyfriend of hers. How soon can you be here?"

"I can be there in an hour, after I've gotten some lunch."

"Come now and I'll give you lunch."

Given that my car was toast, I had Thom sign a requisition form to get me a car from the motor pool, stuffed my feet back in my boots and snagged my coat and headed for the elevator. A few floors down and I was in the garage where I picked up one of the newspaper's cars. According to some of the old timers, the wisest reporters always take the oldest cars from the fleet. They die closer to the paper's garage than the newer ones, so it's easier to get back and pick up another.

I slid behind the wheel of some kind of blue Chevy. A gaping hole stared at me where the cigarette-lighter receptacle had been yanked out, along with the ashtray to prevent anyone from smoking in the paper's car. Given that I quit smoking as a New Year's resolution, and given that the phone charger, which I would have plugged into the cigarette lighter outlet, had succumbed in my del Sol, I didn't much care. I was glad that at least the radio was already tuned to my favorite jazz station.

The high that day was supposed to be zero degrees Fahrenheit. I've lived here my entire life and still the cold of January can reach down my throat and grab my lungs. Minnesotans say the cold keeps the riff-raff out. I find that hard to believe. But it certainly keeps the riff-raff like me awake. The car's vinyl seats were so cold they crackled.

My stomach was beginning to rumble as I pulled into the Berry driveway for the second time in as many days. This lunch better amount to more than bean sprouts and tofu, I thought. A grilled cheese sandwich and glass of milk would do me fine.

Either Cathy Berry had undergone a personality transplant or she was on new meds because the woman who greeted me at the door before I could even ring the bell was entirely different from the one I talked to the day before.

Her raccoon eyes of yesterday had been expertly covered with heavy makeup. She had applied a little blush on her high cheekbones. Her lips, which had looked thin and translucent yesterday, were a bright cherry red. She wore Donna Karan black pleated slacks I remembered from an advertisement, a black pullover sweater that sure looked like cashmere to me, and black ballet slippers. She had faded into the white-on-cream décor of her house twenty-four hours earlier. Today she stood out like an exclamation point.

"I've got lunch ready for you in the kitchen," she said as I reached for the door handle.

No "hello." No "good to see you again." No "cold enough for you?" The slight slur from her morning "coffee" seemed to have gone away too.

"Nice to see you again, Mrs. Berry." She took my coat and I sat on the bench in her foyer to remove my boots. No way was I going to track snow into her home.

She gave a nod and I followed her into the kitchen. This lady may not eat much herself, but she sure could put out a lunch on twenty minutes' notice. All the food groups were covered: grilled chicken with some kind of marinade, rice with sautéed mushrooms, broccoli sprinkled with lemon juice, and fresh, out-of-season strawberries that must have cost a fortune. Being hosted by a control freak isn't all bad.

I briefly wondered if the meal violated the paper's ethics code that says we can't accept anything worth more than five dollars from anybody. No matter. I was hungry and lunch looked good. Besides, it's about forming a bond with the source, right?

"I assume you still haven't heard from Billie?" I said between bites.

"If I had heard from her I wouldn't need to be talking with you, now would I?" She had taken a seat on a kitchen chair, pushed back a bit from the table and crossed her arms over her chest.

"I guess not."

"I had flyers out by yesterday afternoon."

I decided not to rise to her bait. "What do the flyers say?"

"They have a description of Billie and our phone number. We used the picture I showed you, even though it's out of date. The lady at Missing Children suggested that I include a personal note to Billie in case she's just run away."

"What did you put in your note?"

"I thought about it a long time," she replied. "I'll kick her butt if this is just a trick. But I didn't want to scare her off. So I said that I missed her and I loved her and I wanted her to call home."

I asked her what color the flyers were, thinking I'd watch for them when I headed back downtown.

"Orange paper and green print. Those colors together are appalling, but Billie liked them when she was a little girl. Plus, they stand out among all the others."

"Tell me where Billie hangs out," I said.

"All the usual haunts—Gap, Abercrombie & Fitch, Ragstock. Sometimes she'd leave on a Saturday morning before I got up and she'd be there until after midnight."

"That's a long time. Weren't you worried about her?"

"Frankly, I didn't always notice that she was gone. Real estate is a time-consuming business."

The Mall of America is so immense that a girl Billie's age could almost move into the place, I thought. "Did you ever check on where she had been?"

"Are you investigating my mothering skills or writing an article that will bring Billie home?"

"I'm writing an article about Billie," I replied, biting back a more caustic response. "I have no idea whether it will bring her home. Did she ever tell you about anything odd going on there, like older men offering to buy girls clothes?"

She shifted her position in her chair, crossing her legs at the ankle and resting her chin on her hand propped up on the table. "No," she said, her right eyebrow raised a bit. "Of course, there have been rumors about that for years. Something about prostitution, I think. There were stories in the newspaper a while ago about the blond, blue-eyed Minnesota girls being a hot commodity for pimps in New York. But she never said anything to me about that. Why do you ask?"

"I'm just exploring every angle. I have to ask lots of questions."

"What do you need me to do?" There was catch in her voice that made me think just asking the question was hard for her. She was much more comfortable giving orders than asking for them. This was a woman who would go against her natural grain to get her daughter back. I gave her points for that.

"You can be totally honest with me."

"I have been honest with you. Billie didn't come home Friday night. She still hasn't come home. Do you think I'm lying?"

I steeled myself, knowing that the next question would be tough to ask.

"No. But I noticed yesterday that you have a hand-shaped bruise on your arm. Where did you get that, Mrs. Berry?"

She rubbed her left forearm with her right hand. She looked me straight in the eye for a long time, and I could almost see the wheels turning in her brain as she was making a decision. Suddenly she stepped into another room and sat in a leather winged-back chair on the opposite side of the room. I wanted her to think of me as an equal, so I sat in the chair's twin, which was placed next to her.

"When Billie and I tussled Friday she grabbed my arm. I guess she pressed a little too hard. I bruise easily." She pulled her eyes away from mine as she said it, looking instead out the window on the sparkling white snow.

It could have been true, but I didn't believe that story. I thought she had done a quick cost-benefit analysis and decided that was more truth than she was willing to share. The look on her face warned me not to ask any more questions on that topic.

"Mrs. Berry, yesterday you told me you suspected Billie's dad knew where she was. Do you think he might have kidnapped her?"

"I doubt he would do something as stupid as that," she said. "He's an evil man, but he's very bright."

"Why do you say he's evil?"

"Are you going to put all this in the newspaper?"

I gave myself a moment to think before I answered. The story was about Billie, not her mom. Still, if there was abuse in the family it could be a factor in Billie's disappearance.

"I don't know what I'm going to put in the newspaper because I don't know the whole story yet. But you need the newspaper's help. Billie may show up in an hour or you may never see her again. Working with me is the best vehicle you have right now to get your daughter back."

We sat there for a moment, each of us with our arms resting on the leather chairs. Mrs. Berry gripped hers so hard I expected the upholstery tacks would make an indentation on her hands. Neither of us spoke until she said, "Peter bedded half the women in this community, including my best friend and my brother's wife. To make matters worse, the entire neighborhood, even Billie, knew about it before I did. I do not want the matter rehashed in the newspaper."

Follow truth and it will often lead to motivation, I thought. Suddenly, I understood that Cathy Berry had the temperament of a woman scorned because she was a woman scorned.

"The story about Billie is not about Mr. Berry's infidelity," I replied. "I don't see any reason to put that in the newspaper."

She said nothing, but the wash of relief erased ten years from her face and she loosened her grip on the arm of her chair.

"Do you have any more questions for me?" she asked.

"You said in your message that you had more to tell me about Billie. What is it?"

"Oh, that. Yes. I wanted to tell you I put out the flyers."

"That's it? You could have told me that in the message."

"In my business face-to-face contact is always the best," she said.

I looked into her eyes and saw a woman with only the façade of control. Just below that was a terrified mother and I was the strongest link she had to her daughter right now. I could have lit into her for dragging me out here, wasting my time, on a ruse but decided against it. I understood how she could feel that way.

"I probably will have other questions later." I rose and headed for her hall closet, where she had hung my coat. I grabbed it myself and then slipped my stocking feet into my boots. "Thanks for lunch."

She gave me a quick nod, and then stood at the door as I moved down her perfectly shoveled walk. Half way down the path I turned. "Be sure to call me if you hear from Billie."

"Oh, I certainly will," she said before she shut the door.

My next stop was the Hennepin County Government Center in downtown Minneapolis to look up the divorce file of *Berry vs. Berry*. When the government center was built in the mid-1970s, only a chest-high railing separated the mentally unstable from a leap to the stone floor four hundred feet below. It took three jumpers to convince the county to add ceiling-high glass partitions to the railings.

Court documents are stored on the twelfth floor, so I took the elevator up and then a sharp right down to the end of the hall. When one of the computers, probably bought by the county when Bill Gates was still in high school, became free, I typed in *Berry v. Berry* and up popped a case number, which I handed to a pleasant woman standing behind a desk. She stepped into a back room, and minutes later came out with a buff-colored folder about five inches thick and dog-eared.

What a fine mess that divorce was.

Mrs. Berry, it turned out, had sold enough houses and invested in enough real estate to earn a salary upwards of $500,000 a year. When I first met her I had guessed Mrs. Berry was about fifty. I was off by ten years. Mr. Berry listed his wife's hard drinking as one of the complaints. No surprise there.

Peter Berry was a drug salesman who earned about two-thirds of his wife's income. The file included charges of adultery, and mentioned the name of one Allison McNulty, who I bet was the woman who became his wife. At the time of the divorce Mr. Berry was also forty and considerably older than Ms. McNulty, who was listed as a twenty-six-year-old flight attendant for Northwest Airlines.

The Berrys had fought over everything—the house, the furniture, his hunting gear, her jewelry. Mrs. Berry charged that because she had paid for more of the house, it ought to go to her. Mr. Berry argued that he had cut back his business to be home with Billie while Mrs. Berry was out making all that money that bought the house. He deserved at least half the price of the sale, he said.

Saddest of all, Billie had filed an affidavit that sketched a tough home life. Her parents fought daily for two years before they finally filed for divorce.

"I lie in bed at night and listen until I can't listen anymore," she said. "On good nights, I fall asleep from crying. On bad nights, I can't fall asleep, and I just cry."

At the ripe old age of fifteen, Billie said she had come to realize that her parents were never going to get back together again.

"Please, judge," she wrote, "let them get divorced so I can get on with my life."

Perhaps most significant, Billie had called the police to their home on two occasions because her parents' fights had become violent. No charges were filed.

Had Peter caused those bruises on Cathy Berry's arm? Was he volatile? Given to occasional violence? Salesmen can come from a breed that acts first and thinks later. Did his new wife know about the police calls?

I jotted down Billie's dad's address and phone number in my reporter's notebook. It was time to visit Mr. Berry.

According to the file, Peter Berry worked from his home. Hoping he wouldn't be with a client at that exact moment, I opened my cell phone and dialed his number. The fates were with me.

"Mr. Berry, my name is Skeeter Hughes and I'm a reporter for the *Citizen*. I'm working on a story about Billie. Is there any chance

I can come out and speak with you?"

"I was wondering when you would get around to talking with me," he said. "I have an opening at 2:30. Can you come out then?"

Stealing a quick glance at my watch, I figured I had just enough time to make it. Peter Berry lived about a mile away from Cathy Berry, but he may as well have been in a different universe. While the home they had shared when they were married was all about straight lines, ninety-degree angles, and symmetry, his was all about interconnecting circles. Peter Berry lived in a two-story stucco box topped by a geodesic dome.

"Hi, I'm Skeeter," I said offering him my hand when he came to the door.

Peter Berry was close to six feet tall with the hairiest arms I've ever seen sticking out of his short-sleeved red T-shirt. Chest hair poked through the neck too. He wore jeans I suspected he'd had at least since college. There was an impish look about his small brown eyes hidden under bushy brows. What figured to be a constant, slightly crooked smile turned up above a pointed chin.

"Come in, Skeeter."

"Great house." I really meant it. I wasn't trying to establish rapport this time.

"Glad you like it." He took my coat, hat, and mittens. "We bought it from some people who moved to Scottsdale. They couldn't stand the cold here, but we love it. Would you like to look around?"

"Sure would."

Even though it was biting cold outside, the inside of this Berry house was cozy, almost balmy. The first floor was an open design, with a kitchen, living room, and dining area flowing into each other. Blue, red, and yellow rope rugs were scattered over wide-plank oak floors. The furniture tended toward overstuffed traditional.

"Amazing place," I commented. "The dome is very cool."

"Yes, it is," he replied. "Except that it leaks. But we still like it."

He motioned me to one of the chairs. I envisioned a whole

flock of denuded ducks as I sank into several inches of down feather stuffing.

"I thought you worked out of your home," I said, opening my notebook. "Where is your office?"

"How did you know that?"

"I read it in the court file on your divorce."

"So you are a prepared reporter, as well as pesky," he said. "I like that. There's a back room with a separate entrance on the west side. That's where I do my work. Can I get you some coffee?"

I had been trying to cut back on coffee in the afternoons because I suspected it had been keeping me awake at night, but I accepted. Bonding again, you know. "Tell me about Billie."

"Billie is the classic child of an alcoholic mother. In fact, she was the first one, even before me, to recognize her mother's alcoholism."

"How old was she when she figured that out?"

"Pretty young. Probably six or seven. I happened to walk into the laundry room one day as Billie found a fifth of bourbon beneath a pile of laundry. I'll never forget it. She turned to me and said, 'Mom's an alcoholic. That means she's sick. ' "

"Billie was wise beyond her years," I said.

"Yes, she was," he said with a sad shake of his head. "Children of alcoholics often are."

"That was at least ten years ago. Did you try to get Mrs. Berry any help?"

"Certainly. We did interventions and she had two stints in Hazelden in Center City. She'd be dry for a while, then slip back again."

"How does she conduct business with this problem?"

"That's the interesting part about her illness. She drinks while she's working. She's an excellent real estate agent. Her colleagues know she has a drinking problem, but they're reluctant to get too public about it, unless it affects her work. And so far it hasn't."

"Tell me more about Billie. Are you worried about her?"

"Yes, I'm worried that I don't know where she is. I'm worried that she may be in some kind of trouble, or worse, danger. On the other hand, I know she has always been good at taking care of herself. She's nobody's fool."

"Do you have any idea where she is, or what she's doing?"

"None."

"Has she ever disappeared before?"

"No."

"Have you made any effort to find her?"

"One of my friends works at WCCO-TV," he replied. "I asked him if they would put anything on the air about her. He couldn't help. That was about all I could do. Plus, I know Cathy is raising a ruckus about Billie. I figure I'll leave the matter to her."

I spied our newspaper stacked on a table with a half-full cup of coffee and small square plate stacked with chocolate chip cookies. A dozen half melted candles surrounded the indoor Jacuzzi. Clearly this was a man who enjoyed his creature comforts.

"How well do you and Billie get along?" I asked.

"Better than she and her mother do."

"Did Billie have a choice about where she would live or did the court decide?"

"She decided to live with Cathy. Because our homes are so close together it's easy for her to go back and forth."

"How about Billie and your new wife?"

"I suspect she chose to live with her mother because she didn't want to live with Allison. She blames her for our divorce. Actually, it wasn't her fault. I had many affairs while I was married to Cathy."

The place was full of knickknacks and artifacts from Africa to China. I guessed that his flight-attendant wife worked the international trips for Northwest. "Why did you marry Allison?"

"You know, life is short. After trying to fight Cathy's alcoholism for years, I gave up and decided I deserved a little fun. There were many years when Cathy and I were married in name only. Then I met Allison on a flight to Germany, where I went to see some drug manufacturers. We hit it off. We fell in love. It felt good so I decided to make it legal."

"I certainly give you points for honesty," I replied, a little taken aback by his candor. "I noticed Monday that Cathy had some bruises on her arm. Do you know anything about that?"

"Cathy has always bruised easily. She's so fair-skinned, her worst days, she's almost translucent."

"I read in the file that Billie called the police to your house a couple of times before your divorce when the arguments turned violent." Even though he knew I had read his divorce file that seemed to catch him off guard.

"That's true," he said after a moment.

"Did you hurt Cathy physically? Was your relationship violent?"

"Of course not," he replied. "Yes, we fought. But the only violence came from her. She pushed me through sliding glass doors so Billie called the cops."

"And the second call?"

"There was no second call."

"That's what the court documents said."

"They're wrong. Cathy made that up to make it sound worse than it was."

"You're a licensed psychologist with an expertise in eating disorders. Why are you selling pharmaceuticals instead of seeing patients?"

"Boy, you are well prepared. Yes, I have a license as a psychologist. I discovered a few years ago that insurance companies are more willing to pay for drugs than for someone who will listen. I saw how much money Cathy was making in real estate and decided it was time to make some of my own. You aren't going to put all this in the newspaper, are you?" he asked, suddenly aware of how much he had said.

"So far, I don't have anything to put in the newspaper. Just a bunch of suspicions."

"So why are you here, talking to me? Can I sell you some drugs?" he asked with half a laugh, trying to change the subject and lighten the tone of our conversation.

"Spoken like a drug salesman," I replied. That drew a smile from him. "Makes me wonder if Mrs. Berry wanted to sell me a house."

He laughed at that, then turned serious when I asked the next question. "Does she often lace her morning coffee with bourbon?

"Yes." He looked me squarely in the eye, then added sincerely, "She has always tried to douse her pain with alcohol."

"What's her pain about?"

"It goes way back," Peter replied. "She comes from a controlling family that I suspect was alcoholic, but they didn't call it that back then. She was always expected to be successful, rich, and thin. She's managed all three, but it has cost her."

"Did that play into her relationship with Billie?" I asked.

"Yes. And me," he said, and then asked, "I repeat, why are you here?"

"Because I want to find out what happened to Billie. I don't know her, but I'm beginning to feel like I do. I'm getting a picture of a girl, a young woman, who is smart, tough yet creative, insightful, courageous, and sensitive all at one time. I'm thinking she's a rebel too. What about her sense of right and wrong? Justice and injustice? Where does she fall in that continuum?"

"I don't think I know anyone with a stronger desire for justice than Billie," he replied.

"What makes you say that?"

"I've seen her loyalty to her friends."

"For example?"

"For example, her friend Nancy Nguyen. They met when they were in seventh grade, in a peer-mentoring program between native Minnesotans and Vietnamese-born kids. Billie said she couldn't believe Nancy was thirteen when they met."

"Why not?"

"Billie said she looked nine, especially in those little-girl clothes Nancy's mother made her wear. Billie wasn't sure she could be the kid's friend, let alone her mentor."

"What changed her mind?"

"One day the other kids were making fun of Nancy," he said. "Billie told them to shut up, then brought Nancy home and gave her some of her own clothes. They've been friends ever since. She's like the little sister Billie never had."

I told him I'd like to talk to Nancy.

"That might be hard," he replied.

"Why?"

"Nancy's family sent her back to Vietnam."

Chapter 10

I didn't want to leave Peter Berry's warm house. Big, fat snowflakes were starting to float like feathers to the six inches already clogging the roads as I pulled away. The gunmetal gray skies and the air temperature in the upper twenties fit right in with the foot of the white stuff predicted for the afternoon. I would have preferred to make more chocolate chip cookies in his fabulous kitchen and watch the snow pile up. As it was, all I could do was hope the newspaper's car I was driving had good treads on the tires.

It took twice as long as usual to make it back to downtown Minneapolis. Heading east on Highway 62 and trying to negotiate north on 35W is a test of driving skills in good weather. Unlike New Yorkers, who have no inhibitions about getting in your face, Minnesotans pride themselves on being "nice." Until it was redesigned last year, the convergence of Highway 62 and 35W was an impossible bottleneck intended to test that "nice." In snowy weather it was a classic example of the state's unwritten desire to keep the riff-raff out.

Except for Alaska, Minnesota is the northernmost state. Like Alaska, Minnesota can get dark very early in winter. Even though it was only about four o'clock, dusk was setting in as I made my way north on Hennepin Avenue. I was in search of the young man who worked with Billie the night she disappeared. He was on the same shift as Billie and would have started at three, so I decided to swing by the SuperAmerica in Uptown on my way back to the paper. If he was too busy to talk, at least I could get a feel for the place where Billie was before she disappeared.

While most of the buildings on Hennepin Avenue in Uptown are funky and old, this SuperAmerica looks like it was built out of Lego blocks. Dominated by primary colors of red and blue, it's perfectly square with turrets in each of four corners that I swear are plastic. I pulled up to the gas pump, swung my legs through the open car door, and put the nozzle in the car's tank. While the numbers spun around, I gazed through the glass at a young man I hoped was Billie's co-worker. He looked to be in his early twenties, with the translucent skin that came with his fire engine red hair, which was braided into dreadlocks and dyed purple on the ends. He was about five-foot eight and muscular. I pegged him as a wrestler.

After filling up the tank, I wandered around the store awhile, waiting for the customers to pay for their gas. I eyed the cigarette packs behind the counter longingly and remembered I'd given them up. I approached the cash register as the last customer was finishing.

"That'll be $10.23 on pump two," he said, his tongue stud twinkling as he talked. "Thanks. Have a nice day."

"You're Joey Pignatello, aren't you?" I asked as I passed him the newspaper's credit card.

"Yeah. Who are you?"

"I'm Skeeter Hughes from the *Citizen*. I'm working on a story about Billie Berry. Weren't you working with her the night she disappeared?"

"I already told the whole story to that wacko mother of hers," he replied. "The cops don't care. Why do you?"

"I cover Land o' Lakes, and a lot of people in Land o' Lakes know Billie. Her mom would like them to know that she's missing. But there won't be a story in the newspaper unless I can give readers a feel for what she's like, where she might be, and why. Have you got a minute to talk?"

"I can talk until it gets busy. I'm the only one here this afternoon until six."

"How long have you worked with Billie?"

"We started here at about the same time a year ago." He leaned his backside on the counter behind and grabbed of cup of steaming coffee from a shelf in front of him.

"How well do you know her?"

"Our shifts overlap maybe twice a week. We talk."

"How's that?"

"Usually I come in at ten o'clock and work until two in the morning. I go to school at the University of Minnesota during the day, study until I have to work. She starts at three and works until eleven. It gets pretty quiet after about 10:30, so we usually had time to talk then."

"What did you talk about?"

"All kinds of shit. Music, movies, current events, if you can believe that. She reads three newspapers every day: your paper, the St. Paul paper, and the *New York Times*. I never met a girl who knows so much about what's going on. She said she wanted to be a cop someday. First she had to get away from that crazy family of hers."

"How are they crazy?"

"Mom's a big-time drinker. Her dad kept trying to get her to dry out. Finally, he divorced her and married some chick who works for Northwest . . . a flight attendant, I think. For a while Billie was tryin' all the time to fix everything and everyone."

"Does Billie need fixing?"

"She probably has her head screwed on better than any of them. She has goals, ya know? Says she's going to finish high school. Then go to college. She said she's wanted to be an 'enforcement official' ever since she saw Jodie Foster in *Silence of the Lambs*." Joey used his index fingers to put the quotes around 'enforcement official.'

"Did she break up with Nate Whitehorse because he didn't want her to become a cop?" I often ask questions about information I already have to see if that information is true.

"That was one reason, but mostly she dumped him because she was with him for the wrong reason."

"What do you mean?"

"She thought she could fix him."

"Did she?"

"No. He was always fighting with her," he replied. "He'd call her up on her cell phone while she was working and scream at her. Called her a whore and stuff like that. Me 'n Billie talked about him a lot."

"How long was she with him?" I was trying to listen to him without staring at the cigarettes above. God, I really wanted to buy a pack and smoke it in the company car.

"Too long."

"Was it hard for her to break with him?"

"You know, that's what I don't understand about girls. Even the smart, strong ones let guys walk all over them. Yeah, she had trouble cutting him loose."

"Tell me about Friday night."

"It was busy all night. Billie said she had to buy popcorn and take off at eleven on the dot because she was going to watch a movie with her mother. Billie wasn't exactly sure it was going to come off, because she never knew whether her mother was going to be sober or passed out."

"Did you see her leave?"

"Only sorta. We got real busy."

"So you didn't see her leave?"

"There was something wrong with the furnace in here that day and it was damn hot inside, even though it was awful cold outside. I remember watching her walk out the door, but the windows were steamed up. I couldn't see very well, so I don't know for sure. I think she got in some guy's car."

"Do you think Nate Whitehorse was driving the car?"

"Beats me. I've never seen the guy before. Just heard him screaming at her on her cell phone."

"She didn't drive her own car?"

"Nope. It was in the lot when I left at two. I thought it was odd, but you know, she's got a lot of friends. I thought maybe one of them picked her up."

"Did you hear from her after that?"

"Nope. Her car was still here when I came in Saturday night. Sunday morning her mom came to get it. But there was another weird thing."

"What was that?"

"She never bought the popcorn."

"Do you think she ran away? California can look pretty good this time of year."

"I don't think so. She isn't that type of girl."

"What type of girl is she?"

"The tough, resourceful type." There was a hint of admiration in his voice.

"We get some rough characters in here and sometimes they hit on her. One night this old drunk guy was hitting on her. I watched her tell him to pay up and get the hell out of here. Not much scares her. She's more likely to spit in some guy's eye than run away from him."

At that moment a gaggle of kids from the junior high down the block burst through the door of the SuperAmerica, backpacks swinging as they plowed through the aisles, grabbing candy, pop, and corn chips.

"I gotta work now," Joey said.

I handed him my card and invited him to call me if he thought of anything else I should know about Billie, then squeezed in one more question.

"So where do you think she went?"

"I don't know, but I wish she'd come back soon. It's a real bitch working here alone."

Chapter 11

I cranked up the car, continued north on Hennepin, hung a right on Franklin, then north on Fifth Avenue and headed toward downtown and the Haaf Ramp, named for Jerry Haaf, a cop who was murdered as he ate pizza while on his break. I flashed my parking card at the reader, swung up the ramp and into the line where the paper keeps its cars, then trudged to the skyway that connects the ramp to the building. The newspaper is on the eastern edge of downtown, four blocks from the Hubert H. Humphrey Metrodome, which looks like a huge, square marshmallow melting on 20 acres.

Minneapolis straddles the Mississippi River with gleaming office buildings shooting up on the south side like stalagmites jutting toward the sky. Multi-million-dollar condos line both banks. Sometimes I wonder whether the glass-and-concrete boxes would inspire Mark Twain if he were writing about the Mighty Mississipp' today?

I waved at the guard as I entered the building and made straight for the elevator to the newsroom. The editors were huddling to decide what to put in tomorrow's newspaper.

Filling the same chairs they had used for the morning meeting, editors bent their heads over their fifteen-page, single-spaced list of potential stories. Earlier in the day, the section editors had written up a one-paragraph description, called a "budget line," for each of the stories they were proposing for tomorrow's paper. Each budget line was nicknamed with a one-word "slug" and included who would be writing the story, whether there was a photo to go with it, and its length in column inches. Sometimes a budget line with snazzy writing would put a story on page one regardless of the content.

The idea is that all the editors know what all the choices are for tomorrow's snapshot of today's news. Each day a different editor stands before a dry-erase board to lead the discussion. The slugs for the contenders for page one are written on the board. An arrow up or down next to the slug indicates whether it will go in the top half or the bottom half of the newspaper.

They do it every day at this time, and the discussions can get heated. As usual, my attention-deficient editor Thom was dominating the conversation.

"Look, Sweeney's piece about the governor is timely and a good read. It should go above the fold," he said in his usual staccato rhythm.

"That's what you said two days ago, Thom. I think the readers have had enough of the governor this news cycle," said the features editor.

"I gotta agree," piped up the city editor.

"We're the biggest newspaper in the state," Thom argued. "What the governor does is important."

"The governor is staging a publicity stunt," said the photo editor. "Promising a two-bit solution to a million-dollar problem. I don't think we should reward that behavior. Besides, the photos aren't compelling."

After no one said anything else the editor leading the discussion drew an arrow pointing down next to the slug "guv."

The discussion went on for another thirty minutes until the lineup of page-one stories was set. I'd always found it ironic that the editors spent so much energy fighting over whose story went where when the night editor could overrule all their decisions as late as midnight if something worthy of page one happened in the evening. Of course, night editors who changed the day editors' priorities without good reason were usually raked over the coals at the morning meeting, which they didn't attend because they worked nights.

The huddle broke and the editors returned to their desks, making ready to stare at computer screens and edit copy for the next two or three hours. I grabbed Thom as he was on his way back to his area. "We need to talk."

"OK. I'm on my way to another meeting. Walk with me."

"When am I going to get a check for my car?"

"Bad news there, Hughes. I'm afraid the company pays you 41.5 cents a mile to use your car. That includes your payment for car insurance to cover damages. You're responsible for whatever happens to it. But we're gonna make you whole. We'll pay the deductible your insurance company will charge you."

"Shit," was the only word that came to my mind.

"Sorry, kiddo. If we paid for your car we'd have to pay every time this happens."

"Are you trying to tell me reporters get firebombed and shot at all the time?"

"No," he said.

"Let me get this straight. You call me from home on a night that's colder than a Dairy Queen blizzard and send me out to cover a meth explosion. To stay safe I have to leave my car there, and when it's firebombed the newspaper will pay only what my own insurance won't cover. Do you realize the message that sends? Does the paper want to tell its reporters that it won't back them up when they need it the most?"

"That's corporate America for you," he replied with a shrug.

"Do you think that's right?"

"I think we work for a company where the shareholders have expectations," he replied.

"And what about readers' expectations? What about journalism, Thom?"

"We try to meet those demands, too," he replied.

I was so angry with him that I couldn't think of another word to say. Thoughts of the Mall of America and anything more about Billie Berry flew out of my head. I turned on my heel and headed back to my desk, fuming. I spent the rest of the afternoon furiously rearranging the icons on my computer screen. What had happened to Thom? He was once one of the true believers, part of the flock that went into journalism after Watergate to make the world a better place. How did he turn into a corporate hack?

I turned the cursor on my computer to Outlook Express with a plan to write an angry e-mail to Thom when I noticed that I had a dozen e-mails waiting. I scrolled through them, deleting the ones that offered me a better mortgage rate or a larger penis, or both, and clicked on the one that warned, "Watch out" in the subject line.

"Stop asking questions about Billie Berry, bitch. It's none of your business. And stay away from the Mall of America or there may be another fire in your future."

Chapter 12

I highlighted the e-mail address and hit "properties" right away but an error message came back that said the address was unknown. My mind began to race. Great, I thought. Now I've got an anonymous e-mailer who is trying the scare the hell out of me, and doing a pretty good job.

I know it was silly, but I found myself looking around the newsroom to see if anyone noticed that I was terrified. Showing fear in a newsroom is a bad career move. Bravado is rewarded over humanity. Then I told myself I was being ridiculous. I just needed to talk to Michael. I dialed his cell phone, hoping to catch him before he went to whatever it was he had to go to. Instead, I got his recording. "You just missed me," it said. "Leave a message."

"Call me," I said in the most confident voice I could muster. Then I added softly, "Please."

I needed to get out of the newsroom, I decided. Traffic was light and I made it home in record time, pulling into the garage as the winter sun was setting. When I walked in the kitchen, the girls were watching TV and our neighbor, Helmey (rhymes with "tell me") Andersen, had his head stuck under the sink.

"Uncle" Helmey, as the girls call him, had rented the unit above us for twenty years when we bought the duplex. He retired from his job as a butcher about five years ago. When his wife of forty-nine years, Marilyn, died a year ago, he adopted our family and we adopted him.

He's not a very big guy, maybe five foot six or seven, and no more than 140 pounds. He lost most of his blond hair long before we knew him and his face is what the girls call "craggy," with wrinkles that have turned into canyons. The crow's feet around his eyes are deep from many years of smiling. His parents named him Hjelme after the town in Norway where they were born, but no American could figure out the pronunciation so he changed it to Helmey.

"Helmey, what's going on?" I dumped my purse and keys on the kitchen table before hanging up my coat and hat. The house smelled of wet woolen mittens and chicken noodle soup.

"Rebecca called," he said, pulling his head out from under the sink and sitting back down on his heels. His toolbox rested on the floor beside him. "Looks like someone put something too big down the garbage disposal and backed it up. I'll have it working in no time."

"Helmey, I don't know what we'd do without you. Can I persuade you to stay for dinner?"

"I think that's possible," I think he replied. It was hard to tell exactly what he had said because his head was back under the sink. I set a place at the table for him.

Soon we were gathered around our kitchen table, munching on grilled-cheese sandwiches and the soup Rebecca had made. I asked the girls about their day in school and Suzy launched into a lengthy tale about the boy who had thrown up and had to go home.

"You shoulda seen the puke. It was gross."

"How was your math test today, Rebecca?" I asked, trying to turn the conversation to something a little more palatable for the table.

"Fine."

"Fine. Does that mean hard? Easy? You think you aced it?"

"I aced it," she said, before sucking in a long noodle.

All day long I dreaded telling the girls about the del Sol, but I couldn't put it off any longer.

"Ah, girls, something happened at work that you might find troubling. Remember last night when I had to go out and cover that explosion? Well, the car caught fire too."

Rebecca looked up from her soup, startled. "Mom, what happened? Are you all right?"

"I'm fine, but I'm afraid the car is toasted a lot blacker than your grilled-cheese sandwich."

"Do reporters' cars usually burn up?" asked Suzy, my intuitive one.

"I don't know any other reporter whose car caught fire during work."

"Why did it happen to us?" Suzy again.

"Bad luck, I guess."

"What did Dad say?" Rebecca wanted to know.

"I haven't told him yet."

"Boy, wait 'til he hears about this one," Rebecca said.

It was quiet around the table while we chewed over the idea.

"Damn," shouted Rebecca. "I had an Eminem CD in the glove compartment."

Good news, I thought. One less Eminem CD in the world.

"Oh my God," shouted Rebecca. "Our soccer stuff was in the trunk."

I promised her we'd get new equipment.

"You know, I think there are some soccer balls and shin pads in our basement from when our boys played," Helmey said. "You're welcome to use them until you can get your own new ones."

Once again, I offered a prayer to the gods of parents, thanking them for Helmey.

"You were in love with that car." Suzy's voice was sympathetic. "Are you going to get another one?"

"I don't know. Honda doesn't make del Sols any more."

"That sucks seriously awful," Rebecca chimed in. "Paper going to buy us another car?"

"We're talking about that." I didn't want to lie but I didn't want to scare her either.

The only sound in the kitchen was the scrape of spoons on soup bowls as we absorbed what had happened.

"Rebecca said she wanted a loft in her room to give her more space underneath," Helmey said, breaking the somber mood. "You know, I built a loft for one of my boys when he was in college—can't remember which boy it was, now—but it's not that hard to do. Would it be all right if I built one for her?"

"Oh, Uncle Helmey, would you?" Rebecca looked like she was going to jump off her chair and kiss him. "That would be so cool."

"That's a big undertaking, Helmey," I replied. "Are you sure you want to do that?"

"It's winter. I like indoor projects in winter. The girls can help me."

"It's fine with me if you want to do it. Thank you."

Announcing that she had homework to do, Rebecca stood up from the table and went to her room. Suzy was almost falling asleep so I picked her up and put her to bed. When I got back, Helmey was scraping the last dish into the now-working garbage disposal and putting it in the dishwasher.

"Want a cup of coffee, Helmey?"

"Don't mind if I do there, Skeeter," he said. "You know me. Typical Scandinavian. I could drink strong coffee until midnight and still sleep like a baby."

I looked out our kitchen window as Helmey and I sat at the table, sipping coffee. A gentle snow was falling like flour from some giant sifter. The moon was bright and the halo created by the snow around the street lights reminded me of the Christmas cards I used to send out every year BK—before kids.

"So how's the news biz?" Helmey asked.

"Complicated, Helmey. Plenty complicated."

"Sounds like there's a tale to share," he said.

"I can't talk about this part of my work with my girls. Life is scary enough for them without including a threat on Mom among the things to worry about. Michael's busy."

"Too busy to listen to his wife?"

"You know Michael. He's always chasing a story."

"So let good ol' Uncle Helmey lend an ear."

I laid out the whole mess for him, beginning with Billie's disappearance and ending with the e-mail.

"When the newspaper prints your e-mail address and phone number in the paper every day, you get a lot of kooks who see you as a convenient target for their rage. Anyone who hates what I've written can yell at me. And they do. A lot. I usually reply with a polite 'thanks,' and hang up, or if it's e-mail, delete."

"But this e-mailer knew you had been asking about Billie, knew you had been at the Mall of America, knew your car was fire-bombed," Helmey said. "This was personal."

"Yeah, but it is also a sign that I'm on to something with this story about Billie and what I saw at the mall, and the meth lab explosion," I replied. "How are they related? Does it mean Billie is alive and hiding? Or kidnapped and hidden? Or dead? Or a drug dealer?"

"What do you think?"

"She doesn't strike me as the kind who would run away. She's too strong for that. Her co-worker, Joey, said she was a spit-in-your-eye kind of girl. Why would someone kidnap her?"

"Maybe she was dealing drugs and didn't pay somebody," Helmey said. "Those are pretty rough people. When Marilyn and I were young this was a real safe city. We never even locked our doors. If people were smoking funny cigarettes they kept it to themselves. Now you read about some gang shooting every day, and you know it's about drugs."

"Maybe," I replied. "I sure hope I don't have to write a story about a girl who went missing, then turned up dead. The e-mail definitely means Billie was more than just a teenage girl who skipped town to get away from Mom and Dad."

"Why don't you tell the police what you think?" Helmey asked.

It was a reasonable question. "I've thought about that, Helmey, and here's the problem. If I go to the police now, that could make me an active participant in their investigation. Potential sources have good reason to distrust reporters who are working with the police."

"Cops aren't even looking for her," Helmey said. "You said so yourself."

"I know. And instinct tells me there's plenty more here than I've uncovered so far. More coffee?"

As I went to the counter to get Helmey his second cup, I looked out the back window at the garage. It was wicked black out there because neither Michael nor I had replaced the burned out light bulb. I caught myself staring at the garage door, willing it to open as Michael's car came down the drive.

"What are you going to do about your del Sol?"

"I figure if we have to rely on our insurance to replace the car, our rates are going to go up for sure."

"You know, Skeeter, this is dangerous stuff you're playing with." Helmey finished the last sip of his coffee. "Be careful."

Chapter 13

After getting the girls off to school in the morning, I headed for work, arriving about 8:45 when the newsroom was practically empty. Most reporters don't roll in until 9 or 9:30. The few who arrived earlier were reading the paper, surfing the Internet, or reading wire stories on their computer screens, coffee cups in hand.

It looks like they're being lazy, but mostly they're stuffing facts in their heads to be called out later. Anyone who has been in the business for even a few years is a walking file cabinet full of information normal people don't even try to retain. Wanna know how many Republicans have been elected governor of Minnesota? How about the year Spiro Agnew resigned as U.S. vice president, and why? Ask a reporter and odds are good you'll get an answer sooner than you can say Google.

But knowing stuff and thinking are two different skills. And this morning, thinking was high on my to-do list. I needed to talk to someone. I looked around the newsroom, and the only one who didn't appear to be exceptionally busy was Thom. I debated whether to approach him. I was still fuming about his cavalier attitude toward my life.

When I was in journalism school at the University of Minnesota, Thom was an adjunct professor who taught a class on reporting. He had been an editor for only six months, but it was obvious he knew his craft. In between teaching us how to do telephone interviews, face-to-face interviews, and how to question kids, he waxed philosophical about the importance of newspapers to the community. It doesn't matter, he said, whether people buy the newspaper for the comics, the sports page, the bridge column, or news of the latest scandal in city hall. What matters, he said, is that reporters and editors give them context. It's not enough to tell them that the mayor and police chief are fighting, he said. Television can do that. Newspapers have to tell readers that the mayor hates the police chief because he didn't support him in the last election. Then they have to tell them the chief hates the mayor because he ran on a soft-on-crime platform.

"Newspapers that don't give context every day are doomed to fail in direct proportion to the growth of the Internet and television," was his mantra in class. He only had to say that once and I was hooked on journalism. It was Thom who offered me the job in Minneapolis when I was ready to leave the paper in Rochester.

We've wrangled plenty of times, occasionally for fun, often because we tend to see the world differently. As time has gone by Thom has become increasingly tied into the newspaper's corporate line, while every day I see more problems with it. It seems he's begun to think the primary role of newspapers is to give shareholders the best return on their money, while I think newspapers should be keeping their readers informed while making enough profit to stay in business.

I decided to put that philosophical discussion on a shelf and focus on finding Billie. "Got time for a cup of coffee, Thom?"

"I suppose." He's so tall he has to bend to push the button on the elevator to go to the second floor, where we took a right to the skyway.

The common perception is the skyways—essentially glass tubes that cross streets and connect buildings in downtown Minneapolis and St. Paul—were built to allow pedestrians to scurry all of downtown comfortably even in the dead of winter. Actually, that's not true, according to a city planner I once interviewed. Skyways were built to add a second layer of storefront retail to increase the city's tax base and separate pedestrian from auto traffic. It was a side benefit that the skyways are an effective deterrent to frostbite in January.

Whatever the reason, they meant Thom and I could walk to the nearest coffee shop without dressing up like the Michelin Man.

"What's up?" said Thom, gripping his latte with both hands.

"I'm wrestling with this Billie Berry thing."

I told him the whole story—about the guy at the mall, the threatening e-mail. "I'm not sure where to go next."

"Why didn't you tell me about the e-mail, Skeeter? Or any of this?"

"Last night I was too pissed to talk to you after you said you guys weren't going to pay for my car, which, by the way, we still have to talk about."

"OK, I'll try to talk to the publisher about your car. She likes you."

"She does?" I replied. "I never knew that."

"I'll tell the public safety reporters to nose around, find out if there's any more detail from the meth lab explosion or complaints about men hustling girls at the mall."

"What do you mean, she likes me?" I asked, hoping there was a raise in my future. He brushed me off.

"What about the rumor about the guy getting fired by the Land o' Lakes school board? A principal or superintendent? Why'd he get canned? Remember that story out of Fargo a few months ago about an assistant principal getting the ax for having sex with a student? Is that what's going on in Land o' Lakes? Is there any connection between the Land o' Lakes firing and Billie? Context, Hughes. Context. Have you checked on the divorce papers on the Berrys?"

"I looked at *Berry vs. Berry*. What a mess. I forgot to check into the principal. I'll get on it.

First, tell me how you know she's got a soft spot for me."

"Who?"

"The publisher," I replied, raising my voice enough to make the man reading the paper at the next table look up.

" 'Soft spot' is a bit strong," he said with a tiny smile. "I had lunch with her and some of the other editors a month ago and she mentioned that you do good work."

"Did she mention a particular piece? Was it the profile I wrote last month about the mayor of Land o'Lakes? Didn't she go to college with him or something? I bet that was it. He told me to send her his greetings but I never did. Yeah, that was it. The profile. That's the best piece I've done in awhile."

"She didn't mention anything specific. Can we get back to the story here, Skeeter? See what you can find out today, and we'll talk in the morning. Meanwhile, I won't give you any daily assignments until you get this figured out."

The combination of the triple espresso and a chat with Thom got me revved up again. I hauled back into the newsroom like Superwoman trying to make up for lost time. My first task was to call back all my sources on the school board. The possibility that the removed principal was somehow involved in the disappearance of Billie was a long shot, but worth pursuing. Half a dozen phone calls later, I got lucky.

"This is Skeeter Hughes from the *Citizen*. Is Mrs. Peters there?"

"I'll put you right through," said her assistant.

Hmmmm, I thought. Now that was a first.

"Well, hello, Skeeter. It's nice to hear from you," said the newest member of the school board.

Marilyn Peters was a neighborhood activist who paid her dues in years of tedious meetings before running for the Land o' Lakes school board against an incumbent whose family had owned half the farmland that turned corn into housing dollars. It was a squeaker to the finish, with a recount putting her ahead by just twenty votes. I covered her campaign.

"Hi. I'm calling to check on the vote Monday night firing the principal."

"It's considered private unless someone is actually let go," she said.

"So does that mean no one was fired?"

"If someone had been fired it would be a matter of public record. There is no public record on this matter so you can draw your own conclusion."

"Mrs. Peters, please don't be coy with me. If there's a principal who has been fired, or a principal who ought to be fired, readers—especially parents—need to know that. Would I be correct in assuming that there was a vote to get rid of somebody that failed to pass?"

"That would be one interpretation."

"Come on. You know me. You know I always do my best to report fair and square. Verbal acrobatics aren't good for anyone."

"OK. Can we go off the record?"

I hate letting sources go off the record. It usually means one of two things: either they're going to tell a lie, or at least a heavily shaded half-truth, to get back at someone they hate; or they're going to say something true and important but next to impossible to confirm with anyone else.

If I let a source tell me something off the record, it means I have to be willing to go to jail to protect her if I put what she said in the paper and somebody else takes exception. I don't want to go to jail. I'm allergic to cinderblock and the fluorescent lights make me look washed out. Plus my behind is too big for those jumpsuits they make you wear. But Thom was on me to get the information, and no one else was going to help me.

"OK. Shoot."

"We had a report that the principal of one of the middle schools was involved in a prostitution ring. The rumor was that he was picking up high school girls at the Mall of America by buying them clothes. That was all it was. A rumor. The evidence was shaky at best. Certainly not enough to remove him."

"What'd the board do?"

"This is serious stuff. We can't have somebody like that running one of our schools. But if we fire him based on a single report that turns out to be false, or even unproved, we open ourselves up for a huge lawsuit. So we voted to keep him in the job until he is charged and convicted of a crime."

"Who is he?"

"I'm not comfortable telling you that. I trust you will not let anyone know I told you this much. This is a tough matter. We have to protect our students, but we can't jeopardize a police investigation or the reputation of a man who is considered innocent."

"I promise no one will know where I heard it," I said. "I'm curious. Can you tell me why you shared this information with me?"

"Because I know you and trust you. And because there are a few city officials who would like to cover this up. Keep your eyes open, Skeeter. You may pick up hints about this in the future and I want you to know what's going on behind the scenes."

I said thanks and hung up the phone. While talking to Marilyn Peters I had heard the little click on the line that told me there was another call waiting. I checked the caller ID and saw the number for Michael's cell phone. Afraid that if I took his call it would take me forever to get her back again, I let him slide over into voice mail, which I checked immediately.

"You must be yapping away on your phone again," he said. "Hope you aren't beating me on a story."

I called his cell phone right away, but got his recording. Damn.

"Sorry I missed you, sweetie," I said. "Talk to you tonight."

Meanwhile, I got back to thinking about what Marilyn had said. I couldn't help but wonder: Is the guy I saw at the mall the principal with the side business in prostitution? Is this related to Billie Berry's disappearance? Or is there more than one scandal brewing in Land o'Lakes?

Context, Hughes. Context. Think context.

There was only one way to find out if the guy I saw was the principal in hot water. It was time to head to Land o' Lakes again.

Chapter 14

I logged on to the Internet and punched "Land o' Lakes Minnesota middle schools" into Google. Four schools popped up. When I checked for the names of principals I found that two were women. That helped my search. I clicked on the map icon and printed out two sheets of paper with directions to each remaining school. Then I snagged my coat, pulled on my boots, and headed for the elevator.

I zipped along the highway, reveling in the cold but gorgeous day. The high temperature was supposed to make the mid-teens. No self-respecting piece of dirt hangs around in that kind of cold, so the air freezes to crystal clear. Rays of sun shot through the windshield, warming my face. And me without my sun block.

I wanted to eyeball the two principals to see if either was the man I had spied upon at the mall. I never try to interview people without first telling them who I am. I was going to have to tell someone there who I was. But I couldn't sashay up to the office window and say, "Hi, I'm here from the newspaper to find out if your principal is enticing girls into prostitution." I was still working on a plan as I walked into the building.

"Hi, I'm Skeeter Hughes from the *Citizen*," I said to a woman sitting behind a desk. "Is your principal in?"

"He's in the cafeteria. Can I help you?"

"No, I really need to talk to him. Can you direct me to the lunch-room and tell me what he looks like. This won't take a minute."

"I suppose that will be OK. Just go down this hall and take a left. You'll see it from there. He's about six feet tall, wearing a red shirt today. You can't miss him."

My heartbeat was well up into the anaerobic range as I turned and followed the sound of kids laughing and dishes clanking. The smell of boiled hot dogs, orange pop, and wet wool told me I was getting close. I tried to glide unnoticed into the lunchroom and looked around. Most kids were sitting at tables eating. A bunch of boys in the back seemed to be giggling and pointing at a table of girls in front of them. The sight reminded me of my own days in junior high, especially the lunch period when Buzzy Jones, who I thought was the cutest boy on earth, was sitting right behind me. I'd wanted to talk to him all year, and finally, just as I gathered the courage to wave, a boy at another table threw a full carton of chocolate milk, which tipped off my raised hand, spilling the chocolate all over the girl who was sitting next to me. She let out a scream, which drew the attention of the nun who was in charge of keeping order in the lunchroom.

I can still see Sister Rose of Lima striding across the lunchroom at me, feel her grab my shoulder to spin me around, then demand to know who had thrown the carton. I refused to tell, even though I knew exactly who the culprit was. Next thing I knew I was sitting in detention, accused, unfairly I might add, of throwing a carton of milk in the cafeteria. I never did talk to Buzzy, but the incident launched my reputation as tough and trustworthy in the seventh grade. I've been doing my best to maintain that rep ever since.

Gazing across the Land o' Lakes lunchroom, I spied a tall man wearing a red shirt, but he definitely was not the guy. This principal was African American, and the guy was definitely white. My heart rate began to slow as I turned on my heel and hauled out of there.

Moments later, I was in the car, heading east on Highway 5 toward the remaining middle school on my list. Students were milling about outside as I pulled into the parking lot. Even when it's very cold, schools usually try to get the kids to go outside for a few minutes at least during lunch time, to give them a chance to air out. Half the kids I saw on the school lot were hatless and the other half had forgotten to zip up their jackets. There must be some goddess who keeps most kids from catching pneumonia in this kind of weather.

A different goddess was watching over me that day. From my parking spot, I spied a man outside talking with some of the kids. Like them, he was without a hat, but his jacket was zipped. He looked to be about six feet tall, maybe 180 pounds. Blond with a touch of grey at the temples. Big blue eyes. I didn't have to hear his voice to know who he was.

I watched him for a while from the car. Half a dozen boys and girls gathered around him, laughing as though someone had told a great joke. I watched him put his arm around one of the girls and whisper something in her ear. She was a bit chunky and dressed plainly compared to the other girls on the playground. She looked up at him with a smile reminiscent of Monica Lewinsky's greeting President Bill Clinton in that video clip played over and over again in the late 1990s. It was a smile that said, "We have a secret." The sight turned my stomach.

I had to confirm that the man I saw was the principal and look up his name. Then I would have one small piece in the puzzle called finding Billie. I locked the car and headed into the school, once again formulating a plan as I walked. But it turned out the man's ego saved me the trouble. Hanging on a wall in the entrance was a large, framed four-color picture of the man with a sign that said, "Principal Matthew McClintock welcomes you to John F. Kennedy Middle School."

Chapter 15

Mission accomplished, I jumped in the car and headed downtown. As I drove I ran through the facts in my head. McClintock was definitely the guy I saw buying clothes in the mall for what appeared to be a teenage girl he met there for the first time. McClintock was a middle-school principal who likely was suspected of picking up girls in the mall and later turning them into prostitutes. Billie Berry spent a lot of time at the mall, and her wardrobe had expanded dramatically in the past few months. Her mom wondered where Billie got the money for clothes she certainly hadn't bought.

Someone who didn't want me asking questions about Billie knew I was at the mall and that my car was firebombed when a methamphetamine lab blew up. Billie's mom and dad went through a rancorous divorce, and Billie's mom was suspicious that her dad didn't seem upset enough that Billie had been missing since Friday night.

All that thinking made me hungry. News is important, but a girl's gotta eat. I pulled into the newspaper's ramp, locked the car, then hiked a block to Subway, where I ordered a twelve-inch turkey sub on whole wheat with cheese and mayo. Subway bag in hand, I jogged back to the building, headed up in the elevator to the third floor, hung a left, and strolled fifty feet to my desk.

When I fired up my computer the picture of the girls flashed on my desktop screen. I gave a little smile, then turned my head back into reporter mode. Something Marilyn Peters said kept tickling the back of my mind, but I couldn't figure out what it was, so I turned to the pile of releases from the folks of Land o' Lakes that littered my desk. Safety officers wanted us to remind residents that cars illegally parked on snowplow routes would be unceremoniously ticketed and towed during declared snow emergencies. Furthermore, driving on lakes with less than ten inches of ice was a bad idea, they said. Every year, some idiot with slush for brains ignores that little tip. And finally, this hint of spring: all ice-fishing houses had to be off the lakes by the end of February, when the ice begins to thaw. I wrote up a brief on the fishing-house item, then picked up the St. Paul *Courier* to see what the competition was covering.

The Twin Cities is one of the few metropolitan areas in the country that still has more than one major newspaper. The Minneapolis paper has a bigger staff, a bigger circulation, and, I always argue with Michael, is a better newspaper. He comes back with the charge that his newspaper may be smaller but it has more heart. And the *Citizen* is arrogant, he always adds.

I'm told the same argument continues across many kitchen tables, given that both newspapers employ couples. Journalism is a consuming, high stress profession, best understood by other journalists. Relationships among the staff are inevitable, and that can create a different set of problems.

I started in the news business in utero. My mother wrote a weekly column for our neighborhood broadsheet, the paper of record and the beacon for those eager to know about planning and zoning changes, the school lunch menu, and whose kid had broken into whose garage. It was the stuff that held the community together, the stuff big daily newspapers later discarded because studies showed readers in the desirable eighteen-to-thirtyfive demographic didn't care anymore.

Mom always said writing the column was her only chance to sit down while raising me and my five brothers. She said I was born with a genetic instant response to sirens, not only because she liked to chase them, but because my father was a fireman. In fact, that was how they met.

Mom had started writing the column while she attended community college, first because she needed some newspaper experience for a class, later because she liked it and needed the money. One night she was taking her column to her editor—this was when they wrote on paper with a typewriter—when a fire truck passed her, sirens blaring, red and white lights flashing. Her column was done an hour early because she had planned to hit the bar with some girl-friends after turning it in. Instead, she followed the sirens.

As she tells what has become family lore, she came upon a duplex fully engulfed in flame a few blocks away. "We're talking about flames shooting five feet out the windows," she always says at this part of the story. Firemen braced themselves on the sidewalk in front while they shot water through the broken windows, trying to douse the flame. Mother knew she was less than an hour away from deadline. No time to run back to the little storefront office that served as the newsroom to get a camera. "I always wanted to shoot the photos, too," she says at this point.

Instead, she used a neighbor's phone to call the photographer, who she happened to be dating. Then she went to each of the firemen, got their names—"spelled correctly," she says—and garnered as many facts as she could. Just as she got the final name she heard a cry for help. Someone was in the upper duplex window, shouting. One of the firemen dropped his hose and rushed to the spot below just as a huge woman—"She had to be 300 pounds," Mom always says—jumped. The poor fireman had his arms out, ready to break her fall. Instead, the woman caught him in the upper chest, flattening that sucker so bad both their bodies dented a plot of hostas deep enough to dig a six-inch hole. That fireman—and here's where she really winds up the tale—"was NOT your father," she would say, laughing hysterically. "He was home with the flu that night."

In fact, the flattened fireman was married with four kids. My dad was his best buddy, who was visiting him in the hospital when my mom went to interview the hero for a follow up. "I thought he had a cute butt," is how Mom recalls her first meeting with Dad. They dated a year then married. She never tells us what happened with the photographer.

In any event, I was reading the *Courier* closely, as I always do, when I happened upon a short item picked up from the *Portland Oregonian*. It seems the city treasurer of one of the suburbs out there had been indicted on charges of drug trafficking and prostitution. That's when it struck me. Marilyn said that some city officials were trying to quash the investigation into McClintock's extracurricular activities. Who might they be? Why would they care if he were brought up on charges? What were they trying to cover up, I wondered. And then the bigger question: How could I find out?

I sincerely doubted Marilyn would tell me. It was clear she was uncomfortable sharing as much as she had. I would have to plumb my other sources. I thought back to the last election. The mayor and six of the thirteen city council members were all new. Hostilities between winners and losers often linger after the election is over, so I went looking in the losers circle for the folks with the most to gain by talking with me.

Compiling a list of losers and their phone numbers was tedious, but by mid afternoon I had the information and started what I like to call "dialing for the dope." I talked to two answering machines, two office assistants, and two losers. None of them knew what I was talking about. Then I got through to Gladys Swenson, who had run against the mayor, Joe Baldwin.

"Hi, Mrs. Swenson. This is Skeeter Hughes from the *Citizen*. How are you today?"

"I'm fine, Skeeter, but I'm sure you're not calling solely to check on my health." Then she let loose with a slurpy, down-to-the-bottom-of-her-lungs cough, which reminded me she had barely made it through the League of Women Voters debate because she needed a cigarette so badly.

"What can I do for you?" Good old Gladys was as much a straight-shooter now as she had been during the election.

"This is a wild guess," I replied, "but I was wondering if you knew of any connections between Mayor Baldwin and Matthew McClintock, the principal at Kennedy Middle School."

"What kind of connection?"

Here's where my line of questioning got dicey. I didn't want to tell her McClintock was under investigation for possible links to prostitution. She'd probably already heard the rumor, but if she hadn't, I didn't want to be the one to start it. It was a good story and I wanted to keep it to myself until it was time to publish. It wouldn't take much for my competitor from the *Courier* to hear about it if Gladys Swenson knew I was nosing around.

"I was wondering if they were friends, or relatives maybe," I replied, sounding a little lame even to me.

"I'm not sure what your motives are here, Skeeter, but you've always treated me fairly, so I'll tell you what little I know," she said. "When we did our research on Mr. Baldwin before I ran for office, we found that he had some business partnership with McClintock. It was a privately held company, so we got very little information about it. I don't know how big it is, or even what it does, and to tell you the truth I can't remember the name of the outfit. As I recall, it was formed a few years ago."

I thanked her for the information and hung up. Whoa, I said to myself. If the creep procuring girls at the mall was tied to the mayor, my publisher's old college chum, this could be much bigger than I had thought. If that turned out to be true, I hoped the publisher would remember that she likes me. I'd have to dig a little harder and see if there was more I could find out about this company.

That's tough to do without a name. I called the state attorney general's office to see if there was any incorporation listing either one of them. Zip. Whatever "partnership" they had was off the books. Maybe Gladys had her information wrong. It wouldn't be the first time that a candidate for public office operated more on gossip than fact.

Just to try one more shot, I wandered down to the end of the newsroom where the business reporters worked. The market hadn't quite closed yet, so I snagged Laura Billings, a reporter and friend with whom I shared a couple of classes in journalism school. I asked her if there were any other way I could find out what kind of a business connection Baldwin and McClintock might have had. She said that without a name for the company, I was out of luck.

I stopped at the bathroom on my way back, grabbed a cup of the late morning coffee from the newsroom pot—always an act of desperation—and headed back for my desk.

I'd only been gone from my desk for half an hour, but my inbox had twenty-two e-mail messages and the light on my phone was blinking like a firefly. Apparently a lot of people had been trying to get hold of me while I was snooping around middle schools. I decided to go through the phone messages first. The first three were from readers commenting on stuff I wrote last month, and frankly didn't remember very well. The fourth gave me chills.

"I won't warn you again," said what sounded like a woman trying to disguise her voice deep by talking through a hanky over the mouthpiece of her phone. The line went dead.

I took several deep breaths to try to get over my fear. I had never been threatened before, and had certainly never been threatened twice in two days, so I figured yesterday's e-mail and today's voice mails were coming from the same person. The second message told me the person was probably female, and not terribly sophisticated. I wasn't sure if that made me feel more frightened or less. A pro would know that harming a newspaper reporter is right up there with shooting a cop in the stupid-move department.

Chapter 16

Everyone has a different reaction to fear. Mine is food. Actually, food, especially chocolate, is my solution to most of life's problems. Time for lunch, I decided.

Eating at the computer can be risky business. Unfortunately, I do it all the time. I'm now on my fourth keyboard because I keep dropping mayonnaise-covered crumbs between the keys. The people who run our technology department are not among my fans.

I munched on my Subway sandwich while I checked www. minnpost.com, then surfed the online editions of our paper, the St. Paul paper, Minnesota Public Radio, and the TV stations to find out whether I had missed any news from the morning. Some guy who kept a full-grown Bengal tiger in his St. Paul apartment got his hand bitten off. A foot of snow was forecast for the next twenty-four hours. A bank robber in Richfield jumped in the wrong getaway car that happened to be driven by an off-duty cop who drove him to the police station where he was apprehended. Real news is always better than anything I can make up.

I balled up the tissue paper from the sandwich and stuffed it in the now empty milk carton I had bought to go with it, then flicked my wrist to land the whole thing into a waste basket about six feet away. I left the double chocolate-chocolate chip cookie on my desk for later, hoping no one would snatch it if I went to the bathroom.

Meanwhile, I turned the Billie story over in my head. Joey Pignatello, Billie's co-worker, knew more about Billie's life than her own mother. But Joey seemed to be wrong about Billie being such a straight arrow. If what Nate was hearing was true, Billie was somehow involved in prostitution. It's not hard to figure how that squared with her wanting to be a cop. I've often heard police reporters say that the line that divides the cops from the crooks is a very fine one. They're both drawn to the adrenaline rush that comes with dancing close to each other. Maybe Billie was unsure where the line fell for her.

Nate also said he'd heard a rumor that she was involved in methamphetamine. Could he have meant the meth lab that blew up?

I had been trying to forget about that night, but then I flashed back on the girl who had fled. I didn't get a very good look at her in the dark. I only remembered that she had short, blond spiked hair. Then something else occurred to me. I picked up the phone and called Cathy Berry again. It took her eight rings to pick up. The woman needs an answering machine in case Billie calls, I thought.

"Hello," she said very slowly.

"Mrs. Berry, it's Skeeter. I have another question. Does Billie have a belly-button stud?"

"Doesn't every girl her age have one?" I could hear her eyebrow arch.

"So she does have a belly-button stud, right?"

"Yes, she does."

"What does it look like?"

"Well, it's metal. Gold, I think. Oh, yes, I remember now. It's in the shape of a shamrock," she said.

I jetted my fist into the air and mentally shouted, "Yes!"

"Thanks. I'll talk with you again later," I said, hanging up before she could question me.

That meant the girl I saw run away from the meth house was Billie, which meant that she was at least alive and likely in town, thank God. This was a story about disappearance, not death, at least so far. Could the e-mail and phone messages have come from her? That would suggest that she didn't want to be found.

When my phone's caller ID showed Cathy called back, I let it roll over into voice mail, suspecting she was going to ask me about the belly button ring. I wasn't ready to wrangle with her if I had to tell her there was no story there. Which there wasn't if Billie was just a runaway.

But what if Billie was being held against her will? What if she had been enticed into some prostitution ring? The teen prostitutes who had appeared on the "Oprah" show talked about how hard it was to leave the life. One girl said she had been paid $935 for a fifteen-minute topless dance. It would be awfully tough to turn down that kind of money, especially for a girl who had little financial or emotional support at home.

The "father figure" recruiters showed them the only real affection they had ever experienced. Was that what Billie felt? The question led me to wonder about Billie's father, Peter Berry.

The results of my Internet search for Peter Berry surprised me. He held an undergraduate degree in marketing and a master's in sociology from Michigan State University. He also had a Ph.D. in psychology from Berkeley, and a host of academic papers on eating disorders among upwardly mobile girls. I checked to see if he had a criminal record (no), the value of his geodesic dome house ($525,000), whether he voted and paid his taxes (yes to both). A check on his psychologist's license turned up more interesting information: It seems he'd had half a dozen complaints filed against him. The record didn't disclose the nature of the complaints, just that they had been resolved and he was still licensed.

I wondered what prompted the complaints. Were they serious? Did he take advantage of a patient? Was the amiable Peter Berry an abuser? Was he the source of those bruises on Cathy Berry's arm? Or was he just another victim of a litigious society? Because he was still licensed there was no public record that would tell me the specifics about the complaints. If I asked him about the complaints there would be no way that I could verify whether he told me the truth.

As I turned to skimming e-mails, hoping there were no more threats, Thom happened by. "Where have you been?"

"Out tracking down details on the principal."

He said he wanted to hear about it, but he was on his way into a meeting. Then he added that one of the cop reporters was looking for me.

"Something about that meth lab explosion," he said over his shoulder walking away.

I stood up and looked around the newsroom, which is long and narrow. The police reporters sat about half a block away, but I could see that someone was down there, talking on the phone. I ambled toward his desk, catching snippets of conversation on the way.

"Ma'am, I'm going to have to hang up if you continue to use that language with me."

And, "I understand you were eye to eye with her breasts, but how tall are you?"

And, "If you boys don't stop fighting there will be no television for either one of you tonight."

Some of the most tenacious reporters can be the most absent-minded. One day a few years ago I looked up from my computer to see a reporter who has won several awards, including a Pulitzer, walking the length of the newsroom with a six-foot tail of toilet paper flapping from the back of his pants. He came back and sat at his computer, oblivious to the fashion faux pas. Because I like the guy, I shot off a quick e-mail to the reporter who sat opposite him. I put the message simply in the subject line: "You've got to tell him."

In seconds came the reply: "I told him last time. It's someone else's turn."

The stereotypical police reporter is some big, hard-drinking hairy guy whose favorite word is "fuck." While that's true in some cases, the reality is that women are as likely as men to cover public safety. Most of the time, print cops reporters are introspective types who like the work because it gives them an unobstructed view of the human condition. A woman I know who did it for about five years said it was better coursework in sociology then anything she had ever taken in college.

"Hey, Skeeter, how ya doin'?" said Ramon Luiz, his Brooklyn accent still strong six years after he came to the Twin Cities with his wife and two sons. When I asked him once why he left New York City, he said it was because he wanted to live in a state where cities have names like Golden Valley, Eden Prairie and New Hope.

"Good job covering the meth lab explosion Monday night," he said.

"Thanks. Whatcha got there?"

"The report is in and I thought you might be interested because there are some odd details here among the usual stuff," he said.

"Like what?"

"The cops figure the explosion closed down a $2 million operation that had been in business for about four years. They found the charred remains of all the stuff you need to make meth."

"So?"

"So, in the back of the house they found a pristine room with a bed with satin sheets, K-Y jelly left on a bedside table, and lingerie hanging in the closet— the stuff of prostitution."

"So the bad guys were running prostitution and making meth," I said. "So what?"

"That's unusual," he replied. "Usually guys makin' meth don't want the traffic that comes with hookers."

"Does the report say anything about the girl who kicked the cop in the balls and split?"

"What girl? It doesn't say anything about any girl."

"There was a girl, about eighteen, white, short spiked blond hair, kinda chunky, who got beat up by some guys and fled into the night. Is there any mention of that in there?"

"Not a word."

Once again, my antennae were tingling. How could they not mention the girl? Maybe the cop was embarrassed that she got away so easily. Still, it seemed odd that she wasn't even part of the report. I wasn't ready to share my suspicions in the newsroom yet, so I kept my wonderings to myself.

"So, you gettin' a new car, then?"

"That's another piece of my life that's complicated right now. Thom says the official word is that the paper pays us 46½ cents a mile to use our own cars, so whatever happens to it is our responsibility."

"You gotta be kiddin'."

"No, trust me, I would never kid about that. Thom is looking into it, trying to see if the publisher can get around the corporate bean counters."

"Good luck."

"Thanks. If you hear any more about the meth lab thing, let me know, OK?"

"You betcha," he said, Brooklyn accent and all, just as I was hearing my name called in a newsroom-wide page.

"Hughes. Phone call."

I headed back to my desk where my phone was ringing and picked up the receiver, without looking at the caller ID first. Unfortunately.

Chapter 17

"Skeeter Hughes."

"Skeeter, this is Cathy Berry. Why did you ask about Billie's navel ring?"

It was a direct question I couldn't dodge, so I didn't try.

"Because I saw a girl who had one like hers," I said.

"Where did you see this girl?"

"She was involved in a meth lab explosion."

"I can't imagine Billie being involved in methamphetamine. Do you think the girl you saw was Billie?"

"Probably," I replied.

"Have you any idea how many girls have shamrock-shaped belly button rings?" she asked. "I'll tell you. There are lots. I was appalled when Billie wanted to get hers, but she said half her class at school had pierced their belly buttons, and other even more disgusting parts. And their volleyball team is the Fighting Irish, so shamrock is a very popular choice among the girls."

"Now, let's get to something more likely," she said, dismissing the matter for something more important to her. "I was thinking about your questions regarding Billie going to the mall, so I looked through her closet. There's something I want you to see. You need to come out here, now."

"Mrs. Berry, a snowstorm is moving in. There's already six inches on the ground and they're predicting at least six more. Can't you tell me what you found?"

"No, I cannot. If you care about this, you'll come here."

I was beginning to realize why Billie didn't return to her mother's house. The woman knew which buttons to push to get what she wanted. Asking me if I care about a story gets my attention like a slap across the face with a leather glove. I peered across the newsroom trying to see through the window. Darkness was falling as fast as the snow, which created haloes around the streetlights. Plus, it was getting toward rush hour, when the roads from the city to the suburbs would be clogged with drivers, not to mention new snow. I had planned to cut out of the newsroom early and spend a little quality time with my daughters.

"All right," I said. "I'll be out there as soon as I can."

I called the girls to tell them I might be late for dinner. Suzy answered. "Dad called. I told him Uncle Helmey was staying with us and the car burned up. He said he was glad about Uncle Helmey. He wants you to call him."

She didn't see me grimace as I told her I loved her and hung up. That was not the way I wanted him to hear about the car, but what was done, was done. I couldn't talk with him about it right now, thank heaven. Besides, he probably assumed the newspaper would happily cover it.

I grabbed my cell phone, which had been charging for about two minutes, along with my hat, mittens, and jacket, and clunked to the elevator in my Sorel boots. Down to the skyway and over to the Haaf ramp and into the fleet car. I dialed the radio to 88.5 FM so I could be sure to get traffic updates as I drove—or, more accurately, crawled—to Cathy Berry's house. Twenty-five minutes later, I was sitting at the ramp, trying to get to 35W south. Many of the two-lane ramps have meters that allow alternating drivers on the road in twenty-second intervals. The system is supposed to make traffic flow more easily, and I suppose it does, but the effect for me is teeth grinding.

I had been slip-sliding my way on the highway for about ten minutes when the radio announcer said the Minnesota Department of Transportation was advising drivers to stay off the roads. Great. Here I was, in the middle of a snowstorm, headed away from home to see a lady who was beginning to piss me off. I pushed on for another forty-five minutes, thinking with every swipe of the windshield wipers that she had better have something important to share.

All around me, drivers were peeling off, taking exit ramps to their warm homes and loving families. By the time I got to the exit into Land o' Lakes, the last snowplow had passed me ten minutes before and I was the only one on the road. Every year somebody dies while following a snowplow too closely or, worse yet, trying to pass one. Meanwhile, snow that is plowed to the side of the road can turn granite hard if it's been sitting a few days, accumulating dirt from the road.

People who grow up driving in Minnesota winters can get complacent about deep snow. We figure once you've driven through fifteen inches with a ten-mile-an-hour wind and arrived on time, you've earned your mark. The intimidation is gone. But that can also breed a false security, and I was about to fall into it.

County Road 212 and Highway 5 meet with I-494 in a perfect cloverleaf formation with sharp curves. Many times, to keep from getting bored with the trip to Land o' Lakes, I had played a little game with myself, where I try to see how fast I can take the curve without screeching my wheels. That had always been in good weather. Heaven only knows what I was thinking this time, but for some reason I played the game, and lost.

I swear my speed was no more than twenty-five miles per hour— OK, maybe thirty-five or forty—when the wheels pulled away from the road, putting the car into a swerve. Gripping as tightly as I could in my mittens, I turned the wheel sharply into the curve. A little too sharply, I guess. Suddenly I was spinning a 360, my heart pumping even faster than the spin. I jerked the wheel in the other direction. That threw me into an even faster spin. As the car scraped along the guard rail I heard the sickening screech of metal on metal. The car careened to the left curb, then the right. I glanced in my rear view mirror praying no one was there.

The next thing I knew the car had flipped off the ramp. The last thing I heard before blacking out was an earsplitting whoosh.

When I woke up my face was planted in the car's airbag. A moment later it deflated and I had the odd sensation of a funny smell. My eyes burned when I brushed my hair away from my forehead.

The car had landed on the driver's side with its nose pointing in the air and the tail stuck in a pile of snow. My left shoulder jammed into the driver side door and my collarbone was sore from where my seatbelt had rubbed. My head hurt and within moments I could feel a goose egg growing above my left eyebrow. Slowly moving my neck, shoulders, arms, wrists, fingers, legs, and feet, I determined I hadn't broken any bones.

My whole face and neck began to burn. I looked more closely at my mittens and saw a powder residue that also covered the airbags. Ahh, I thought, it's the stuff they put on the plastic to keep it from cracking before its deployed.

I pounded the dashboard with my fist, shouting "Shit,shit,shit!" which made my head hurt more.

Then I heaved three big sighs and mentally ran through the rules of winter survival. Stay in the car. Call for help.

I grabbed my cell phone. The tiny battery icon in the corner was just about empty. Hoping I had enough juice to call for help, I dialed the number for the garage at the paper. I wasn't so far from the newsroom that someone couldn't come out to pick me up. The old timers who had said to take one of the junkier cars had been right.

It rang four times, and just as Pete answered, "Garage," the battery made its little bloop sound and the phone shut off. I looked to the cigarette lighter where I could recharge, then remembered that, even if I had a charger—which I didn't because it had burned up in the car the paper refused to pay for—the place to plug it in had been removed from the newspaper's car because the company didn't want people smoking. Damn, I thought.

Looked like I was going to have to wait for help to find me.

Another inch of snow piled up on the windshield. It wouldn't be long before the entire car became a pillow under a white fleece blanket, camouflaging it from any possible Good Samaritan.

Inside, the car was getting cold as a morgue, so I turned on the engine and pumped up the heater. Then it dawned on me that since the back of the car was stuck in the snow, it was likely that the tailpipe was clogged. I vaguely remembered reading an article last winter about a couple who died of carbon monoxide poisoning after running their car with a clogged tailpipe. There was no way that I could be sure of the condition of the tailpipe without getting out and looking. I was going to have to break rule number one.

My daughters have always made fun of my hat. It's a brown woolly helmet that covers my head from my hairline to down well below my ears and ties under my chin. The tips were a much lighter tan, causing Rebecca to tell me once, "Mom, when you stand up wearing that hat, you look like a dandelion gone to seed."

The car door, barricaded with snow, opened only a couple of inches. Because it hurt my shoulder to try to push it, I lay on my back sideways in the driver's seat and kicked hard with both heels. It opened another six inches, enough for me to slide out, into snow up to my knees. The next step put me in snow to the middle of my thighs. Caught off guard, I inhaled with surprise, filling my lungs with icy crystalline air, which felt oddly pleasant. Getting out on the driver's side meant the tail pipe was on the opposite side of the car, so I had to slog my way almost half around the car before I could confirm that the tail pipe was indeed packed solid with snow.

Before I climbed back into the car I stopped a moment to look around, hoping to see another car or some other sign of salvation. No such luck. The sky was a dome of white. The wind had died down. There wasn't a sound to be heard, just the muffled plop of flakes piling up, one on top of another. If I hadn't been so terrified I might have appreciated the beauty of the scene.

I sat in the car for a while, clapping my mittens together trying to warm up from my scouting trip. The snow that had stuck to my slacks on my trip to examine the tailpipe began to melt against my body, reminding me of the story I once wrote quoting an expert who said wet clothes drained heat from the body core.

So this was how I was going to die.

Chapter 18

They say freezing to death isn't so bad. You start to hallucinate that you're hot and you take all your clothes off, then just go to sleep and never wake up. I made a mental note to keep my clothes on. I'd be embarrassed to have someone find me naked and dead.

I had always pictured myself dying of old age, trying to remember the names of all my great grandchildren. I saw myself surrounded by family and friends as I slipped away, not alone, frozen in the newspaper's car that didn't have a cigarette lighter for a phone charger.

As I envisioned those surrounding my death bed, I saw the girls and their husbands, sobbing. I didn't see Michael there.

Would Michael remarry? Probably. Would his new wife be good to my girls? He wouldn't marry someone who would become a wicked stepmother, I hoped.

Would she repaint my living room? Probably, the bitch.

That cinched it. I had made too many trips to the paint store to come up with the perfect dusky rose color for my living room. The only hue that flawlessly complemented the carnelian stonework around the fireplace. The best possible choice to set off the wide-planked oak floors. Nope. Not gonna leave that color to some blousy woman who no doubt would change it to chartreuse, and that was final.

Watching my thoughts, because there wasn't much else to watch, I realized that my worry about the color of the living room was my version of whistling while walking past a graveyard.

Then I got serious. What was I doing with my life? Why was I working so hard to find the daughter of a woman I didn't even like, while spending too much time away from my own daughters? Did I really believe in what I was doing? What if I did die here? And what was going on with Michael and me? It felt like so long since we'd talked. Not just talked about the debris of life, but talked about our lives. Was this what I really wanted in a marriage?

Examining your life is tough, especially when you're really cold. At thirty-six, I haven't accomplished anywhere near what I want to accomplish. My girls still needed me—I could even argue that Billie Berry needed me.

It wasn't my time to die yet, I decided.

I had to figure a way out so I tried the cell phone again. I pushed the button that said "end"—I've never understood why "end" should turn a cell phone on, but no matter—causing it to vibrate while a windmill spun on the screen and a bell chimed. Just as I was about to dial 911, the damn thing gave off three beeps, then another message: "battery low. Recharge." Then it went dead.

OK, I thought. Plan B. What is Plan B? It was hard to think as I began to shiver uncontrollably. I would have shouted, but I knew I was totally alone, and no one would hear.

At the beginning of every winter, the *Citizen* tells Minnesota drivers they should carry survival kits in their cars, packed with handy items like a flashlight, jumper cables, blankets, and flares or reflective triangles. For good measure, I remember reading, drivers are supposed to pack kitty litter for traction and a small shovel for digging out of snow, an ice-scraper, water and food, and a first-aid kit. I wondered if the folks who run the newspaper's fleet of cars actually read the newspaper and heeded the advice.

Finding no survival kit in the back seat, I hoped there would be one in the trunk. I didn't want to go outside again, so I climbed over the back of the front seat, hoping I could pull a latch on the back seat and get into the trunk that way. Fortunately, that worked and I found myself crawling, exhausted, into the filthy trunk, which was packed with big, thick Sunday editions. If I didn't find a blanket,

I could always make a warm nest of the newspaper, I figured. That wouldn't be so bad. I love the smell of ink-to-paper and our printing plant uses soy-based ink, which doesn't smudge on clothes.

It had been a long day in what was already a long week. I was plenty tired. I toyed with the idea of taking a little nap. Then I gave myself a quick slap in the face and remembered the living room walls. The thought got me moving again.

The only light came from highway overheads that reflected off the snow and through the backseat windows. It wasn't much as I began to grope around the trunk with bare hands. I had taken off my mittens because I wanted to improve my sense of touch. Just as my fingers were starting to turn to ice, I put my hand on a metal box. Lying on my side in the trunk, I opened it with a prayer that it would contain some kind of a reflective square, and some food. Half my prayer was answered. A Day-Glo square piece of cardboard with the words "SEND HELP" printed on both sides glistened in the box. Apparently there had been food in there at one time. I found empty wrappers from three Mars Bars.

As I cursed the previous user of the car who had eaten my candy bars, I heard a thumping on the trunk and voice shouting, "Hello—anybody here?"

I flipped the latch on the trunk, the door opened, and I found myself on my back looking up at the most handsome state trooper I'd seen in my entire life.

"Hello, Gorgeous," I said, giving the line from *Funny Girl* my best Streisand impression.

"Why are you lying in the trunk, Ma'am?" he asked.

"It's a long story. God, I'm glad to see you. How did you find me?" I asked before he could ask me to tell him that story.

"Someone called the state patrol," he said. "The person said a woman might be lost somewhere between Minneapolis and Land o' Lakes. We've been looking for you for about four hours."

"Has it only been four hours?" It felt more like ten.

"Who are you?"

"I'm Skeeter Hughes from the *Citizen*," I said. "Didn't the caller tell you my name?"

"No, Ma'am," he said.

"What's your name?"

"Trooper Trevor Johnson," he replied with a smile and a hand to help me out of the trunk.

"Thank you, Trooper Trevor Johnson," I replied.

He invited me into his nice, warm patrol car, where he gave me a blanket and a cup of hot chocolate from his Thermos while he radioed his headquarters to say he had found me. Wrapped in the blanket, I rested my head, eyes closed, on the passenger side window. My head was pounding and my shoulder ached. My legs ached. My back ached. My arms ached. I was so tired my eyes felt like kitty litter had been dumped in them. Even my hair felt tired.

The cold of the pane was in direct contrast to the warmth inside his car. After about thirty seconds, my breath steamed the window. I wiped it away with my hand and looked at the car I had exited. It was nothing more than a pile of snow. I knew that traffic would easily pass it in the morning with no idea that there could have been a dead reporter inside.

The storm had run its course and the flakes had stopped their downward drift. The temperature was falling, fast. If he hadn't come along when he did, I might not have seen my family, or my dusky rose living room, again.

"What kind of a name is Skeeter?" Trooper Johnson wanted to know.

"That's another story."

Chapter 19

It was well after midnight when Trooper Trevor took me home and I looked in on the girls. Rebecca's purple hair splayed against the white pillowcase. She had her thumb in her mouth. Suzy was curled up with her green pillow embroidered with a frog and the question, "just how many do I have to kiss?" Soft snores wafted out of their rooms, as comforting as the steam on a pot of boiling water.

The phone indicated Michael had called home three times while I was wondering if he'd remarry after I'd turned into a Popsicle. The last call was 10:30.

"Where have you been?" Michael said from the living room. He was wearing grey sweat pants and his "WILL WRITE FOR FOOD" t-shirt. He had a bottle of beer in his hand and the newsletter from Investigative Reporters and Editors was open on his lap.

"I'm wondering the same about you," I said. "Looks like you haven't been home long."

"And the girls were left alone – again," he said.

"Yes, Michael, they were. Whose fault is that?"

"Are we going to fight about this?" he asked. "Just tell me where you were."

I told him the whole story, ending with Trooper Trevor. "And my car was fire-bombed."

"Heard that from Suzy. Paper's going to pay, right?"

"That's my plan," I replied. "Now tell me where you've been

and why you haven't returned my phone calls."

"Working. Didn't have time to call."

"Jesus, Michael. What's going on here? Remember when we were both on the Rochester paper?"

"What do you mean?" As he took another swig of his beer I noticed two empties next to his chair.

"I mean, remember how we worked together on that sports cheating story."

"And you got the lead byline," he growled.

"We flipped a coin," I reminded him. "How many beers have you had, Michael?"

"Since when do you care?"

"I'm going to bed." There was no point in even trying to carry on a conversation with him, I decided.

Instead, I lay in bed fuming. What was up with him? Was he having his mid-life crisis a little early?

I thought about how we first met. He was a sports reporter and I was covering education. Classic male/female reporter type jobs. We had both been working there about a year when I learned that a high school coach was skimming money off the football budget and paying a local woman to write papers for some of his star players. The newspaper editor told us to work together on the story.

It was not love at first sight.

We worked on the story all season and I guess we were a good team. I was always doing the gritty work, digging through the coach's trash looking for incriminating evidence, while Michael was searching the Internet putting together the guy's track record at schools where he had worked earlier. One of us would come up with a theory about what was going on and call the other one at midnight. We'd argue for hours about how to frame the story. I wanted to show the coach for the scumbag he was. Michael wanted to make sure that the context was right. He saw a coach just trying to win. I saw an authority figure teaching kids to cheat.

We had our last argument when the story was done and it was time to put our names on it. I argued that the bylines should be alphabetical, which meant mine should go first. He thought the honors should go to him because it was basically a sports story, not an education story. Finally, our editor flipped a coin and I won. It was almost morning when I fell asleep dreaming about quarters falling on my head.

The girls had gotten off to school and Michael was gone when I awoke to the muffled drone of my neighbors' snow blowers rattling the walls of my bedroom. I dragged my body out of bed and over to the window. Outside, people shoveled and blew their way through huge drifts, their bright red, blue, orange, green winter jackets stark against the white. The snow that had threatened my life the night before was pure, fluffy, and beautiful this morning.

The girls had left me some coffee that was almost warm, so I popped a cup in the microwave and threw a piece of bread in the toaster. The newspaper's car was still buried under a foot of snow at the exit into Land o' Lakes, so I had to call Thom to tell him I'd be a little late getting into work. The city bus stops about two blocks from my house, but its schedule can be unpredictable in this much snow.

Half an hour later I was crammed into the Number 4 bus heading down Hennepin Avenue toward Fourth Street. Holding on to the strap above me, I jostled along, feeling every bump and turn. The perfume of wet boots, coats, and woolen mittens filled the bus. Melted snow sloshed from one end of the bus floor to the other with every start and stop.

I transferred to the Number 16 bus and headed east about six blocks to where the newspaper is headquartered. Being careful not to slip with my wet boots on the granite tiles that had been polished smooth as glass in the Grain Exchange building lobby, I made for the elevator and pushed the button to take me to the third floor newsroom.

After jamming my hat and mittens in the sleeves of my coat and hanging it in the metal closets off the elevator, I clomped in my boots to my desk. The bump on my head was now invisible under my hair. Once again, the message light on my phone was blinking fast and furiously.

I punched in my code and heard Mrs. Berry's shrill voice.

"Skeeter, it's Cathy Berry. Had you made it to my house last night I would have shown you what I found, but since you didn't, I guess I'll have to tell you.

"I kept thinking about your questions about Billie's clothes and the Mall of America, so I went looking in her closet to see if there were any clues. I found a pair of cargo pants I'd never seen before and a sweater. The pants were a size ten, and Billie wears a twelve, so either they would be quite tight on her, if they're hers, or they belong to somebody else."

"Anyway, I went through her room again and opened her laptop. Facebook is her home page. A note said 'Billie is on a mission to A & F—same time, same place.' It was written two hours ago. Please call me ASAP."

Well, well, well. Looks like Billie is not only alive and in town, she's involved in something that's probably much bigger than she realizes, I thought.

As I was hanging up the phone, Thom brushed past my desk.

"Cold enough for you?" he asked, without waiting for an answer. "I heard you had a chilly night."

The man's charm never ends, I thought. Had he said something a little supportive I might have told him about the note Mrs. Berry found. As it was, I kept my mouth shut as I logged on to the computer.

Dialing Cathy Berry, I mentally ran through what I was going to say. She picked up the phone before I even heard it ring.

"Billie?" she said.

"No, Mrs. Berry. It's Skeeter. How are you?"

"I'm the same as I have been all week—nervous, pissed off at Billie for putting me through all this. What happened to you? I thought you were coming out here last night?"

I told her what happened and thanked her for calling about me.

"If the state patrol hadn't found me, I would still be sitting out there, probably frozen stiff." Hope that isn't how we're going to find Billie, I thought.

"I never called the state patrol," she said.

"You didn't? Then who did?"

"Don't know, but I've got a couple of things I need to talk to you about," she said. "First, somebody has taken down the flyers from coffee shops and street corners."

"That's odd," I replied. "Did you tell the people at Missing Children about that?"

"They said it happens once in a while and told us to post more," she said.

"Why would somebody take them down?" I wondered.

"They didn't know for sure," Cathy replied. "It could mean that somebody doesn't want us looking for her."

That didn't sound like good news to me, but I had no answer, so I continued to press her. "I'm guessing the second thing you want to talk about is this note you found on Facebook."

"Yes. It was dated yesterday. How can she post a note on Facebook if she doesn't have her computer with her?"

"She can do anything to her Facebook page from any computer as long as she knows the password." I learned that from Rebecca.

"What's A&F?"

"Abercrombie & Fitch would be my guess," I replied.

I debated with myself about whether to tell her what I had seen at the mall, and what I had heard about the middle school principal, then quickly decided to keep my counsel. So far, I had few facts, just a lot of suspicions. Mrs. Berry was unstable, at best. I decided it wasn't time yet to fill her in. It could all be smoke at this point.

"I'm getting another call," I lied. "Gotta go."

I turned my attention to my computer. Scrolling and deleting through the usual e-mail spam, I came upon a message with the subject line, "Wanna know more about Billie?"

Yeah, I do, I thought. I also want the paper to pay for my car, I want Michael to be like he used to be, and I want to clone myself so I can be home with my girls and work my job at the same time. A Pulitzer would be nice too. Not to mention a raise and a new wardrobe. Oh yeah, and I'd like to lose fifty pounds.

Figuring I'd have to settle for learning more about Billie, I clicked on the e-mail: "Meet me at the Uncommon Grounds in Uptown. 9 tonight."

Chapter 20

The editors were gathering for the morning meeting as Ramon Luiz, the police reporter, strolled by my desk.

"Hey, Skeeter, cold enough for you?" he asked, with a smile.

Gossip is the most liquid currency in any newsroom. Doesn't matter if you're talking about the *New York Times* or the *Toledo Blade*. Small town gossip is a mere molecule in the mountain that is gossip in a newsroom. I often think that's because journalists are wired to notice details then try to make sense of them. Sometimes, the patterns journalists see have no basis in fact. They're conjecture dressed up to look like fact.

"I'm fine, Ramon," I said smiling back at him. "Thanks for asking."

"That's good, because we all know skeeters die off as soon as it gets cold," he said with a wink. "While you were hibernating yesterday I was asking around the cop house about the girl who kicked the cop in the balls the night of the meth lab explosion. At first, I got these blank stares, but then this sergeant heard me talking about it and got a funny look on her face."

According to Ramon, the sergeant wanted to know where he had gotten his information. When he told her, she started asking a bunch of questions—how long I had been at the paper, what I covered, how trustworthy I was.

"That's when I started to get suspicious," he said. "Of course, I told her you hadn't gotten a fact right in five years. Just kidding.

Anyway, I hate to give out more information than I'm getting, so I told her you were the gold standard for an honest, accurate reporter. Then I started asking her questions. All of a sudden she got lockjaw."

"What's her name?" I asked.

"Sergeant Victoria Olson," he said.

"How old is she?"

"Forty, maybe."

"How long has she been a cop?"

"Maybe fifteen years."

"What does she do?"

"She's been investigating teen prostitution for the past couple of years."

"Is she trustworthy?"

"Good question," he said. "The other cops think she's a rogue. There've been rumors about her being a bit overzealous."

"What do you mean?"

"They say she's not above unconventional tactics if it will nail the bad guy. She'll do anything it takes."

"Like what?"

"They didn't give specifics," he replied.

"Thanks, Ramon," I said. "I don't suppose you have a phone number for her, would you?"

"The things I do for you, Skeeter," he said, as he scribbled it down on a piece of scrap paper. "You owe me."

"As always."

I dialed her number and let the phone ring four times before the message machine kicked in.

"Hello, this is Sergeant Victoria Olson," said a smoker's deep, raspy voice. "I'm either on my phone or away from my desk right now. Please speak clearly and slowly and leave me a message with your phone number, the date, and the time. I'll call you back."

It's always the controlling types who tell callers how to speak and what to say in their answering machine messages. I wasn't going to let some cop manage my message, so I hung up without a word. That meant I had the rest of the day to think about Billie and the

Big, Bad Wolf before meeting with my anonymous e-mailer tonight. It was time to nail down some facts.

People think that journalists have some magic underground system to ferret out every dark, dirty little secret there is. Or that we have electronic listening devices installed in every nook and cranny. Or that the holder of a degree in journalism is smarter than most folks, or at least meaner and nosier.

They couldn't be more wrong, except for the nosy part. The fact is that journalists use mostly a telephone and a notepad and pen. Sometimes we use computers, to track down information such as names and phone numbers of people, and sometimes we use computers to sort data such as home sales or arrest records. But the true business of journalism is much more prosaic than that.

So, what were my options for the rest of today? I wanted to know more about Matthew McClintock, the sleazy principal of Kennedy Middle School. I wondered how long he had been principal. How long at Kennedy? Presumably, he had been a teacher somewhere first. Where had that been? What had he taught? What grades? Had there ever been any charges filed against him? Or complaints? Was he married? Children? If he was connected somehow to Billie, did he have some kind of a connection with the meth lab? Was he a druggie? Or was the meth/prostitution gig some kind of a funding mechanism?

That got me to thinking about his finances. How much do principals earn, anyway? Did he own a house? What was the mortgage on it? Were there any liens against his property? He seemed so slick when I saw him operating at the mall. He didn't fit the stereotype of the dirty old man, if there is such a thing. More like a salesman.

In *All the President's Men*, about the *Washington Post*'s Pulitzer Prize-winning investigation into the Watergate scandal, Deep Throat, the undercover source, repeatedly tells the young reporters to "follow the money." That was good advice then, and good advice now. Reaching for my best high-tech tool, the telephone, I put through a call to the Hennepin County clerk of court.

"Hi, this is Skeeter Hughes from the *Citizen*," I said to the pleasant voice that answered. "Could you please check the computer to see if there are any judgments or active lawsuits filed against a Matthew McClintock? That's M-C-C-L-I-N-T-O-C-K. First name M-A-T-T-H-E-W."

I was on hold maybe thirty seconds, tops, while the clerk checked.

"Is he in Land o' Lakes?" she asked.

"That would be him. Is there a file there?"

"There's quite a bit here, actually. About half a dozen suits have been filed, but nothing has been resolved yet. There are liens on a house, a boat, and what appears to be a vacation home. Looks like there's a divorce suit filed here as well. Would you like the case numbers?"

"That would be terrific," I replied, jotting them down. "I'll be right over. Thank you. "

"That's quite all right, honey," she said. "Just doin' my job."

Court files can be a gold mine of information, and there's nothing like a divorce to make public what some people would like to keep secret.

Grabbing my purse, I snagged an elevator to the basement, hung a left through the double doors to the limestone sub basement of Minneapolis City Hall. Then up six steps to the tunnel to Hennepin County Government Center. Up two escalators to the atrium, then an elevator to the 12th floor. The whole trip took me 10 minutes.

"Hi, I'm a reporter with the *Citizen* and I'm looking for these," I said as I showed the case numbers to the woman behind the desk.

"You must be the one who called," said a woman who appeared as pleasant and grandmotherly as she had on the phone. "I have them right here."

The stack wasn't terribly high, as legal files can go. There were four cases, each about four or five inches thick. Still, all put together, there was about a foot and half of reading material there. I knew how I would be spending my afternoon.

I assembled the files according to date filed on the large wooden table in front of me and grabbed a handful of paper clips to mark the pages I would need photocopied. Then I pulled another wooden chair beside me, kicked off my shoes, and propped up my stocking feet. I read better when I'm settled in.

It looked like the good principal's life had started to fall apart. A boat manufacturer that wanted to foreclose on a $70,000 loan for a twenty-eight-foot Donzi Scorpion fiberglass powerboat filed the oldest suit. McClintock had paid $30,000 in cash for the boat, financing the rest through the manufacturer. Within six months he was making payments a week or two late. Not much later, he was paying $763 every other month, and then, not at all. Included in the file were letters between the manufacturer, looking for the money, and McClintock promising to pay. The case closed with the manufacturer reclaiming the boat.

Then came a lawsuit filed by the bank to foreclose on Mc-Clintock's $619,000 summer home on Potato Lake just north of Park Rapids, Minnesota, where my family had vacationed many summers when I was a kid. Located sort of in the middle of the state, Potato Lake is shaped like a fish hook and is north of Fish Hook Lake, which is shaped like a potato. We always figured the map had been drawn by a dyslexic cartographer. About the same time he bought the boat, McClintock put 10 percent down on the twenty-five-acre home with nine hundred feet of sandy lakeshore.

I had to hand it to him, the guy had taste. The home was on a point into the lake with a long, asphalt drive. It had a two-sided fireplace, a sauna house, a steel outbuilding, probably to store the boat in winter, and an attached garage. An all-new, $90,000 kitchen and a dining/living room area with huge windows looked out on the lake. Three bedrooms, full bath and powder room. Monthly payments: $3,500.

Judging by the dates on his payment schedule, McClintock alternated one month paying for the boat, the next month paying for the home. The bank foreclosed on the home the month before the manufacturer hauled away the speedboat.

Apparently, that was the last straw for Mary McClintock, his wife, who divorced him months later. According to Mary's affidavit, Matthew J. McClintock had a gambling addiction. She said Mc-Clintock spent four nights a week, and untold thousands of dollars, at Mystic Lake Casino in Shakopee, Minnesota, about five miles from Land o' Lakes, where the McClintocks had lived. Fortunately, there were no children.

Mary, a partner in the Minneapolis office of a national accounting firm, said she began to wonder about her husband's finances when he bought his first Lamborghini. Because they maintained separate checking accounts for personal purchases, she decided not to pry. When he bought the boat and the lake home, she started asking questions.

At her urging, McClintock started attending a gamblers' anonymous program, and seemed to be doing better for a while. Every morning he read twelve-step anti-gambling literature, called his sponsor, and attended meetings twice a week. But after a couple of months he made fewer phone calls and started coming home late without an explanation about where he had been. Apparently, she said, he had been back at the casino. She filed for divorce after he lost the Potato Lake property.

McClintock didn't deny her claims and the divorce went through in a matter of weeks. Mary kept their $250,000 home in Land o' Lakes, which she said she had paid for.

I pushed the files to one side and stretched both arms in the air, then rose from my chair to touch my toes. Reading long files like that always makes my muscles stiff, and I needed to get the blood circulating to my feet again. I twisted my head sharply to the right, then sharply to the left, and noticed the clock on the wall that said the clerk's office would close in thirty-five minutes. I had just enough time to have the clerk photocopy the twenty-three pages I had marked with paper clips. Those pages gave the names and addresses for Mary and Matthew McClintock, their former Park Rapids home, their lawyers, and the critical details of the lawsuits. At fifty cents a page, I was glad the newspaper ran a tab for photocopies at the clerk's office.

Judging from what I had read, McClintock lost house, home, and marriage to a gambling problem. I wasn't sure how much money principals made, but it probably wasn't enough for him. I wondered if he had other predilections. Say, for example, high school girls.

The former Mrs. McClintock would probably know. The question was, would she talk to me?

Outside, it was starting to get dark, but the tunnel back to the newsroom is always well lit and open until 6:00 p.m. I put my shoes back on, gathered my photocopies from the clerk, and headed back to the newspaper. I figured I'd call Mary McClintock to see if she would talk with me about her ex-husband sometime tomorrow.

I had planned—needed—to go home a little early and have dinner with the girls before heading out to my 9:00 p.m. meeting to "find out more about Billie," as the e-mailer had promised. What did that mean? The needle on my this-is-creepy meter was beginning to quiver.

That plan, it turned out, was doomed.

Chapter 21

It was almost 5 p.m. when I got back to the office to call Mary McClintock. As I was dialing her number it occurred to me that I didn't know what to call her. Mrs. McClintock? No. Mary? Not a good idea. As she picked up the phone I decided to go with no name at all.

"Hi, I'm Skeeter Hughes with the *Citizen*," I said. "I cover Land o' Lakes. I'm working on an article about a missing girl who might have a tie to your ex-husband. I was wondering if I could ask you a few questions."

I said it all pretty fast, hoping that I would get my whole request in before she hung up on me. I need not have hurried. There was a long silence before she replied.

"How did you get my phone number?" she replied in a voice that sounded like an accountant not in the mood for jokes.

"From the court documents."

"I'm divorced. I have no more contact with Mr. McClintock."

"I know that. I was hoping you could help me understand whether there is any connection between him and Billie Berry, the girl I'm writing about."

Another long silence.

"I don't know that I could help you."

"Maybe not. But maybe you can."

"I don't like reporters."

"Some people don't."

I let the thought hang on the wire between us for a moment while I considered what to say next. She was right. It was altogether possible that she would not be any help and I would be wasting my time and hers. This was clearly a long shot. Still, my antennae were vibrating again. I sensed there was connection between Billie and McClintock. The former Mrs. McClintock was my only connection with him, tenuous as it was.

"If you would be more comfortable we could talk totally off the record," I said.

Another silence.

"Why should I talk to you?" she asked.

Good question, I thought. At least she was softening. I knew that my next words would either scare her off completely or convince her to talk with me. "Because you might be helping a girl who has been missing since Friday."

Still more silence, then a sigh that sounded like a slow leak on a radiator.

"Alright," she said. "But it's got to be here, in my office, face to face. And it's either now or in a month. I'm leaving on a Mexican vacation tomorrow morning."

So much for dinner at home with the girls tonight, I thought.

"I see you have your office in the IDS Center. What floor are you on?"

"I'm on the forty-second floor. The entrance closes in five minutes. I'll call down to the guard and tell him you're coming."

"I'll be there in twenty minutes," I said.

I had just enough time to call the girls. Rebecca picked up on the first ring, quickly filling me in on her day and why soccer tomorrow was going to be lame, and how she and Suzy were fighting over who was going to empty the dishwasher. Then Suzy was on the phone to say it wasn't her turn, no matter what Rebecca said, and besides, she wanted to watch television. Then she put Rebecca back on the line.

"Oh, and Dad called. I was having trouble with my algebra, so I e-mailed the problems to him. He called me back and asked me questions until I had figured it out. We probably talked an hour."

Michael has always been very good with the girls, and as they get older they seem to rely on him more and more. I've seen other fathers distance themselves from their teenage daughters and it can lead to trouble. I am lucky Michael is a good dad, I thought.

"Did he want me to call him?"

"No. He said he was in meetings until very late at night. He said he missed us. When are you coming home, Mom?"

"It's going to be late. I have to work tonight."

"Again?" Suzy wailed. "Moooommm, this is getting to be too much. You weren't home last night and you weren't here when we left for school this morning."

"I know, honey. I'll make it up to you. I promise. Would you like me to see if Uncle Helmey can come over?"

She thought that would be great, so I dialed his number.

"Hi, Helmey. It's Skeeter. Are you busy?"

"Hi, Skeeter. No. I'm sitting here watching CNN. You know, I voted for President Bush, but I've got to tell you, I'm real glad he's almost gone. I don't like what's going on in Iraq. Too many kids dying."

"I know, Helmey." I agreed with him, but I didn't have the time to get into a lengthy conversation about the war. "I'm going to have to work tonight and I was wondering if you'd like to spend a little time with the girls."

"Well, you know, that's just the ticket for me. I had no plans for tonight anyway."

"That's great, Helmey. Thanks. Michael and I owe you."

Chapter 22

The IDS Center is fifty stories tall, the highest in the Twin Cities. At its base is the Crystal Court, made famous by the opening shot of the 1970s TV program, the *Mary Tyler Moore Show*, which showed Mary lunching at a railing-side table. At the end of the day, the Crystal Court is swamped with workers who pour from the IDS Center elevators before heading for home. I felt like a fish swimming against the current trying to make my way through the skyway to the IDS. Finally, I pushed my way to the guard who stood at a lectern at the base of the elevator banks. Still not knowing what to call McClintock's ex, I couldn't tell him whom I was going to see.

"I believe you're expecting me," I said. "I'm Skeeter Hughes."

"Yes, I got a call from Ms. McClintock," he said. "You're cleared to go up."

I stepped on to the second elevator bank for floors forty to fifty and stepped off at the forty-second floor seconds later. I hung a right on the gold-speckled carpeting and found myself looking through a glass wall at the conference table in a room with a spectacular view of the western portion of the city and the suburbs beyond. No one was sitting at the receptionist's desk, so I stopped in the lobby area for a few minutes trying to figure out what to do.

Within moments, a woman of about forty-five dressed in a navy pant suit and white silk blouse open at the neck approached me with her right hand extended.

"I'm Mary McClintock," she said with a shake of my hand.

"You must be Skeeter. Please follow me."

She turned on her heel and strode down the hallway with a quick, confident step. Because of its zigzag shape, the IDS Tower has thirty-two corner offices on each floor. One of them belonged to Mary McClintock. Her taste in office décor was far better than her taste in husbands. A silvery grey carpet and grass cloth wallpaper with a stunning metal sculpture of a woman's torso covered the wall behind her oak desk. From her leather-padded, high-back desk chair she could look through two floor-to-ceiling windows at the cityscape, where office lights were twinkling along with the stars.

Blond hair clipped short and tucked back behind her ears. Angular face. Tired-looking hazel eyes. Yellow gold-framed reading glasses set to the side of her desk, which was devoid of any personal items, except a mother-of-pearl Mont Blanc pen, which she twirled with long, slender fingers.

"I understand this will be off the record," she said. "That means you will not use in print anything I tell you and you will not tell anyone we talked, correct?"

"That's right," I said. "I'm hoping that after we've spoken I'll have a better handle on what may have happened to Billie Berry, the girl I mentioned on the phone."

"What do you want to know?"

I gave the lady points for being direct. "Let's start with some basics. How long were you married?"

"Two years, six months, three weeks, four days," she said.

"But who's counting?" I joked. She didn't laugh.

Awkward moment.

"How did you meet?" I continued.

"My firm was hired to audit the Land o' Lakes school system. They do an audit every five years. I went to Kennedy Middle School to look at the books. Matthew was the principal."

"Did you date long?"

"Not really. Maybe five months. We were past our mid-thirties. We had both been around the dating circuit for a while and we were sick of it. We both knew what we wanted in a spouse."

"And for you, he was it?"

"That's what I thought at the time," she said ruefully. "And, of course, he was attractive."

"When did the marriage begin to fall apart?"

"It was great at first. We were compatible. We liked to have fun. We dined at restaurants and attended the theater. We had season's tickets to the Vikings, the Twins, and the Timberwolves. We traveled, too. There were half a dozen trips to the Bahamas to scuba dive. We also spent a lot of time—and money—at the casino."

"Which casinos?"

"Mystic Lake, mostly," she said, her voice getting soft and wistful. "We gambled a lot in the Bahamas too."

"What happened?"

"We gambled for entertainment. I liked the lights, the sound when someone hit a jackpot. The cheap drinks, cheap dinners. But after a while it was more than that for him. We'd say we were going to spend no more than $100 each, and I would stop at that. He couldn't. He kept saying he'd just bet $50 more. Pretty soon he was down $500. There were nights when I left him there."

"Did he ever win?"

"Yes. He was a great blackjack player. Played on the edge. Often taking another hit when most folks would have held. One night he walked away with $9,000."

"How long did that last him?"

"Not very long. Junior high school principals don't make a lot of money. And he had grown up poor. His mom left him and his dad when he was a kid. His dad was dead by the time I met Matthew. He managed to graduate from high school, then worked his way through St. Cloud State University selling cutlery door-to-door. He's one hell of a salesman. Very smooth talker. Good looking. It made him a great teacher. When he talks, kids listen."

"When did you know there was a problem?"

"Not soon enough. I wondered, though, when he bought the boat and house on Potato Lake. His aunt died about the same time. He told me she had left him a lot of money. Said she was one of those little old spinster ladies you read about who bought stock in

Microsoft early on and never spent a penny. I guess I wanted to believe that was what happened."

"When did you find out otherwise?"

"When they hauled the boat away and the bank changed the locks on the doors of the lake house. You know, I loved that house. We had some great times there. Water-skiing all day in the summers. Cross-country skiing in the winters, then back at the house for drinks around the fireplace. I hosted parties for my partners at that place. I was mortified when the bank foreclosed."

"That's when you decided to file for divorce?"

"Yes. I couldn't live a lie anymore."

"In the course of your marriage, did you ever have any hints that he might have been involved in anything illegal?"

"Such as?"

"Such as drugs or prostitution?"

She stopped to think for a moment, rubbing the bridge of her nose with her right thumb and forefinger. Then she gazed at something behind me. For a moment, I thought someone else had walked into the room, so I turned around quickly. There was no one there.

"Sometimes he got phone calls from young girls. He told me they were students who needed help."

"Didn't it seem strange to you that young girls would call him at odd hours?"

"I did wonder when they called at one or two in the morning, so I asked a few more questions," she replied. "He said teenage girls often stay awake long into the night. That fit with what I had heard parents at work say, so I left it alone."

"What about drugs?"

"He certainly has an addictive personality. He's much too smart to actually use drugs himself, although he once mentioned a colleague who had been arrested for methamphetamine use."

"What did he say about him?"

"He talked about how stupid the guy was for getting caught."

"Did you ever see drugs in the house or his car?"

"No," she said, slowly drawing out the word. "But I traveled a lot. He could easily have done all kinds of illegal things when I was out of town and I would never have known about it."

"Now I want to ask you a question," she said, sitting straighter in her chair, looking every bit like an accountant. "What has this got to do with the girl you're writing about?"

I always hate it when I get to this point in the interview. Experience has taught me that some of what I suspect always turns out to be wrong, and some is often only half true. If I told her all my suspicions, it would feed the gossip mill. But she had spilled her guts to me, so I felt a certain obligation to leave her with something.

"I saw Matthew buying some clothes for a teenaged girl at the Mall of America earlier this week," I said. "Billie Berry, the girl I'm writing about, in the past came home with some clothes that made her mother suspicious. Billie disappeared Friday night. I'm wondering if there's a connection."

"What does that have to do with prostitution or drugs?"

"I'm not sure," I replied, honestly.

She pushed back the left sleeve of her jacket with her right hand, looked at her wristwatch, and said, "Time's up. I've got to go now." Her brisk manner made it very clear I was not going to be allowed to ask any more questions.

Indicating I should follow, she stood and walked toward her office door. The interview was over.

The doors parted on an empty elevator and I stepped in. As it dropped I wondered if any of those late night calls to McClintock came from Billie. The idea left me with a funny feeling in my stomach. Of course, the forty-two-floor drop may have contributed to it.

Chapter 23

I quickly made my way back to the newspaper via deserted skyway. Grabbing my coat, I made a mental checklist of the things I needed to take with me. Notebook, pen, cell phone, and a tape recorder. I didn't know who was going to meet me, or what this person was going to have to say about Billie, but I figured a tape recorder might be helpful if I needed to double check quotes.

Once again in the newspaper's car, which the guys who maintain the garage retrieved, I headed west on Franklin Avenue, then south on Hennepin Avenue until I got to Uptown, my favorite twenty-something stomping grounds and the neighborhood where Billie worked.

Even though the Twin Cities is home to large populations of Southeast Asian and Somali immigrants, most Minnesotans still have a Scandinavian sameness about them. But not in downtown Minneapolis' funky cousin, Uptown.

Stretching about six blocks along Hennepin Avenue, Uptown is the best place in town to wear anything studded. Micro skirts over black leggings and knee-high boots are de rigueur for women with purple hair while men often sport enough chain metal to make a fence.

It had been a long time since lunch, so I pulled off Hennepin, parked in the lot behind McDonalds and headed inside to place my order. I was enjoying the parade of diversity from my seat by the window as I ate my zillion-calorie double cheeseburger with onions when, from the corner of my eye, I saw someone moving toward me. I pulled my purse closer to my side and looked more closely. Charles Manson's clone was twitching a couple tables over. He had long stringy brown hair and wore a dirty, torn jacket not warm enough for this weather. Crazed brown eyes, which bracketed a scar in the shape of a cross on his forehead, were staring at me. I gulped the last couple of bites of my burger and tossed the balled wrapper in the trash with a shaking hand. It was time to move on. Already this week I'd had my car firebombed, nearly died in a snow storm and had too many threatening messages. Was there a pattern forming here? I didn't know.

I pulled myself together and walked a couple of blocks up Hennepin toward Uncommon Grounds, which is a few doors from my favorite store in the heart of Uptown, Saint Sabrina's Parlor in Purgatory, where shoppers are provided with a big platter of chocolate cookies and condoms, both free. The Grounds is in a Victorian-era house, where light classical music plays in the background and ceiling fans swirl softly over faux marble tables, rose-colored chairs, and booths covered in green velour scattered among many small, romantic rooms. It's listed as a not-to-miss spot on many Twin Cities gay and lesbian Web sites, the perfect scene for an intimate chat in a public place.

I ordered a decaf coffee and pulled up a chair at the table for two next to the gas fireplace. Sometimes I marvel at how this business of journalism ever gets done. I had no idea who I was meeting, male or female, or how this person would know who I was. Nonetheless, there I was, sipping my coffee, waiting for this encounter to play out.

I had been watching the clientele for about twenty minutes when a deep, female voice coming from behind me made me jump.

"What kind of a name is Skeeter, anyway?"

I looked over my left shoulder to see a woman of about thirty. She wore jeans, a chambray shirt, work boots, and a bright yellow North Face down jacket, unzipped. Her feet were planted like the roots of an oak tree. A cup of coffee steamed in her right hand. Her left hand was tucked in the pocket of her jeans.

"Actually, it's Marguerite," I replied.

"So how did you get to Skeeter from Marguerite?"

"I'm the youngest of six kids, and the only girl, in the last Catholic family in Minneapolis to do something as stupid as skip birth control," I replied. "My brothers called me The Pest because I was always buzzing around, making them crazy. One day, one of my brothers swatted at me, saying I was worse than a mosquito. My other brothers started calling me Skeeter. The name stuck."

"So you've been a reporter since birth," she said with a chuckle while sliding into the chair across the table from me.

"It was good training. Who are you?"

"Victoria Olson."

I did a quick brain scan to remember where I had heard the name before.

"You're the cop who was asking one of our reporters about me."

"Yep."

I took a closer look. Full, round face. Blue-green eyes. A little mascara and eyebrow pencil on her blond lashes and brows would have brought her eyes out better, but she struck me as the kind of woman who thinks Estee Lauder would be a good name for a hooker. I put her at almost two hundred pounds, most of it muscle—a lady who likes to lift weights and eat.

"How tall are you?" I asked, unconsciously verbalizing my thoughts.

"Five-eleven and a half," she replied, proudly.

"You said I could learn more about Billie Berry if I came here," I said. "So talk."

"First, I have some questions for you," she replied.

Here it comes, I thought. I hate answering questions. Especially from cops. Cops and reporters are often variations on the same theme. They have the same built-in skepticism, which I figure comes from seeing too much reality, up close and personal. To be a good cop, or a good reporter, you've got to have a piece of DNA that builds the enzymes for a bullshit detector. But I wanted to learn more about Billie. If I were going to play ball with Officer Olson, I'd need to do a little negotiating first.

"I'm willing to answer your questions, Officer Olson, if you'll answer mine."

"First, it's Sergeant Olson," came the reply. "Second, I'm prepared to tell you some things, but you have to understand that I'm working on a police investigation. I'm not at liberty to share everything."

Hmmmm, I thought. So Billie is somehow mixed up with this cop. Suddenly her disappearance was a lot more interesting. This was the toehold I needed to get this story in the paper. My brain started to burn. This could be good for a Sunday piece. Maybe 1A, depending on what Sergeant Olson had to say.

"OK, shoot," I said.

"Why are you asking so many questions about Billie Berry?" she said with a sharpness that made it sound like I was doing something illegal, which I clearly was not.

"I cover Land o' Lakes. Billie's mother called Monday after she didn't come home Friday night. The cops had written her off as a runaway and her mom wanted us to look for her. So that's what I'm doing."

"Since when is the *Citizen* interested in a runaway?" Olson asked. "They're a dime a dozen."

This line of questioning was getting less and less comfortable for me. If I had balls, I'd have thought this woman was out to bust them. I realized she wanted to scare me, another sign I was on to something interesting. If she could be a hard ass, so could I.

"Lookit, Sergeant," I said, "We need to rearrange our footing. You called me out here, remember? I don't appreciate your tone, which implies I'm some kind of criminal. I'm a reporter, doing my job, which right now is to ask questions about Billie Berry. There's no law against that, last I checked. So lighten up. I came here to have a conversation, not to be a bull's eye for your verbal target practice."

She leaned back on her chair, surveying me for what seemed like a full minute. I could almost peek through her left squinting eye to see the synapses sparking in her head.

"OK, Skeeter," she said with a half smile. "You can call me Victoria."

"I may have come on a little strong," she said after a beat or two. "I've been working on a case for a couple of years now and it's about ready to pop. I do not want to see it fall apart because a reporter is asking questions."

"You'll have to get used to me nosing around, Victoria," I replied. "Because that's what I'm going to do, whether you like it or not."

"As a cop, I've always been taught that reporters are assholes and our worst enemies," she replied. "I don't know you. Until you prove otherwise, I have no intention of trusting you."

"Yeah, and cops aren't my favorite folk either," I said, thinking we're off to a fine start here. Then I remembered State Trooper Trevor Johnson hauling me out of the trunk of the car in the snow, and mentally adjusted my opinion, just a bit.

"The way I see it, we've both got a job to do. We can go our separate ways and avoid each other, but odds are we're going to intersect again somewhere. We can snarl and pass. Or we can look for a way to work together."

"I don't work with reporters," she replied.

"That's too bad, because, within certain limits, I could be a help to you."

"How?" she replied.

This woman keeps asking the questions because she is used to being in the power position, I decided. I had to change this relationship quickly if I was going to find anything productive in this evening I was spending away from my daughters.

Then I remembered a lesson I had learned early in my career while lifting beers with police reporters. Cops really love publicity. The kind that makes them the hero—or heroine—fighting to rid the world of evil.

"If you let me in on what's going on, I'll try to get a story in the paper after the bust. If you'd like, I can write it so you have a prominent position."

"Going for the ego massage?" she replied.

"Whatever works," I said with a small smile.

"You're good, Skeeter, I'll give you that."

"Can we find common ground here at Uncommon Grounds?" I asked, returning the same half smile.

"I suppose."

Even though we had taken a step closer, I sensed that I was going to have to keep my guard up with this woman, which was OK. I like a verbal thrust and parry from time to time. That guy in McDonalds scared me, but she sure as hell didn't.

"Tell me about your case," I said.

"I work in vice," she said. "Ever hear of the Martin family? They ran a prostitution ring between here and in Texas. I busted them about three years ago. It was a federal case because they were transporting girls across state lines. Two of the brothers went away for a very long time."

"I bet you're proud," I said.

"Yeah, I am. Prostitution is the worst of the worst in my book. It takes young girls' very souls."

No kidding. When I was in college working on the student newspaper, I wrote a series about prostitution. Anyone who says it's a victimless crime has never known a teenage hooker. The guys who run them know how to read body language, know which girls have the lowest self-esteem, just by looking at them. Often their fathers or uncles were in the same business. They prey upon these girls, who usually have no family, no support system of their own. They treat them well, at first, make them their girlfriend. After a while, they'll ask them to have sex with a friend of theirs. "Just a quick blow job," they'll say. "It's not a big deal." When she does it, because she wants to please her boyfriend, he'll tell her to do another friend. After a while, she's done a dozen guys and her "man" will tell her to start charging and to bring her earnings to him. If she tries to run away, he tells her nobody's going to take her because she's just a whore.

"What's your case got to do with Billie Berry?" I asked.

"I'm still working vice. Prostitution. Teen prostitution."

"Are you telling me that Billie Berry is a prostitute?" I asked.

"I'm telling you she may or may not be involved in a case I'm working on now," she said. "Now it's my turn to ask questions. Why were you asking about a girl who disappeared the night of the meth explosion, when your car was firebombed?"

"You know about my car, huh?"

"Word gets around in the precinct. What did you see that night?"

"I didn't see much," I replied. "There was a girl who was getting her head kicked before Mohamed hauled her into his shop. I was in there waiting for the cavalry to arrive. Her nose was bleeding and at first her eyes didn't seem to be focusing. I knew she was pretending to have a head injury when she executed this great karate kick in the crotch to some poor cop. I thought it was odd that they let her go."

"They didn't 'let her go,' " she chuckled. "She got away."

"Why wasn't she mentioned in the report?"

"Cops like to forget the embarrassing parts of a bust," she responded.

That made sense, but I still wanted to know why Victoria was asking about Billie.

"Because she may, or may not, be involved in the case I'm working on now," the sergeant repeated. I bet she learned to say that at the police academy, I thought.

"The girl I saw that night was Billie Berry?" I said. I needed confirmation. Besides, something told me the most direct way to Sergeant Olson's confidence was to play dumb.

"So now you know my secret." Patronizing. Very patronizing.

"Yeah, but that's not much," I said. "All I know now is Billie may be a prostitute, may be involved in meth, and you may be working on a case that's somehow related. That's not enough, Victoria."

"Enough for what?"

"Enough to make me stop asking questions," I said. "In fact, it makes me want to ask more. If you know so much about Billie Berry, do you know why she didn't come home Friday night?"

Another long silence hung between us as we stared each other in the eye. After a moment, she said, "I'm getting more coffee. You?"

I shook my head and watched her rise, taking her cup to the counter. She moved gracefully, especially for someone her size. Each muscle seemed to fire a fraction of a nanosecond earlier than expected. If she were an animal, she would have been a racehorse.

She must have been working the night shift because it was approaching ten o'clock and she ordered a double espresso before returning to our table, while I continued to sip my decaf.

"If you're only interested in Billie Berry, why were you spending so much time at the Mall of America earlier this week?" she asked.

Now this was getting a bit spooky. I didn't like that she knew where I had been. Cops watching reporters sounds like other countries that don't have a free press. Apparently I wasn't blending in among the other shoppers. Did that mean McClintock spotted me too?

"How do you know where I have been spending my time?" I asked. "Were you tailing me?"

"It doesn't matter. Just tell me why you were at the mall, outside of Abercrombie & Fitch."

"We had a call about the Ferris wheel getting stuck, so I went out there to check it out. Cathy Berry, Billie's mom, told me Billie had spent a lot of time at the mall," I replied. "I thought it would be a good idea to look around."

"And what did you see?"

"If you know I was there, you probably know what I saw," I said.

"I want to hear it from you."

"I saw an older man buy some clothes for a teenager who could have been a poster girl for vulnerable adolescents." I didn't like revealing the crux of the matter, but she had backed me into a corner. She'd make a great reporter.

"Did you find out who either of them was?" she asked.

This was getting downright obnoxious. This woman was grilling me, yet she seemed to know the answers to her own questions before I did.

"He was Matthew McClintock, principal of Kennedy Middle School," I said. "I don't know who the girl was."

"What do you plan to do with that information?" she asked.

"Right now, nothing, because that's all it is: information. It's not a story. At least not yet. It's plenty interesting, but not a story."

"Good," was her only reply.

"Wait a minute, here," I said. "That's all you're going to say? 'Good?' What if I were going to do more with it? What if I were to go back to my editor and tell him we should run a story that says a Land o' Lakes middle school principal bought clothes for some girl he picked up at the mall?"

"That would be a stupid mistake, and you're smarter than that," she said.

"Why would it be a mistake?"

"Because the story is much bigger than that."

"What do you mean, bigger?" I asked, as my heart began to beat faster and I leaned across the table to be closer to her.

A smile crept across her face. With just a little twinkle in her eye, she replied, "We're going to have to come to an agreement here, Skeeter. If I tell you what is about to go down, you have to promise not to breathe a word and I certainly don't want to see it in the newspaper until I say so."

"I need to be able to tell my editor."

"Is your editor trustworthy?"

Now we're talking about Thom, at least, and probably a couple of editors above him too, I thought. Were they trustworthy?

There was a case in the 1980s in which editors at both newspapers in town overruled their reporters, who had promised a source they would keep his name out of the paper. The U.S. Supreme Court ruled the editors had been wrong to break the reporters' promises and the newspapers paid the source lots of money. Thom and I were in high school at the time, but the lesson was well learned in the newsroom. People still talk about it.

"Actually, I'll probably have to tell a couple of my editors, but, yeah, I think they're trustworthy," I said.

"Just thinking they're trustworthy isn't good enough. I need to know they are trustworthy."

"OK, OK—I trust them," I said finally, surrendering with my

hands in the air like a bad hombre looking down the barrel of a six-shooter. "Tell me what's going on."

I couldn't take my eyes off Victoria as she spun her tale. She said the police had been following McClintock for about two years after they first heard reports that he was buying clothes for girls at the mall, then, gradually, enticing them into prostitution. His girls were not streetwalkers. Rather, he set them up in hotel rooms near the Mall of America. Their customers were carefully screened—men with a lot of money to spend who would not take the risk of picking up girls in cars. Doctors, lawyers, business executives—all men McClintock knew from the Land o' Lakes community.

"He's smart about his business," she said. "He never works out of any hotel for long, and he doesn't run the service all the time. So he's hard to track."

Instead, she said, he'll take a couple of rooms under different names for a few days of the month, then shut down, and weeks later set up in another hotel.

"He's got a good job. He's a respected member of the community. Why he would jeopardize that?"

"We're not sure," she said, "but we think he's using the money from prostitution to fund a side business in meth. That's why we haven't busted him yet. We want to get him on all his activities. And, we suspect he has a partner or two."

I flashed back on Mary McClintock telling me about what a good time she had at the home on Potato Lake. About all the parties. Could some of the prostitution have been going on up there? Were some of the friends she said they had entertained also customers, or even partners?

"I presume you know about his gambling issues," I said to Victoria.

She gave her head a slight shake. "Our sex crimes and drug units don't coordinate very well with gambling investigations. What makes you think he's into gambling?"

I filled her in on what Mary McClintock said about their trips to Mystic Lake. His fish tale about the dead aunt who supposedly left him a big chunk of change, the house, the boat, the divorce.

"We'll look into that," Victoria said. "Meanwhile, you remember our agreement."

I assured her I would, and then asked, "What's Billie got to do with this?"

"McClintock is smart, but he made a big mistake," Victoria said. "He approached Billie at the mall. She was outraged that he would try to prey upon her."

"What does that have to do with her not showing up since Friday night?"

"She's working for us," Victoria said.

I was shocked. That was one scenario that had not occurred to me.

"Is she in danger?" I asked.

"Hope not," she said, ruefully.

Chapter 24

"What do you mean, you 'hope not'?" A couple at the next table turned to look at us.

"Keep your voice down....We don't know where she is."

"You're going to have to explain this to me," I said.

"I'm not at liberty to discuss any more details."

Oh, boy, I thought. What would Woodward and Bernstein do?

"Sergeant Olson," I said. "What I have here is a story where the cops are using a young girl to break up a prostitution ring and possibly a drug business that may have a gambling component, tied to a junior high school principal. And the cops have lost touch with that girl. Readers are going to wonder what the hell is going on. I'm willing to wait, but you've got to give me good reason to sit on this story.

"Now, let's start again," I said. "When did McClintock approach Billie and why did she go with you?"

If Olson could have reared at me like a horse, she would have. She clearly did not like the situation. But she needed my promise to delay putting anything in the paper that might botch her investigation. I, on the other hand, needed her help to get accurate detail on what could be the story of my career, so far. I wasn't about to tell her that, however.

I could almost see the gears of her brain doing the same calculus I had done. She stared at me for a long time before starting in.

According to Sergeant Olson, Billie was shopping, alone, in the mall one day last fall, trying to forget a fight with her mother. She was sitting on a bench on the first level outside the entrance to Nordstrom, crying, when McClintock approached her. Although he didn't recognize her, she remembered that he had been her junior high school principal. She said that when she was in the seventh grade he would sometimes call girls into his office for what she thought were bogus reasons. Billie pretended she didn't know who he was and let him talk to her for a while.

"He gave her some song and dance about missing his own daughter who lived far away. Then he offered to buy her some clothes. Billie told us she was looking for something to distract her from thinking about her mother, so she went with him. He bought her a new outfit, then told her he would be back at the mall the following Saturday, if she wanted more clothes."

"The girl has great instincts, I'll give her that," Olson said. "Before returning to the mall, she came to us. She said his advances felt weird."

"I find it hard to believe you would work with a teenage girl in that kind of situation," I said.

"We were very reluctant," Olson replied. "But we had been watching him for months. We were getting nowhere. We had to get special permission from the chief to let her work for us."

"You didn't need permission from a parent?"

"Not after she turned eighteen," she said.

"She's only been working for you since Friday?" I was incredulous.

"That's right," she said. "Before that we were just talking."

"About what?"

"This and that," she replied. "He contacted her again Friday. Asked her to meet him. She was supposed to wear a wire and drive there after she got off work at the SuperAmerica. But she must have taken it off because we lost her. Then she showed up at the meth explosion. I knew it was Billie when I heard about the karate kick to the crotch. I taught her that move."

The expression on Olson's face was a mixture of pride and consternation. For all her bravado, Sergeant Olson was clearly a cop who cared about people.

"What was she doing at the meth lab?"

"We had talked about the possibility that McClintock is involved in drugs," she said. "I'm afraid she's decided to break away from us and investigate on her own."

"She told her ex-boyfriend she always wanted to be a cop," I said. "This could be her way of fulfilling a fantasy."

For the first time since our conversation began, Sgt. Olson looked me squarely in the eye. "If that's what she's doing, she's not as smart as I thought she was."

We sat there and looked at each other for a few more seconds, both of us trying to absorb what we had just shared. My mental picture of Billie was coming into better focus. She likes the excitement of the chase. That she went to the cops, without telling either of her parents, indicated a fearless, independent streak. Why didn't she put on the wire? Was this independence run amuck? Had something untoward happened?

While I was trying to formulate a plan for my next step, my antennae were vibrating again. Something didn't feel right, but I couldn't quite put my finger on it.

"I've got to talk to my editors about this," I told Olson. "What's your next move?"

"Billie has got to surface somewhere, and soon," Olson said. "Meanwhile, I'm going to touch base with our gambling unit. See what they know about McClintock."

"You know how to get in touch with me," I replied. "How do I reach you?"

She took a card from the pocket of her jacket and scribbled a number on the back. "Here are my office and cell numbers. My home phone is on the back. If you find out anything more, you contact me, understand?"

"Likewise," I replied.

It was almost midnight when I dragged myself to my car which I had left in the McDonalds parking lot. My body was exhausted. My joints ached. My head ached. My muscles ached. I felt as though all my energy had drained from my torso and limbs and somehow dumped into my brain, which was buzzing from the potency of a news story that had grabbed me by the throat and wouldn't let go.

As I drove home, street sounds muffled by new-fallen snow, my mind chewed through everything that had happened this week. I was closer to answering the question that had started my week: Where is Billie Berry? But now I was more worried about her than ever. Was she adult enough to get into serious trouble, yet a child with no idea of her own mortality? Or did she have the maturity combined with physical agility that would keep her safe?

What's more, I was facing a completely new set of issues. I had promised to sit on the story. How was I going to convince my editors to back me up on that decision? They hate keeping news quiet. The notion runs contrary to every journalist's being. If an editor or reporter knows something that would interest readers, the job is to share.

We have a spotlight with a motion detector on our driveway that's supposed to flash on when a car pulls in. The bulb had burned out before Christmas and neither Michael nor I had had time to replace it. As I walked thirty feet from the garage to the back door in pitch dark I heard a car approaching. It's a subtle sound in the snow, but unmistakable, especially in a quiet neighborhood that late at night. I stopped dead and listened closely, straining my ears, then tucked behind the arborvitae against the house. A deep blue rusty Saturn cruised by very slowly, with the lights off.

I pasted myself to the stucco of the house until the car turned the corner, then I dashed inside. What was that about? Had I been followed home? Or was I so tired that I imagined I had been followed?

Breathing hard, I pulled off my warm jacket and headed for our bedroom where I stripped, then climbed into bed. I lay there staring at the ceiling for a long time, wishing Michael were home.

Bump. Scratch. Bump. Scratch. There was a noise I had never heard before. It came from the living room. I picked up the phone and hit the speed dial.

"Helmey," I whispered. "Someone's in the house."

Chapter 25

Helmey came down right away, God love him, carrying a baseball bat. "Don't worry, Skeeter. I'll get him."

Helmey, in his saggy boxers and a ratty bathrobe, and I, in my long t-shirt that says "SHOW /DON'T TELL," tiptoed through the house, turning on every light. I didn't want to wake the girls, so I just peeked in their rooms. Both were asleep so soundly that they didn't hear us.

"I don't see anybody," Helmey said after checking every possible hiding place. I had to agree with him.

"I'm sorry I woke you, Helmey," I said. "I must be hearing things."

"That's OK, now," he said. "You know you can call me any time."

I turned off all the lights and we both went back to bed.

What seemed like minutes later Suzy was jumping on me.

"Mom, where were you last night?" she asked. "I was worried about you."

"I had a late interview, honey," I said. "I'm really sorry I didn't make it home until after you were in bed. How was your evening? Did you get your homework all done?"

She launched into a twenty-minute monologue about how she and Rebecca had made sandwiches for dinner and then watched only one TV program. Then Rebecca "talked, talked, talked" on the phone while Suzy read her book. Yes, they got their homework done, she said.

"A clown came to school and gave us balloons. I brought mine home and Rebecca wanted to suck in the helium to make her voice sound funny, but I wouldn't let her."

"Good. Come here," I said to her, and pulled her down on the pillow beside me. We lay like that for a long time, cuddling, listening to each other's breathing, feeling the restorative power of being close.

We were both almost asleep again when Rebecca came to my door.

"Mo-THER," she said archly. "Where have you been?"

"Working on a story about a girl like you who may be in big trouble," I replied. "She hasn't come home in a week and the cops think she's in danger."

"Are you going to find her?" Rebecca wanted to know.

That's one of the things I love about my girls. They get right to the point. They don't get caught up in side issues, personalities or ethical quandaries.

"Hope so," I said.

"You'd better get up and get to work, then," Rebecca said. "Suzy, the bus will be at the corner in fifteen minutes. I'm not telling the driver to wait for you. If you aren't out there when the bus pulls away you'll have to walk to school. It's going to be cold today—the high is zero—so move it."

With that, Rebecca turned on her heel and left, the scent of her plumeria perfume hanging in the threshold. Suzy scrambled out of bed and trotted off behind her. There I was, alone in bed, thinking about my daughters and Billie Berry. If a creep had approached my daughters, would they have had the sense to tell to me, or Michael, or the cops? I hoped they would.

I dragged my ragged body out of bed, managed to take a shower and brush my teeth. Dressed in my underwear, I was peering into the bathroom mirror, trying to throw on some makeup when I heard bump, scratch, bump, scratch, the same sound as last night. It was coming from Suzy's bedroom.

Grabbing my makeup brush as a weapon, I stepped down the

hall and into her room, where her red helium-filled balloon made the bump, scratch, bump, scratch I had heard as it glided across the ceiling along with the hot air current from furnace. I fell backward on her bed and laughed until I cried. Catharsis at last.

A glass of orange juice and a slice of toast with peanut butter later, I was in the car, coffee steaming from my travel cup as I headed back into the newsroom. The editors were out of their morning meeting when I slid into my seat and fired up the old computer.

I was punching "Peter Pickle" into my log-on when Thom happened by.

"We need to talk, Thom," I said. "I think we should have George in on this, too."

George Ralston, also known as Curious George, was Thom's boss. Newsroom lore had it that the actor Ed Asner had based his Lou Grant TV series character on him.

"It so happens that I have a moment free, and I see that George is doing nothing more productive than staring at his computer screen, so why don't we meet in the conference room in ten minutes?" he said.

That gave me time to run to the coffee shop to grab a cappuccino. This was going to be a meeting that demanded caffeine and protein. And a cookie. Chocolate chip. Big.

Once Thom and George were seated at the small round table, I closed the door to the kitchenette/conference room. I didn't want my colleagues interrupting our conversation. Somebody standing around while heating up soup would have no choice but to listen, and then my tale would be all over the newsroom. Like I said, gossip is a liquid currency in any newsroom.

"Guys, I promised last night to sit on what could be an explosive story and I need to fill you in on the details," I said.

Like people who grow to look like their dogs, or married couples who start to resemble each, Thom and George, who had worked together for years, had taken on the same mannerisms. Thom arched his right eyebrow and squinted through his left eye. George arched his left eyebrow and squinted through his right eye.

"Yessssss," said Thom. "Go on."

I wished they had listened quietly while I went through the story, point by point, but they didn't. Journalists have an awful habit of jumping in with questions. It took me about half an hour to lay out the scenario about Billie, the Big, Bad Wolf in the guise of a junior high principal, his gambling, drug, and prostitution businesses, and finally my agreement with Sergeant Olson. The silence lasted about twenty seconds after I'd finished.

"Did you ever read the newspaper's policy on promises to sources?" Thom said. "It says clearly that a reporter should not promise anything without talking to an editor first."

"I know," I said. "And, yes, I have read the policy. What did you want me to do? Call you at home at 11o'clock to get permission?"

"You know I'm always open to calls at home." He said this with a miffed air, as though not calling him at home were an insult. As though I was trying to keep him out of the loop, an especially bad move in front of his boss.

Was I doing that, I wondered? Maybe on a certain level I was. This was a story I wanted all to myself.

"It would have made me look weak, and believe me, I have to be working with this woman from a position of strength," I said. "Anyway, I've already made the agreement."

That didn't sit well with George, who said he'd have to take the matter a couple of rungs higher.

"Don't promise anything more to anybody until we've talked," he said, rising from his chair. Thom also stood up and walked out, saying nothing.

It looked to me like the meeting was over, so I got up to leave just as my cell phone rang.

"This is Skeeter," I said.

"Where'd you get a name like that?" said a young woman.

"It's a long story," I replied. "Who's this?"

"Billie Berry," she said.

Chapter 26

"I need you to promise me something," she said.

"Where are you?"

"I'll tell you, but not until you promise you won't let anyone know I called you," she whispered.

This had to be some kind of a record, I thought. It hadn't been ten minutes since my editors forbade me from making any more promises, and here I was doing it again.

"OK. Where are you?"

"I'm in the Caribou coffee shop on the skyway over Third Street."

"Don't move. I'll be right there."

I grabbed my notebook, pen, and purse and was three steps from the elevator when Thom shouted, "Hey, Skeeter!"

"Can't talk now," I said over my shoulder without breaking my stride.

I must have looked like I was running a marathon as I pushed my way through the crowds on the skyway. I was delighted, and relieved, to hear she was alive.

I knew her as soon as I walked into the coffee shop. She was sitting in a booth with her back to the door. Even though I couldn't see her face, the short, spiked blond hair gave her away. Her shoulders were slightly rounded and she was stirring a cup of coffee. I slid in the booth across from her.

"Nice to meet you, finally," I said.

She looked up with a tired smile. The bruise on her forehead had turned a lovely shade of green since I saw her the night of the meth lab explosion. She wore a red hooded sweatshirt, which I swore I had seen on a table in Abercrombie & Fitch, unzipped to just above her bra. Her left wrist was tattooed with a thorny vine of roses. Her fingernails were bitten to the quick, a couple of her cuticles were bleeding, and her eyes darted around the room, as though beyond her control. She looked like she could use a hug.

"Are you OK?" I asked, before remembering that I was supposed to be in reporter mode, not mother mode.

"You were the reporter on the street the night the lab blew, weren't you?"

"And you were the girl with the shamrock belly-button ring."

"Now that we've established who we are, let's talk business," she said with a command that exceeded her years.

"Your mother's worried sick about you," I said.

"But not my dad." It was a statement, not a question.

"No, not as much," I said.

"My mother should start worrying about her own issues and leave mine alone." Her voice cracked at that comment, and suddenly she wasn't so tough. When I looked into her eyes, I saw a girl who was hurt, sad and defiant all at the same time. "Dad will get over it."

"Sounds to me like you're angry with both of them," I said. "Why?"

"Why?" Her voice went up an octave making her sound like a whiny child, not the heroine she imagined. "Why? Because he has Allison, that's why. His flight attendant. He's with a chick practically my age. Talk about a mid-life crisis."

"You'd prefer he bought a Jaguar?"

"Yeah."

"Anything else?" I was still wondering about Peter Berry. Had he crossed a line with Billie?

"Isn't that enough?"

I let the silence hang between us in hopes she would fill it with more insight into her relationship with her father. Instead, she repeated, "Dad will get over it."

"Get over what?"

"That I'm not the sweet, innocent Land o' Lakes girl he would like me to be."

"What are you?"

"A crime fighter."

Oh, boy, I thought. Now we're in trouble. She's taking this working-with-the-cops thing seriously.

"Like Jodie Foster in *Silence of the Lambs*?" I asked.

"Yeah, something like that."

"Listen," I said. "That was a movie. A good movie, but a movie, nonetheless. Jodie Foster wasn't going to get killed. You might. You are in danger."

"How is that any of your concern?"

"Good question." My job was to write about her, not advise her. It was time to take a different tack. "Why did you call me?"

"I want you to quit asking questions about me."

"Sorry, Billie, no can do. My editors already know there's a good story there. They aren't going to let me shut down my investigations. And I wouldn't, anyway."

"What business is it of anyone's?"

"From what I can tell, a middle school principal is picking up girls at the mall and turning them to prostitution to cover his gambling debts and drug problems. A high school girl is working with the cops to bring him down, but they seem to have lost track of her. And she hasn't been home since Friday night. Don't you think that's something people of the Twin Cities should read about?"

"Sounds to me like a story that would boost your career," she said.

"I don't deny that," I replied. "But it's true."

"Not exactly," she said.

"Enlighten me."

"Why should I? So you can put it in the *Citizen* and ruin my plan?"

"Look, Billie, this is serious stuff. You're going to get hurt."

"Not if you keep your ugly nose out of it," she said.

I pulled a business card from my purse. "I'm going to write a story about this." I wrote my home phone number on the back and tucked it in the pocket of her sweat shirt. "I need your help to make it accurate. Please contact me if you're willing to talk."

"Why did I even bother to call you?"

With that she pushed herself out of the booth with such force that she bumped the table, spilling a full cup of coffee all over me, then strode off, her boots hitting the hardwood floor with a defiant slap. As she marched away I noticed a piece of paper partially hanging from her purse, which she had slung over her shoulder. The paper was orange and looked like it had green printing on it.

I could see why she would want me to stay away from the story, I thought, as I mopped up the coffee, but there was no way that was going to happen. The stakes were too high. People who should have been protecting her—her principal and the cops—were using her. Not to mention McClintock's customers. Sooner, rather than later, it was going to be my job to let the newspaper's readers in on the secret.

But when? And what exactly was I going to write? Was it about a runaway girl hell bent on exposing the people who were supposed to be her role models? Was it a story of a principal who was a menace to students? Was it law enforcement's blithely using a girl who deserved better? All three?

Conflicting emotions gripped me. As a human being, as a mom, I was worried for her. Her fantasies were dragging her into a real-life, dangerous plot. Should I at least tell Victoria Olson that I had met with Billie? What could she do? And what about her parents? Didn't they deserve to know I had seen her?

I was obligated to keep my promise to Billie and tell no one. And then there was the cardinal rule of journalism: don't let yourself become an actor in the story. There were professional reasons why I had to hold my objectivity, and my tongue.

I headed back to the newsroom with a heavy heart. When I got back to my desk the message-waiting light was blinking on my phone and there were two Post-it notes stuck to my computer screen. One from Thom, one from George. Thom's said, "See me."

George's said, "See me ASAP." I figured picking up the phone to retrieve my messages would buy me some time.

"Skeeter, this is Cathy Berry," said the voice on the machine. "It's been a week today since Billie didn't come home. I'm getting a little panicked. Call me as soon as you can."

Beep.

"Skeeter, this is Sergeant Victoria Olson," said the next message. "I want to follow up on our conversation. You have my numbers. Contact me."

Beep.

"Skeeter, this is Billie's dad, Peter Berry. I was wondering if you had heard anything more about Billie. When you have a moment, could you call me, please?"

Beep.

"Ms. Hughes? This is Joey Pignatello, Billie Berry's co-worker? You asked me to call you if I thought of anything else about Billie. I start work at 3:30, if you want to come by the store and hear what I remembered."

Beep.

"Yo, Skeeter: This is Whitehorse, Billie's ex. Uh, I think she owes me money. Tell her to call me.

Beep.

"If you know what's good for you, you'll drop the Berry story," said a deep, smooth male voice.

Click.

Another creep heard from. I had to get out of the newsroom to think over my options. Before anyone extracted any more promises from me.

Thom was in the morning meeting for about another five minutes, so I knew I had to move fast. I made a dash for the women's room—which bosses seldom frequent, because few are women—and hid in a stall. Now what?

I read a lot of mysteries. Whenever the protagonist found herself puzzled in one of my favorites she'd get a pack of three-inch by five-inch cards, write down facts on each, then lay them out on a table in different orders, trying to discern a pattern. Sounded like a good idea to me, in a pre-computer 1980s sort of way.

Making sure that my cell phone and pager were turned off, I made a beeline for the elevator, then headed to the basement of the building, where I took a right into the tunnel under city hall and the county building, then up the escalator to the skyway. I hiked along through the skyway at a good clip until I reached Nicollet Avenue, where there's a Walgreen's. I bought a fifty-seven-cent packet of three-by-five note cards, stuffed it in my purse, then headed back by skyway until I had almost reached the old Milwaukee train depot, which has been turned into a lovely indoor ice skating rink. About half a block away sits the building that had been used as storage for the train station in the 1800s. Dunn Bros. has since turned it into a coffee shop. People from the newspaper seldom go there because it's not connected to the skyway. That's why it's my favorite place to sip coffee and think.

The moment I stepped into the two-story brick building, imbued with the smell of roasting coffee beans and the ghosts of old leather satchels, I knew I was in the right spot. My punch card showed I had knocked back enough caffeine to qualify for half off my next cup, so I ordered a triple cappuccino, with a little more milk than foam, and biscotti.

I slid into a table for two, unwrapped the cellophane and started to write down one fact per card. It was such a charming exercise in these days of computer-think that I actually started to feel my thoughts move from my fingers to the heavy paper. If I couldn't figure out what to do, maybe my pen would.

The easiest move would be to call Cathy and Peter Berry and lie to both of them, telling them I knew nothing more about Billie, then get off the phone as quickly as possible. I definitely needed to talk to Joey Pignatello, but he didn't start work for several more hours, so that would have to wait. I would ignore Nate. Neither Billie nor I needed him confusing the issue right now. Victoria Olson would be tougher to dodge. I had to keep her in the loop if I expected her to do the same for me.

I knew the threatening caller was McClintock. I could never forget the deep, rumbling timbre of the voice I had overheard seducing that poor girl at the mall. I glanced at my watch. It was a little after 1:00 p.m. Odds were Principal McClintock would be in his office at Kennedy Middle School. I could shake in my boots or I could deal with him head on.

I stuffed my note cards in my purse and bused my table, carefully brushing biscotti crumbs into the palm of my hand before dropping them in the trash receptacle. I'd worked at a coffee shop in high school and it always irritated me when people left messy tables. At sixteen, I vowed never to do the same to anyone else.

On the way back to the newsroom, I wondered what McClintock would actually have to say. How did he know I was working on a story about Billie? Would he acknowledge making the call? Would he even acknowledge knowing me? Would he try harder to scare me off the story?

As the elevator doors opened, I stuck my head out carefully, hoping to avoid Thom and George, then dashed to my desk and grabbed a notebook. The light signaling messages on my phone was blinking again, but I ignored it. If necessary, I could check them using my cell phone.

Traffic was light in mid-morning so I glided along easily on westbound Highway 62, slickly executing the exit to Land o' Lakes, and tipped a silent salute to the snow pile where I had spent Wednesday night. I took a parking spot on the street across from Kennedy Middle School and hiked in. An attractive woman with a buzz haircut sat at her desk near the entrance. She was talking on the phone to someone who seemed to be calling to complain about students smoking behind a garage. Rolling her no-nonsense brown eyes while handling the call diplomatically, she motioned for me to wait a moment. Five minutes later, the caller was gone and she turned her attention to me with an exasperated sigh.

"Is Principal McClintock in?" I asked as sweetly as I could. "I'm Skeeter Hughes from the *Citizen*."

"He's with some students now," she replied. "You can take a seat if you'd like. I don't know how long he will be."

I sat on a bench opposite her desk, feeling every bit like the kid who had been caught carving my initials in a school desk, which, by the way, I did absentmindedly when I was in the fourth grade. I still remember the gnawing volcano of fear in my gut while trying to explain to Sister Rose of Lima that I didn't do it on purpose; I was just doodling and my pen slipped off my paper.

Finally, the door to McClintock's office opened, and two girls, who looked about twelve, skipped out.

"Oh, Mr. McClintock!" one of them flirted with a toss of her long blond hair. Clearly, she hadn't been in there for some transgression.

McClintock flashed them a smile, then told them to get to class. He didn't see me sitting on the bench. But I watched his eyes follow them as they sashayed from his office. I didn't like that look of lust.

"This is Stephanie from the *Citizen*, Mr. McClintock," said his assistant.

He reacted with a surprised blink before he could ease his facial expression into neutral. The guy had the uncanny ability of a TV anchor who could feign whatever emotion was necessary.

I stood, and held out my hand. "Actually, it's Skeeter. Skeeter Hughes."

"Come in," he said, his voice soft and dark as black velvet.

He closed the office door behind me and eased himself into a chair in the corner of his office.

"Be seated."

I took the adjacent leather sofa, which was still warm from where the girls had been sitting.

It was the closest I had gotten to him and I was taken aback. He was gorgeous. Almost white blond hair with a tiny bit of curl. Piercing, grey-blue eyes topped by thick blond eyebrows and lashes. A broad forehead, broad cheekbones. A healthy tinge of pink to his white, flawless skin. Square jaw, but not so square that he looked like a comic book character. Perhaps most striking was the perfect symmetry to his face. Draw a line straight down the middle from his hairline to the tip of his chin and both sides would be exact reflections of each other. The only way to tell them apart would be the diamond stud in his right ear.

His shoulders were broad and held back straight, military-style. He wore a short-sleeved white shirt that appeared to be fresh from the dry cleaners and a navy blue tie decorated with red, blue, and yellow children holding hands. Navy slacks with a leather woven belt and black penny loafers. His attire was the perfect mix of authority and casual approachability. I caught myself wishing my junior high school principal had been more like him.

He leaned back in his chair slightly with his hands placed comfortably on either knee, then tilted his head a tad to the left to look at me.

"What can I do for you, Ms. Hughes?" I'd expected him to ask me where I'd gotten the name Skeeter, like everybody else, but he didn't. His thought process had already moved beyond that.

I changed my tack a bit. He was clearly a sly one. I'd have to go about this carefully. "Do you remember a girl named Billie Berry?"

"Let me think," he said. "Billie is not a common name for a girl. I find it interesting that names go through cycles. Twenty years ago, it seemed every other girl was named Jennifer. Then we went through the Joshua and Benjamin phase. Parents who were giving birth ten or twelve years ago seem to like Amber and Lindsey. I'm waiting for them to get back to Johnny and Mary."

"So you don't remember Billie Berry?" I asked.

"I'm afraid not," he said, looking deeply into my eyes. "Why do you ask?"

"I'm working on a story about why she has been missing for a week."

"Girls go missing all the time. Why write about this one?"

"It appears she's mixed up in something more nefarious than running away," I said. My plan was to hint that I knew a lot more without giving anything away. I wanted to draw him out, see if he would contribute anything.

"That's too bad," he said.

There was a moment of silence between us. I had hoped that if I sat quietly he would jump into the breach, just to make conversation. He didn't. Eventually I cleared my throat and looked him dead in the eye.

"I've been getting messages that I should walk away from this story," I said, keeping my voice low and level. "It's not going to happen. My editors know what I'm working on, and I plan to see it to the end."

He reached to the sofa and grabbed my right wrist, causing a spark of static electricity to jump between us. "Is that why you came here, Ms. Hughes? To tell me you plan to stay with the story about some runaway?"

I pulled away from his tight grip and squared my shoulders, cleared my throat, again, and summoned the most commanding voice I could. "Important messages are best delivered face to face."

"Very well, then," he said, rising.

He opened his door, then returned to his desk, pretending to shuffle some papers. "Now you can return to your newsroom satisfied that you've accomplished your goal. If you'll excuse me, I have students who need my attention."

As I left his office I gave a small wave to the office receptionist, then headed to my car, snow under my feet crunching with every step. I let the engine run for a few minutes while I took several deep, cleansing breaths, trying to calm down.

The interview didn't give me any more information that I could use in the article beginning to take shape in my head. His reactions to my questions convinced me of two things: this was one smart guy, and I wanted to nail the bastard.

Chapter 27

My cell phone and pager chimed in disharmony the moment I turned them back on. Everyone, it seemed, wanted to get hold of me.

One message came from Michael. "Call me," was all he said. I hit the reply button and got his voice mail, again. Try as I might, I couldn't get through to Michael.

The next message lit a fire under my fanny. Suzy had been throwing up all morning, the school nurse said. Could I please come and get her?

I threw the car in gear and hightailed it to Suzy's school in Minneapolis. It took a couple of turns around the school parking lot before I found a place to park, but finally I was climbing the eighty-year-old stone steps and almost running down the well-trod hardwood floor in the main corridor to the nurse's office.

When I got there, Suzy was holding a barf bucket with both hands. Her nose was red and running and there were tears in her eyes. She had pulled her hair back into a ponytail to keep it out of the way of her vomit. As I walked in she said, "Mom!" then put her head down and puked her guts out.

"Oh, honey, I'm sorry," I said, on the verge of tears myself.

"I want to go home," was all she could get out before beginning another round of retching.

The nurse asked me to sign a release form and get Suzy to "a more comfortable" setting. "If Suzy has siblings, you might want to wipe down your house with a solution of 5 percent Clorox and water. This bug is working its way through whole families."

Was I imaging a note of criticism in her voice? I bit back a retort about exactly how much time I had to swab the decks of my house and what she could do with her barf bucket while I bundled Suzy in her coat, hat, boots, scarf, and mittens and hustled her off to the car. As we drove home, Suzy leaned her cheek against the window on the passenger side, which we had cracked about half an inch so she could get some air and hopefully make it all the way without throwing up again.

Once in the house she dropped her outer clothes in a pile on the mudroom floor and headed straight for the bathroom. I left her in there for a while as I opened a can of chicken soup, poured it in a bowl, and popped it in the microwave. I had no idea if it would help her, but it made me feel better.

I brought the soup to her room and helped her pull on clean pajamas and scramble into bed.

"I'm sorry, Mom," she said.

"Sorry about what?"

"Sorry the nurse had to call you at work. I know it makes you angry when one of us gets sick, but I couldn't help it."

I would have felt a lot better if she had said I was an awful mother who had left her to get sick and when she grew up she would never treat her children the way I had treated her.

"Shhhhh, honey," was all I could say, fighting back tears. "I'm not angry. It's not your fault you got sick. It's not anybody's fault. Now sip some soup and try to get some rest."

I held her until she was sleeping softly and then tiptoed out of the room, closing her bedroom door quietly behind me.

This was the week from hell, and being the mom without Michael's help was getting old, fast. Not having him as backup only deepened my guilt that the girls didn't have a parent when they needed one. At that moment I was furious with him for never being around when we needed him.

At least Suzy was asleep now. Due to the wonders of mass communications, I could just as easily work from home, which, actually, was better than being in the newsroom. It meant I could avoid editors altogether. With my eight-cup pot of coffee gurgling in the kitchen, I hauled my laptop computer from my closet and set up my office on the living room couch. I put my pager and cell phone in front of me on the coffee table, where I propped my feet. I fired up the old computer, punched in my password, and, voila, I was in the newsroom, without being in the newsroom.

Because it was early afternoon, the beginnings of the stories that would likely show up in tomorrow's paper were posted on the newspaper's Intranet. I scrolled through the offerings: another foot of snow expected; the mayor was about to contradict half his campaign promises. A report from the Hazelden Foundation that said last year forty-seven Minnesota children lived in homes with working meth labs, which are highly volatile because it takes household ammonia, drain cleaner, battery acid, and antifreeze to make meth. The deadly combination can—and does—explode without warning. I had a vision of McClintock in a shack way in the back of some undeveloped parcel in Land o' Lakes, ordering his high-school hookers to get to work mixing up that great big vat of crystals that would make him even more money.

I glanced at the clock and realized it was time for the afternoon newsroom meeting, which meant Thom was likely away from his desk. Since I didn't want to talk to him, it was a good time to call his phone and leave a message that I had a sick kid and would be working from home for the rest of the afternoon.

With Suzy's raucous snores as backdrop, I checked my phone messages again. Cathy Berry had left two more increasingly emphatic messages that she wanted me to call her. There was also another message from Victoria Olson expressing the same sentiment.

I decided to put them both off while I rang Joey, Billie's coworker.

"Hi, this is Skeeter. You said you remembered something you wanted to tell me."

"Ah, yeah," he said, slightly out of breath. Cars and trucks rushing by played in the background. "I'm running across campus to catch a bus to work, so I've got to talk fast."

"So talk," I said.

"I was thinking about last Friday night and I remembered that Billie got a call on her cell phone about half an hour after her mom called. Billie said something like she'd be there and not to worry. Then she said something about 'crown jewel.' I thought her mom was getting anal about her bringing home the right popcorn. Then I thought about it some more. I don't think she was talking to her mom again. It didn't seem like she was talking about popcorn. "

"Why not?" I asked.

"I don't know . . . um . . . I guess it's because I think she said something about the mall too," he said. "Here comes the bus. Gotta go."

Thoughts chased through my brain. Crown Jewel. Was she talking about popcorn or something else? The name didn't ring any bells for me, so I typed it into the newspaper's archives. Only one hit appeared, a two-inch item from 2000 that said a developer planned a small, exclusive hotel called Crown Jewel to be built a mile down Interstate-494 from the Mall of America.

I figured it was time I returned Cathy Berry's call.

"Skeeter, so glad you finally got back to me," Mrs. Berry said. "Do you have any more news about Billie?"

"I'm afraid not," I lied. "But I have a question for you. Have you ever heard of Crown Jewel popcorn?"

"Why are you asking me about popcorn at a time like this?" she asked.

"Believe me, Mrs. Berry, it's important. Did you talk to Billie on her cell phone the night she disappeared? Did you two have a discussion about what kind of popcorn she was going to bring home?"

"No, we did not talk about popcorn," she said. "In fact, we did not talk at all. If it matters, Crown Jewel is her favorite popcorn. I believe I told you that before."

"OK, thanks," I said quickly, and hung up before she could interrogate me further.

Apparently I was speaking a bit too loudly, because Suzy woke and stumbled out of her bed and into the living room.

She looked so cute with her tussled hair and cheeks as pink as her footed PJs. She resembled Rebecca at that age. Same curls, same eyes and nose. As she cuddled next to me on the couch I could feel the heat radiating from her body. We sat like that for a long while, and then she asked me with a scratchy voice what I was working on.

"A story about a girl who hasn't been home in a while," I said. "I think she met a bad man at the Mall of America. He bought her some clothes to try to trick her into being his friend."

"I don't think he was trying to trick her," Suzy said. "I think he was trying to be nice to her. Just like the man who bought those clothes from Abercrombie's for Rebecca."

Chapter 28

My heart stopped.

"What man?" I asked Suzy, struggling to keep my voice calm. If I had screamed, like I wanted to, it would have scared her, or she might have thought I was mad at her, and she wouldn't have given me as much information. Still, it was tough to maintain my composure. "Did Rebecca come home with some new clothes?"

"Yeah, a really cool pair of pants," Suzy said. "They're too tight on her, but she likes 'em that way."

"When did you see them?"

"That night you were out so late," she whispered, casting her eyes away from mine.

"Which night was that?" There had been so many lately, I thought, guilt gripping my chest again.

"Don't remember," Suzy said. "Long time ago."

"Did Rebecca tell you where she got them?"

"She said she was at the mall and a man wanted to buy her some pants to make her feel better."

"What else did she tell you?"

"She didn't really tell me at first," Suzy said, sheepishly. "I heard her talking about it on the phone."

"Who was she talking to?" Please, God, I thought, don't let it be that bastard.

"Stacy, I think," Suzy replied. "She called me a snoop for listening. Am I a snoop, Mom?"

"No, honey, you're not, especially if she was speaking loud enough for you to hear. I'm concerned, though, that she let a strange man buy the pants for her. What happened next?"

I was plenty more than concerned. I was furious. But I didn't want to frighten Suzy. In my head I said a small prayer of thanks that Rebecca has a sister like Suzy who could report on her. What if I had never known?

"She showed me the pants. They've got buttons instead of a zipper and they fit kinda low so her belly shows. Is she going to get in trouble?"

"Not if she tells me everything that happened and promises to never do it again," I said, mentally grounding her for life.

I heard Rebecca's key jingle in the door, then felt a rush of cold air fill the room. She was wearing the knit cap I gave her for Christmas, a testament to the below-zero temperature outside. Her hair was sticking out in a halo around her face. Her nose was a bright frosty pink and she gave a little sniffle as she threw her mittens down on the dining room table.

"Jesus, it's cold out there," she said to no one in particular, then stopped and looked up, surprised to see us. "What are you guys doing here?"

"I'm sick," Suzy said. "Mommy wants to know about the man who bought you pants at the mall."

So much for the subtle approach.

"I can't believe you told Mom about that, you little snitch," Rebecca said.

"That's enough, Rebecca," I said. "I'm glad Suzy told me. I want to talk to you about it."

Heaving a huge sigh, she plopped down on our overstuffed, well-worn orange velvet chair. With a sour look on her face, she began to pick at the cuticle on her left thumb.

"What?" she said.

"Tell me about the pants from Abercrombie," I said, my blood pumping double time through my body.

"I don't want to talk about it." There was a long silence while her thumb cuticle captured her full attention.

"Rebecca, this conversation is not optional," I said, doing my best to keep my voice gentle. Wide-eyed Suzy was taking in every word.

"Why do I have to talk about it?" She stuck out her bottom lip, reminding me of when she was two years old.

"Because it's important," I said. "Tell me."

"You're always trying to butt into my life. I'm fourteen, Mom. You made your own decisions and ran your own life when you were my age. Uncle Steve said you were hell on wheels."

That's the problem with having a wild and woolly youth. It can come back to bite you, especially if you have big-mouth older brothers.

"Whatever Uncle Steve said, he exaggerated," I told Rebecca. "More important, this is about you, not me. I know you're old enough to make many of your own decisions, but part of that is making good choices."

I doubted Rebecca heard my statement because she was in a defensive mode. I hoped she would reflect on what I had said after she calmed down.

"Now tell me how you got the pants," I continued.

"I was at the mall," she said, sarcastically "This guy came up to me. Said he wanted to buy me some clothes. I thought, what the hell, I want new pants. We went to Abercrombie's. I picked some out. He paid for them. I left. He left. End of story."

"When was this?"

"I don't know. Before Christmas. Remember? Stacy and I went to the movies. Her mom dropped us off."

"Was Stacy with you when you met the guy?"

"No, her mom picked her up."

"Why didn't you go home with them?"

"You were going to meet me there," Rebecca said, avoiding eye contact with me. "But you didn't. I was pissed. Took the bus home."

I could hear my heart beating and my palms went wet. I had a problem much bigger than Rebecca getting free clothes from someone I feared was McClintock, a man who should be jailed. Michael and I absolutely had to address what our absences were doing to the girls. This couldn't go on. I didn't know the solution, but that didn't mean there wasn't one. I would find the answer, I vowed.

Meanwhile, I needed to know more from Rebecca. "What did he look like?"

"Like a guy."

"Black? White? Hispanic? How old? How tall?"

"White. Blond. Old. Maybe forty. Taller than Dad."

Oh my God, I thought. It was McClintock. "What did he say to you?"

"I got a cup of coffee outside Nordstrom on the first floor. He sat across from me …smiled. I smiled back."

"Then what?"

"I don't see why this is important, Mother," she pouted, jutting out her jaw.

"Rebecca, I'm working on a story about a guy who tricks girls into prostitution after he buys them clothes at the mall."

"Oh, I get it," she sneered. "This is about your story. It isn't about me."

Her last comment moved me from fear to rage. It was all I could do not to slap her. She wasn't going to divert the attention away from her by playing the guilt card with me. I do guilt too well myself, I thought. I didn't need her to add to the pile.

"Of course this is about you!" I shouted. Out of the corner of my eye, I saw Suzy jump. "The idea of you being anywhere near that creep scares me to death. You were in serious danger. Now tell me what happened."

That got her attention. She continued, with a sigh.

"He asked if he could sit at my table. I said OK, then he said he thought I looked sad. I said, 'Yeah, so what?' Then he said he had a daughter who moved away and he missed her and hoped she wasn't sad. We talked some more and then he said he had some extra money and wanted to buy me something to make me feel better. He said I was beautiful."

He said she was beautiful! Oh my God, I wanted to kill him. Did she have to hear that from sleazeball McClintock? Hadn't she heard it enough from us?

"Then what?"

"We went up the escalator to Abercrombie's and I picked out pants. He paid. Then he gave me a hug and we said goodbye."

"Did he pay with a credit card?" I was hoping this might be a way to get some evidence on him.

"Cash. Had a huge wad in his pocket."

"How much were the pants?"

"Eighty bucks." She started to suck her thumb, ostensibly because her cuticle had begun to bleed, but she didn't fool me. It has always been her way of relieving tension.

"Rebecca, didn't this make you wonder? Why would a perfect stranger spend eighty dollars on a girl he didn't even know?"

"I didn't think about that. At first, I pretended I was Cinderella and he was the prince. He was gorgeous, even if he was old. But there was something about him that made me think he was scum. So it felt pretty good to take his money. It was cool that I could get a new pair of pants for free."

"Didn't it occur to you that what you were doing was dangerous?" I couldn't believe that this tough young woman, my daughter, was such easy prey for this guy. If he could entice her with a stupid line, no wonder other girls were falling for him.

"Mom, we were in a public place. There were people everywhere. The guy didn't lay a hand on me. I'll never see him again. It's no biggie. Trust me."

"What makes you think that?"

"He asked my name. I told him it was Heidi. Heidi Hood," she said with a chuckle.

"Did he tell you his name?"

"Gieriger Wolf," she replied.

"What kind of a name is that?"

"That's what I wondered so I looked it up on the Internet," she said, with a sly smile. "It's German for ravenous wolf."

The little joke didn't calm my fears. My heart still in my throat, I asked Rebecca to show me the pants. We went to her room, Suzy trailing us like our dog, Gus, who died of old age a year ago.

Rebecca was five when we bought this house and the first thing we did was wallpaper her room in a print that she chose: soccer balls bouncing all over the room. It took me a year to walk in there without getting dizzy, but she loved it.

She went to her closet, which was painted to look like a goal, and pulled out a pair of grey narrow-wale corduroy pants. Leaning against the soccer ball wall, she held them out to me. I wistfully thought back to when she was a five-year-old in pigtails and shin guards.

"Put them on," I said.

She gave a shrug, unzipped her jeans, and dropped them to the floor.

"Since when have you been wearing thong underpants?"

"It's not 'thong underpants,' Mom. It's just a thong." She looked me square in the eye for the first time since the beginning of this conversation. "You might want to try it. I've noticed visible panty line on you."

So it has come to this, I thought. My daughter is advising me on my underwear, which I buy at Target in packages of five and is too tight most of the time as it is. I could have gotten into a discussion about the relative merits of thongs versus white cotton underpants, but I wanted to keep the conversation on point.

Suzy was right. The pants were too small and hung low on Rebecca's hips. The tight little T-shirt she was wearing left about four inches of her flat belly exposed. If she were eighteen she'd have looked sexy. But at fourteen she looked pathetic. With her weight shifted to her left hip she gave me a look that was a mix of defiance and a plea for approval. I took solace that my opinion still mattered to her.

"Rebecca, take the pants off and put them in the give-away bag," I said. "And promise you will never accept gifts from strangers again."

"Yeah, fine," she said. "Get out of my room."

I returned to the kitchen, steaming, and made a fresh pot of coffee, banging cupboard doors while I looked for filters. I needed to talk to Michael about this. I dialed his cell phone number and got his recording. Damn. "Call me, for Chrissake," I shouted into the phone. Unable to reach him, my anger bubbled even harder.

I had held on to my sanity just enough to recognize that Rebecca had handled herself pretty well, even though she should never have talked to McClintock in the first place, let alone accepted the pants. I wished she had called a security officer, but I know most are undercover, and not easy to spot at the mall. The police obviously were not protecting these girls. How many more would McClintock lure away? I wanted to destroy him. It was time to get a story in the newspaper. The Crown Jewel was my best lead. I had to get back to work.

Chapter 29

Suzy had stopped vomiting and seemed a little better. The irony of having to leave my daughter to protect someone else's stuck in my mind but the best I could do was to prevail upon Helmey to stay with her. I dialed his number.

"Hi, Helmey. What's goin' on?"

"I'm feeling a bit lonely today," he said. "I miss Marilyn. I miss my boys. They have their own families now and they can't always include me."

Helmey is a remarkable man in many ways. Besides being a charmer, he's got to be the only Norwegian on record who expresses his feeling at a mere ring of the phone. That's one of the reasons I love him.

"I'm sorry you feel lonely," I replied. "I may have something to help. Suzy came home sick this afternoon. She seems better now, but ..."

"Ya, sure. I'll be right over."

Not five minutes later Helmey was standing in my front hall. "I remember when my boys were sick. Marilyn was in such a tizzy. I told her not to worry. Kids can be sick, sick, sick one minute, then up and running around the next. Don't you worry, now. She'll be fine."

Feeling only marginally better myself, I bundled up and headed out the door. "I'll have my cell phone turned on. Call me if you need anything. Have a cup of coffee."

I turned the key on the newspaper's car, let it warm up for a minute, then threw it into reverse. I was out of the drive and headed south on 35W for the I-494 strip in a matter of moments. Fifteen minutes later I pulled into the parking lot of the Crown Jewel Hotel. The black of winter late afternoon had dropped on a couple of Audis, a Lexus, and a bright red new Thunderbird tucked among five-foot high piles of snow left from the plows. Perfect camouflage for someone who didn't want his car noticed. I sat in the parking lot for awhile copying down the license plate numbers and then called Ramon Luiz, my favorite cops reporter, to ask him to run a check on the licenses.

"Hey, where are you?" Ramon asked. "Thom is looking all over for you."

"I'm still working on the Billie Berry story," I replied. "Can you run these license numbers and call me back, please?"

I went back to watching and waiting. After about an hour I wished I had gone to the bathroom before I left, so I locked the car and headed inside the hotel in search of relief.

On my salary, I don't spend a lot of time in fancy hotels, which is too bad, because I could become accustomed to places like the Crown Jewel. It was, indeed, a jewel of a place. Built in the shape of a diamond, the inner courtyard afforded each room a view of a landscape, dressed in evergreens covered with snow, like marshmallow frosting. The carpet was the color of merlot and about two inches thick. Creamy overstuffed leather chairs sat in groupings of twos and fours around a roaring fireplace. It felt clubby and discreet.

I ran to ask the desk clerk for directions to the ladies' room. On my way in, I passed two young women freshening up in front of mirrors. They were so absorbed they didn't noticed this thirty-something woman heading into a stall.

They could have been sixteen or nineteen, but judging chronology on young women can be tricky. They both had long hair. The blond wore a slinky black knit dress that hugged her curves like an Audi TT takes to the road. She leaned into the mirror and reapplied her mascara while talking to her friend. The brunette wore a slip while she hand-steamed wrinkles from a bright red silk dress draped from a hook on the wall by a hanger.

"So was he at least nice?" the blond asked Bambi.

"He was older than my father," she moaned.

"Did he like the dress?"

"I suppose. I didn't have it on that long."

Thoughts of Rebecca flashed through my mind and I got angry all over again.

"Oh, stop complaining," the blond said. "We're making more money than we're ever going to make in our lives. We're young and pretty. Why not enjoy it while we still can?"

"I hope this doesn't go on too long," Bambi replied. "I've got a big chemistry test to study for."

I stayed in the stall for a few minutes after the girls left while I thought through what they had said. At first I couldn't believe they would be so stupid as to talk about what they were doing when I could obviously overhear. Then I thought about the time Rebecca had some girlfriends for a sleepover at our house a few months ago. They gathered around our kitchen table discussing who was dealing drugs at school. I was at the kitchen sink, but I could have been on another planet. They were so wrapped up in themselves they forgot I was there.

If I went back to my editors with what I had heard, they would likely agree that the conversation implied there was prostitution going on at a hotel. That's hardly news. I had to find a way to tie it to McClintock. How?

The answer came in the guise of a funny feeling in my pocket when my cell phone began to vibrate.

"Yo, Skeeter," Ramon said. "I've got the names for you from the license plates."

"Thanks, Ramon," I replied. "Can you read them to me?"

He reeled off a list that included the mayor, a judge, a banker, a couple of CEOs, a doctor and a lawyer, and some other names I didn't recognize.

"Are you at some convention for the rich and famous?" he asked when he was done.

"Sounds like it, doesn't it?" I replied, thanking him as I said goodbye.

What were they all doing here on a Friday night? Maybe it was something as innocent as a business meeting. For months, Twin Cities' movers and shakers who were jockeying to build a new stadium for the Vikings had been meeting secretly. Maybe that was why they were all here. Or maybe it was something more sinister. This was going to take a little detective work. I hoped my anonymity, like Harry Potter's invisibility cloak, would continue to work for me as I nosed around the hotel.

The hotel's restaurant seemed the best place to start, and besides, I was getting hungry. I found my way to the front desk and asked directions to the dining room. This time an officious-looking man of about thirty-five with ramrod-straight posture pointed me down an oak-paneled hallway.

Considering how cold it was outside, I was surprised to see so many people in the dining room. A sweet young woman with her hair pulled up in a knot and a low-cut sweater showed me to a table near the kitchen. All the better for watching the diners.

"It seems busy tonight," I said to her as she handed me a menu.

"Yes, it is," she said, smiling. "Usually Friday nights are pretty quiet. Most of our guests are business travelers because we're close to the airport. They're usually on their way home by now."

I perused the pricey menu mentally savoring each juicy description, then set it down to take a good look about the room. The twenty-something couple in the corner was clearly having a romantic dinner. I detected some thigh-pinching in the rustle of their tablecloth. A couple in their sixties across from them ate in the silence of married folks who needed only to hear each other breathe to feel comfortable. In another corner a table of four women appeared to be sharing either juicy gossip or the plot of a good movie. None of the faces in the room looked familiar.

"I'm Katie and I'll be your server tonight," said the young woman who was suddenly standing by my side. "Would you like to hear the specials?"

I didn't care about the specials, but I asked her to list them anyway. Getting people talking is always a good way to establish rapport before asking nosey questions, so I listened intently, then ordered the shrimp drowning in butter.

"The parking lot is full tonight," I said in my most nonchalant voice. "Is there another party going on somewhere in the hotel, Katie?"

"Oh, yes," she said sweetly. "We've got a private dining room."

She hesitated a beat, then whispered conspiratorially. "About twenty men are in there. I saw an easel with some diagrams on it."

That must mean they were talking about the stadium yet again. Hardly a news story.

After finishing my coffee—and the flourless chocolate cake for dessert—I paid my bill with the newspaper's credit card, then headed for the door. I was reaching into the bowl of after-dinner mints when I heard a laugh and looked up to see the doors on the elevator across from the entrance to the dining room had opened. Standing there looking like a poster for a sleazy movie were the two girls I had seen in the restroom. Matthew McClintock stood between, an arm draped over each teen.

My first thought was outrage, quickly followed by a fear of Mc-Clintock recognizing me. I faked a sneeze, unfortunately into the bowl of mints, in an attempt to hide my face. It seemed to work. The doors closed and the light indicating the next stop for the elevator held at the fifth floor.

Thoughts of Rebecca and Billie swirled. Who did this guy think he was? How could he take advantage of girls like that? And go to school in the morning? This had to stop, I thought.

So what was I to do? Get him, that's what. How? I could hear my editor talking in my ear. Context, Hughes, context. I needed to be able to see McClintock somehow handing these girls off to a "client," preferably a high-profile one.

"Where are the stairs?" I asked the dining room hostess. "I'm on a new exercise program."

I followed her directions down the hall and to the left, then ducked into the stairwell, which I took to the second floor. A tad out of breath—damn, I wished I'd lost those twenty pounds—I opened the door to the hallway a crack in time to see McClintock closing the door to Room 213W.

"We'll be right back," I heard him. Then he stepped across the hall and knocked on room 211W. Bambi, opened the door wearing the wrinkle-free red dress.

"Everything OK?"

"It's all fine," she said in a kittenish voice. "Is he here yet?"

"A few more minutes," McClintock replied. "You just sit tight."

"I can't be late tonight," she whined. "I've got to study."

"This is the last friend for tonight," he said in that soft-as-well-tanned-leather voice of his.

He closed the door and headed for the elevator.

I leaned back against the wall and closed my eyes. What to do? What to do? Think. My brain was slowly evolving a plan when I heard the elevator ping and cracked the stairwell door again. Mc-Clintock stepped into the hallway with the governor's latest appointment to the bench.

They looked like a couple of schoolboys on their way to a dirty movie. There was a hint of a swagger in their gait that made me want to throw up. His Honor, a right-wing, God-and-family Bible thumper, seemed particularly giddy.

"Is she buxom?" he asked McClintock.

"As buxom as they come," McClintock said.

"I fully expect her to come," the good judge replied with a tipsy giggle.

"That was a good one, your Honor," McClintock guffawed.

"Can we come in?" he asked.

"Of course." Her voice was sing-songy.

"This is Mr. Jones," I heard McClintock say as he closed the door.

Ten minutes later McClintock left and made his way to the elevator. The next time the elevator pinged he was with a guy whose picture I had seen in the paper many times: a bank president who had recently beaten charges of embezzlement.

The two men went straight to room 213W. McClintock repeated the same routine, knocking on the door and introducing Mr. Smith. He didn't go in this time, just ushered his "client" into the room, then turned and left. I waited fifteen minutes, then slowly walked down the stairs to the ground floor, then out to my car, being careful the whole time to avoid running into the evil bastard.

The notion of Rebecca even near that man sickened me. I could write a story about pillars of the community having sex with teens for money, but that wouldn't be the whole picture. I needed more. I had to nail McClintock.

Chapter 30

I don't like to call editors at home on a Friday night. In fact, I'd never done it before. But Thom, who picked up on the first ring, had insisted I could call him at home anytime. A movie was playing in the background.

"This is Skeeter. We need to talk."

"It's Friday night and Chuck and I just got the kids to bed," he said, sounding tired. "Is it important?"

"Yeah, it's important," I said. "We need to talk about this face-to-face."

"OK, come over," he sighed. "I'll have the porch light on."

Fortunately, Thom lived near the hotel, so I pulled up to the curb in front of his house about ten minutes later. He lives in what's now called a "mid-century classic," a one-floor, three-bedroom, brick-front home with an attached double garage, like Cathy Berry's. A couple of years ago, Thom had given me a nail-by-nail description of the wood-paneled rumpus room his partner, Chuck, built in the basement for their adopted kids.

Chuck threw me a quick wave from the couch and continued to watch the movie while Thom ushered me into his cramped but homey kitchen. Coffee was already brewing. An editor who knows how much his reporters need coffee can't be all bad, I thought.

"OK, what's so important we need to talk right now?" he asked, once we were seated at the kitchen table. I warmed my hands on a hot mug of coffee printed with pictures of his two boys.

I laid out everything I had, including Rebecca's gift from Mc-Clintock.

"I could have this written up in time for Sunday's paper," I said. "But I know there's more to it."

"Whoa, slow down, Skeeter. I see some problems."

"Problems?" I heard myself yell. Suddenly all the tension of the last week began to spill over.

"What problems? I've been busting my butt to nail this guy. Who knows how many other girls this scumbag is going to use? The cops obviously aren't doing the job. Why not put the story in the paper? That's our job."

"You've demonstrated one of the problems I've got with this story," he said. "You. You're emotionally involved."

"You know what?" I replied. "I am emotionally involved. That's because I'm a human being, not some computer who can absorb the facts, then spit them out in a readable fashion."

"What's going on here, Skeeter?" he said in an even tone. "This isn't like you."

"I'm having the week from hell and it's not over yet. Suzy is sick. Rebecca is playing with fire. Michael is God knows where. I feel responsible for a girl I don't even know. I could have died in a tomb of snow. My car was firebombed! So if I'm not quite myself, that's why."

"You're usually the calm, cool professional," was his reply.

"Is that what I'm supposed to be? Some automaton that doesn't care about what it sees and hears while you're sitting in your nice little newsroom, waiting for slugs like me to turn in the stories you can ship to a computer that turns them into signals that bounce off a satellite, then down to a printing plant that turns them into print? Some robot that turns around and does the exact same thing the next day? A mere drone that feeds the gaping maw that fills in around the ads?"

I could hear my voice getting louder. "If that's what I've been reduced to, then it's time for me to get out of journalism. I didn't go into this business to risk my life and freeze my ass off covering outdoor art installations. And by the way, when are you bastards going to pay for my car?"

After that little Mount-St.-Helen's exercise I leaned back in my chair, feeling like a deflated balloon that had been blown up almost to bursting. I cupped both hands on my coffee and took a sip, eyeing Thom while he eyed me, for what seemed like a long time.

"Your car is what I was trying to reach you about today," he said, quietly. "According to the publisher, company policy says your per-mile reimbursement covers wear and tear on your car. However, she thinks this is an extreme case and she's taking the matter to the owner. You may be getting a check soon."

"Now, as far as your status, no, you are not a robot. If you were I'd have fired you a long time ago," he said. "It's your willingness to throw yourself into your stories that makes you a fine journalist. I don't want you ever to lose that.

"What I meant, however, is that you need to be careful that your emotional involvement doesn't cloud your judgment," he said, kindly. "The minute you learned Rebecca was involved, you should have asked yourself if you were too close to the story."

"You may be right," I told him. "But I'm sure as hell not giving this story to another reporter."

"I don't want you to give it away," he said. "You've already done most of the work. But you also have to realize that you're talking about some heavyweights in town. You've got to have some hard evidence to back up what you saw."

"Like what?"

"I don't suppose you got any shots or video on your cell phone of McCormick and the judge?"

I poured a little more half and half into my coffee. "Had the paper's bean counter who bought these phones spent a couple extra dollars for the kind with phone and video, instead of the Fred Flintstone version, I would have." I stirred in another spoonful of sugar.

"You've got documentation from his divorce that McClintock has money problems, right? So that's taken care of." Thom stirred his coffee while he thought. "Why don't we set up someone with a wire and get him to act like a client and record McClintock?"

"A wire, Thom?" I asked. "Think about it. Prostitution means getting naked. Where is some guy going to hide a wire when he's naked? And even if we could somehow jump that technological hurdle, who would do it? McClintock is no dummy. He'd know right away if we used some reporter."

Thom looked down at his coffee cup while pulling at his mustache. The Thom I used to know was resurfacing. I remembered the first couple of days that I worked at the paper when I had to write about a new city budget. Those things are hugely complicated to write, even for experienced reporters. I barely knew what a tax levy was, let alone all the intricacies of how it fit into the budget overall. Just to make it tougher, the city didn't release the final numbers until four o'clock in the afternoon, and half the politicians disagreed with what it said. By five o'clock I was hyperventilating and looking at a six o'clock deadline. Thom came by my desk and asked how it was going. I burst into tears, which is not a good move in a newsroom that expects reporters to be as calm as the pilot of a 747 in a tailspin. Thom took one look at the information and stood behind me dictating the story. As I typed his words it all began to make sense to me. It had my byline on it, but it was his work. I called him my hero. I wanted to work for him forever. I wondered where that Thom had been earlier this week.

"I saw that McClintock does his business in rooms 211W and 213W. Maybe we should figure out a way to bug those rooms," I suggested.

"No can do," he replied. "Without a warrant, that's illegal. If the paper found out we did that you and I would be looking for jobs yanking the guts out of turkeys for Jennie-O."

"Then what?"

"Remember the story a year or so ago about the cops videotaping a drug bust and then getting a lip reader to translate what was said?" Thom said while stirring his coffee. "We could do the same thing. We could rent a room across the courtyard from where McClintock has his dates and set up a video camera. We can film what they're saying, then have it translated."

"So it's illegal to bug a room but not video a room?"

"Right. We'd be observing what anyone would see if they watched from their own room. Granted, it's window peeping, but it's not illegal."

"How do we figure out where to set up the camera?"

Thom went to his home computer in the den and looked up the Web site for the Crown Jewel. After a few clicks he found a schematic designed to help customers reserve a room on line.

"According to this, there's a 211 East to go with 211 West," he said. "That would probably be a good spot to set up the camera. We'll get you a reservation in 211 East."

"That's an interesting idea, but do you think that a newspaper that is having trouble paying for a firebombed car is going to spring for a hotel room, a videographer, and a lip reader?"

"They come out of different budgets," he said. "One is operating, one is personnel. The paper is always more willing to pay for story expenses than its people."

"Who would we get to do it?" Then I chuckled. "You're not volunteering, are you?"

"Ahhh, no."

"Let's think," I said. "We need a guy who is fairly open-minded, someone who would be interested enough in the story to take the risk. A guy who can think on his feet. A good talker. It would help if he looked like McClintock's other clients. Somebody with a little grey hair."

Another long silence. Then it dawned on me. "How about Billie's dad? He certainly fits all the criteria. He's also got a big interest in the story."

"Would he do it?"

"I don't know," I replied. "Cathy Berry is suspicious of him. For a while there I got the impression she thought he might even know where she is."

"Do you think he snatched her? Or helped her run away?"

"I don't know. I suppose we could get a better idea of how badly he wants Billie back by asking him to help us get to McClintock. It couldn't hurt to ask."

I finished my coffee and looked at the clock. It was getting late. Time to go home to my girls and let Thom finish his movie with Chuck.

"Thanks, Thom," I said as I set my coffee cup on his kitchen counter. "I'll call Peter Berry in the morning."

As I tugged on my hat, coat, gloves, and mittens in preparation to go out into the minus-thirty-two degrees wind chill, Thom put his hands on my shoulders.

"I meant what I said about how important you are to this newspaper," he said. "You're somebody who buys in. That's what makes you good."

Then he tucked a strand of hair behind his ear.

Chapter 31

Saturday morning dawned bright and cold and clear. The predicted high in the Twin Cities was minus five degrees, with a wind chill of minus thirty-four. Because she seemed fine, I decided that Suzy's flu had been of the twenty-four-hour variety. The girls would be with their soccer teams all day. I was grateful they played indoor soccer, instead of outdoor hockey.

Next on my agenda was a call to Peter Berry.

"Mr. Berry," I said when I got him on the phone. "This is Skeeter from the *Citizen*. How are you this morning?"

"I just got back from yoga class. I am serene," he said. "What can I do for you?"

"I wanted you to know that I got your message," I said. Then I took a deep breath. I wasn't sure how he would react to my next question. "I ran a Google on you and found there have been complaints about you to the state licensing board. Could you tell me what they were about?"

"No, I'm afraid I can't, Skeeter." I was relieved that he spoke calmly. "The matter remains confidential. But I can tell you the charges were filed by a delusional patient. I'm sure you noted that the board found no reason to discipline me. Is there another matter we can discuss?"

"Actually, there is," I replied. "I have an idea about what has been going on with Billie. There might be a way that you can help track her down."

"Do you know where she is?"

"Not exactly."

"Then how can you say you have an idea about what she's been doing?"

As I filled him in on McClintock and my coffee shop encounter with Billie, I imagined him nodding his head, taking it all in. I wondered if he already knew much of what I was telling him, or if he was in his good-listener shrink mode. Either way, he didn't ask any specific questions about the scenario I laid out. But he was willing to help.

"What have you got in mind?" he asked.

It sounded far-fetched, even to me. In the light of morning I could only wonder what Thom had been thinking last night when he proposed this idea. Would Peter Berry be part of the subterfuge or laugh at the insanity of it all?

"That's a pretty bizarre idea," he said. "You know, I already tried to get a friend to put something on the TV news about Billie. Now you want me to pose as someone looking for a hooker?"

"If you're not comfortable with this, we can get someone else," I said. "We thought you fit the description we were looking for."

"Do I strike you as the kind of guy who goes to hookers?" he asked, half laughing, half indignant.

"I meant that you're smart, interested in the story—I think—and about the right age."

There was a long silence on the phone line while he considered my request.

"I'll do it," he finally replied.

Maybe Peter Berry really did care about Billie. Hadn't seen that one coming. Then he hit me with the next question.

"How do I get in touch with this McClintock?"

That took me aback. I hadn't expected him to agree so readily, and I certainly hadn't thought about how we would execute this.

"I don't know," I replied.

"I bet my wife would know," he said. "Flight attendants hear a lot. I'll ask her and call you back."

I gave him my home number, and ten minutes later the phone rang. It was Peter Berry.

"As I suspected, it won't be that difficult to get in touch with him. Allison says a few pilots use his, umm, service."

"Hold on here," I said. "You don't mind if some of your wife's co-workers know you're looking for a teenage hooker? And what does Allison make of that?"

I expected him to laugh at my question, but he didn't.

"I'll do whatever it takes to get Billie back home," he said, seriously. I could hear him breathing on the phone while he formulated his next thought. "I don't care what anybody thinks, and neither does Allison. She's appalled at what the pilots have been doing anyway. I'll get a time and a place and get back to you."

He called back within half an hour. "I have a 'date.' "

"You're kidding. That's quick."

"Only took a couple of phone calls," he said. "It is amazing how fast commerce works, isn't it? Delivery is scheduled for tonight at the Crown Jewel. Isn't that the name of some kind of popcorn?"

"Actually, it is," I replied. "How do you know that?"

"It's Billie's favorite brand," he replied. "Anyway, I'm supposed to sit at the hotel bar at 10:30, order a martini, and specify three olives. Sure hope the bartender doesn't put three olives in everybody's martini."

"What's McClintock charging?" I asked.

"He didn't say," Peter replied. "It was a strange conversation. Almost like he thought there might have been a wiretap. He said he'd meet me at the bar then we'd go from there."

"So you don't know what room he's going to take you to?"

"Sorry," he replied.

"OK," I said. "We'll just have to figure this out as we go along."

I called Thom and filled him in. As I heard myself explain what had transpired, the whole thing felt odd to me. Here was this shrink/drug salesman who lives in a geodesic dome, willing to pose as a john for a pimp whose other clients worked with his wife. And I was the one who had asked him to do it. Was I nuts? Would the publisher accept my explanation that it seemed like a good idea at the time?

"I am getting paid overtime, right?" After the hassle with the car I was going to check with the boss on every move.

"Of course," Thom said.

It was going to take some serious hustle to rent a room across the courtyard from where McClintock set up his "dates" and get a videographer in place to capture one of them. Fortunately, Thom had a friend recently fired from a TV station, who started his own freelance video business. It happened that the guy had no life and was actually free on this Saturday night, for a per-hour rate triple what I would be getting.

While Thom set up the videographer, I returned phone calls to Sergeant Victoria Olson and Cathy Berry. I didn't want to talk to either one, but figured that if I rang on a Saturday morning they might not be around to answer. It worked. I got answering machines. "This is Skeeter returning your call," was all I said.

With Suzy and Rebecca gone to soccer, I had a little time to clean up the house, or at least a lick and a promise. I was scrubbing the kitchen sink when the phone rang. I answered without looking at the caller ID, hoping it was Michael. Instead, it was Cathy Berry.

"It was good to get a return phone call from you finally," said the ever-charming Mrs. Berry. "Where have you been?"

I wondered how she had my home phone number, then realized she probably had caller ID. Curses.

"I've been pretty busy, Mrs. Berry," I said. "What can I do for you?

"First, return my calls promptly," she said. I resisted the temptation to tell her she was not my boss and I had no obligation to talk to her at all. I hoped this one instance of keeping my mouth shut would work toward canceling out all the black marks on my ledger of caustic episodes. "Then you can tell me if you're any closer to putting an article in the paper about Billie."

"I'm working on that. Possibly next week. But things can change fast. I never know for sure what's going in the paper until I see it in the morning."

"Then tell me this: Is there any truth to the rumors I'm hearing about Matthew McClintock?"

That knocked me back on my fuzzy pink slippers.

"What have you heard?" I asked.

"I was in the grocery store yesterday where I bumped into the mom of a girl who goes to Kennedy Junior High. She said the school board was investigating McClintock. Something to do with gambling and womanizing."

"Did you believe her?"

"You know, I can't believe it. I've always thought he was the nicest man. And soooo good looking. I must say I took special note when I heard that horrible wife of his divorced him."

"What could be motivating an investigation?"

"There are people in this community who don't like him," she replied. "They think he's too, I don't know, flashy, the way he throws money around. It's not the Minnesota way, you know. People who have a lot of money usually spend it when they're visiting somewhere else. Not here. I think the folks in town are jealous. He could sure lavish some cash on me, I'll tell you. This whole inquisition is the fault of that Marilyn Peters."

It seemed like it had been a year since I talked to school board member Marilyn Peters, but it was only a few days ago when she told me about the vote to remove McClintock. She was right when she said I would probably hear about it.

"Marilyn Peters is involved?" I asked.

"She was having an affair with him," Mrs. Berry replied with a haughty laugh. "That's why his first wife divorced him. Then he dumped Marilyn."

"How do you know that?" I was stunned.

"Honey, everybody in town knows that."

"Are you saying the school board is investigating McClintock because he dumped Marilyn Peters?'

"Of course. What other reason could there be?"

"Maybe he's doing something illegal."

"Do you think so?" was her comeback.

I was so busted. I had backed myself into a quandary because of my own line of questioning. When would I ever learn? I sure didn't want to tell her what I knew if she would be spreading it all over Land o' Lakes. On the other hand, I felt an obligation to leave her with at least something.

"Well, do you?" she repeated. There was a catch in her voice and I could almost hear the wheels turning in her brain. "Does this relate in any way to Billie?"

"The school board's actions are private until they actually remove McClintock," I said. "There is no way that I can know whether the investigation, if there is one, has anything to do with Billie."

It was the truth, or at least, a part of the truth. You may not believe this, but I hate to lie. Truly. I always feel bad afterward. Sometimes I feel so bad I go back and set things right. But not this time. At least not now. I was too afraid of what this lunatic woman would do if she knew what was really going on.

"Sorry, Mrs. Berry, I've got a call on the other line. Gotta go," I lied again.

All thoughts of cleaning the house flew out of my head as I stared at the phone after hanging up. I had to check this out with Marilyn immediately.

Home phone numbers are gold to reporters. I know a reporter who was invited to the home of former vice president Hubert Humphrey for a party. On her way to the bathroom, she stopped at the master bedroom and copied down the private number. That came in plenty handy years later when she needed to reach him fast.

Good thing I covered Marilyn Peters when she ran for school board. I hold on to the cell phone numbers, pager numbers, and e-mail addresses of just about everyone I call. You never know when they'll come in handy. That habit meant I could reach Marilyn Peters to ask her about Mrs. Berry's conjecture.

This is not to say I relished calling her. I dreaded it. Generally, newspapers don't report on trysts. If we ran stories about every infidelity, there would be no room in the newspaper for anything else. But when it involves an elected official and her subordinate, also a public employee, it's a different matter. I've never been one to turn a deaf ear to juicy gossip, but it makes me uncomfortable to ask about an affair. I almost hoped Marilyn wouldn't be home so I could leave a message as I'd done for Cathy Berry and Victoria Olson. Alas, my luck didn't hold. She picked up on the first ring.

"Hi, Mrs. Peters, this is Skeeter from the *Citizen*."

"What can I do for you on this chilly Saturday morning, Skeeter?" she said, skipping any chitchat that would give me a chance to warm up to the subject.

"Has there been any progress on the McClintock investigation?"

"Why do you ask?" Her tone was cautious.

"I heard you had an affair with McClintock." I blurted it out. No preamble. Nothing.

"Where did you hear that, and what business is it of yours?" she asked.

"Where I heard it is irrelevant," I said. "Did you?"

"I repeat, what business is it of yours?" she asked.

"Normally, it would be none of my business," I replied. "But there's a rumor you have started the investigation because of an affair that went bad."

I expected her to lash out. Instead, she let loose a deep, throaty smoker's laugh.

"I love to watch the rumor mill at work," she finally said. "I have never had an affair with Matthew McClintock. I did, however, have dinner with him, once, shortly after my husband died and his wife divorced him. My salad was only half gone when I knew that man had deep, serious issues, and I wanted nothing to do with him."

I would never again accept anything Cathy Berry told me at face value.

"However, I find it funny you should ask about all this today," she continued. "There have been phone calls flying back and forth this morning among the board members. Apparently, the police are close to arresting him."

"How do you know that?" I asked.

"One of the board members is married to a cop," she replied.

She had another call, so she ended our conversation before I could ask about the impending bust. If she was right, the deadline was nearing on our own sting operation.

I called Thom to see if everything was in place with the videographer and the hotel room.

"I talked with the publisher and she's squeamish about paying for this gig," he said.

"You told me it came out of a different budget," I replied.

"Yeah, I know. That budget is running a bit dry," Thom replied.

"Don't tell me you're backing out on this, Thom."

"That's not what I'm saying," he replied. "But if this doesn't work, I don't think we'll get a second chance."

"I'll do my best, Chief," was the best retort I could conjure.

I looked at my watch and realized check-in was not long off. I made a big pot of spaghetti, asked Helmey to pick up the girls and left a note that said I loved them and would be home as soon as possible. "Don't wait up for me," I added, along with two hearts.

Chapter 32

When this is over, I vowed, the paper would be giving me some serious time off, which I would spend entirely with the girls to make up for being gone so much this week.

I hopped in the paper's car, wondering again when I was going to get a check to replace my briquette. I headed for the Crown Jewel. Traffic was light on a Saturday so I got there quickly and parked next to a twelve-foot pile of dirty snow that had been plowed to the back of the hotel's parking lot. I didn't want anyone to see the markings on the car and wonder what someone from the *Citizen* was doing there.

This time I marched right up to the front desk to check in. With his never-ending twisted sense of humor, Thom had reserved room 211 East on the courtyard under the name Ms. L. Lane. I gave the woman cash, took the pass card, and strode to my room as though I were any other hotel guest. The only difference, which I hoped wouldn't show, was my heart was beating so fast it felt like I was there for some illicit affair. In a way, I guess I was.

I read a survey somewhere that said travelers' top three priorities in a hotel room are a big, comfortable bed, a great TV, and a way cool bathroom. Apparently the owners of the Crown Jewel read the same survey, because this expensive room was tops in all those areas. The bed was a pillow-top king. There was a forty-two-inch plasma screen TV on the wall, and an eleven-inch version of the same in the bathroom across from the toilet and next to a second phone. The bathroom sink was a huge, solid glass bowl on a glass pedestal.

I knew this was going to take a while, so I called home to see how things were going. Helmey answered. "Suzy is taking a hot bath. Rebecca is in her room. I wouldn't be surprised if she was grabbing a little shut-eye herself, don't ya know. They both came home pretty tired."

"I'm afraid this is going to be a long night," I replied.

"Do you want to talk about what you're doing?" Helmey asked.

It all sounded so improbable as I listened to myself. "Am I nuts, Helmey?"

"I wouldn't say exactly nuts," he replied. "Maybe a little fool-hardy."

"What do you mean?"

"Why are you doing this, Skeeter?"

"Because we need some evidence that this bastard is preying on girls."

"Is that the only reason?"

"What do you mean?"

"Is this about him, or about you?"

"About me? How can you say this is about me?"

"It seems to me you're going some to get this guy. You aren't even a police officer. Why can't you leave it to the cops?"

"The police have not protected these girls. Their parents obviously haven't protected these girls. If I don't do it, who will?"

Helmey let the thought hang on the telephone wire for a second or two. Then he spoke slowly and softly.

"You're a good woman, Skeeter," he said. "Just remember that you've got daughters of your own to protect. If you're hurt you can't do right by them. Be careful."

"I promise. Thanks for helping me out here, Helmey."

I hung up the phone, but my thoughts kept running. Helmey was right. If I were killed or maimed, my girls would suffer, no doubt about it. Was this story worth that? Is any story worth that? I certainly wasn't about to take a bullet for the *Citizen*. But how far would I go to expose adults who were threatening young women, or should be protecting them and weren't? Pretty far.

I was in the room for an hour, nervously channel surfing on the plasma TV. What had I gotten myself into, I wondered. Would this really work? Would my colleagues laugh at me when they heard about the plan? I had run through all of the stations many times when I got a call from the videographer, who wanted to know where I was and how he could get in without drawing undue attention to all his equipment. I was glad he called about that detail. It meant he understood the assignment. When I let him in I realized he was higher than my hopes. The guy smelled like a marijuana stash. Well, I thought, maybe he had been with friends partaking of the illegal weed. Maybe he joined them, but didn't inhale.

He blew that idea away when he stepped outside to enjoy a joint after setting up his equipment. No wonder he had been fired. Unfortunately, it was too late to request a cogent videographer. I hoped the guy did his best work high.

Moments later, my cell phone rang.

"This is Peter. I'm in the bar, nursing my three-olive martini."

"When you get in the room, be sure to open the drapes so we can get a good view of what's going on," I said.

I described McClintock for him. "Do you see him?"

"Not yet. But there sure are a lot of movers and shakers in here. I see the mayor sitting over in the corner with a council member. There's a table in the back with four guys who look like Vikings, or at least guys big enough to play pro-football."

"But no McClintock?" I was antsy.

"No. Oh, wait a minute. I think I see the bastard now. Gotta go."

With the lights off in our room and the curtains open, the videographer and I scanned the rooms across the courtyard. After about thirty minutes, we saw Peter open the heavy curtains just as the hotel room door was closing. McClintock must have left the room for some reason and Peter took the opportunity to let us see what was going on.

The décor was a mirror reflection of the room we occupied, except Bambi, the brunette I had seen in the ladies' room, was sitting primly on the side of a bed and picking at a thread on the bedspread. Peter was standing beside her.

I had never witnessed a setup for prostitution before, and it felt a bit like watching one of those wildlife TV shows shot in some African jungle. I imagined David Attenborough telling the audience that the male of the species often paces about while the female, in full coloration, watches her potential mates. Eventually the males begin rutting behavior, pawing and bellowing.

My imaginary episode of Planet Earth was almost to an end when I realized McClintock had reentered the room. He was pointing to the open drapes.

"What the hell are you doing?" he said, facing the window squarely and making it easy to read his lips.

Peter was gesticulating wildly and McClintock's Germanic face was bright red. They shouted at each other for a couple of minutes, then Peter pulled back his fist and landed a big one on McClintock's perfect nose.

Chapter 33

We captured the whole gory mess on video. McClintock reached for his nose, which spattered blood all over the grey carpeting, and Bambi jumped up to minister to him with a pure white bathroom towel. Peter stood there, shaking so badly we could see it from across the courtyard, and then he ran out the door. Seconds later, my cell phone rang.

"Skeeter, I'm sorry," Peter whispered into the phone, breathlessly. I looked down in the courtyard, barely able to make out his shadow behind a snow-covered pine tree. He must have dashed out a nearby exit. I hoped he hadn't tripped an alarm. "I didn't intend to hit him."

"Well, you did," I said. "What happened?"

"He's such an arrogant bastard."

"I know that, but tell me what pushed you to break his nose?" And ruin what little hope I had of getting the proof I needed, I said to myself.

Peter said that he had been sitting at the bar, sipping his martini when McClintock slid onto the bar stool next to him. To identify himself, Peter turned to McClintock and commented that he'd never had a three-olive martini before.

"You must be the man I talked with this morning," McClintock told Peter. "Jim, I think you said your name was."

As Peter told it, McClintock ordered his own martini and talked about the tough winter and mused about the buckets of money snowmobile makers were shoveling in. After a bit more chatter, McClintock told Peter he would be taking him to his room in a few minutes. He said he expected to be paid $400 for a half-hour "visit," and that Peter could slip him the money once they got to the room.

"He said she was all mine. That made me think of Billie," Peter said. "I knew I was angry, but I thought I had myself under control."

When they got to the room, one look at the girl and he flashed a mental picture that nauseated him, Peter said. "She could have been one of the friends Billie used to bring home from school."

Peter said he began to imagine what her life was like, what McClintock had been doing to her. He thought about Billie as a little girl, and remembered her first day of kindergarten. How she had a blue lunch box that she dragged behind her as she lifted her tiny legs against the big steps of the school bus. He remembered when she came home from school with a D on a math test, and how she had stayed up most of the night going over the test, vowing to retake it and get every answer right. Then he thought about McClintock as a school principal, and how he violated the trust that parents and kids put in him.

"His cell phone rang and he said he had to make another 'delivery,'" Peter said. "That pushed me over the edge. When he returned, I erupted. I told him he was slime. I told him he didn't deserve to be walking the Earth. He asked me what made me think I was so high and mighty. That hit home. I realized that if ever there was going to be a time to stand up for Billie, this was it. Then I hit him."

"How did it feel?" I asked.

"I haven't had this much fun since the Twins won the pennant. I'm sorry about what this means for your story."

"The good news is that McClintock can't exactly call the cops, or even the hotel management, so I guess we're safe on that score," I said. "He didn't pick up any hint that you were more than a dissatisfied customer, did he?"

"I don't think so."

"OK, go home," I said. "I'll figure out something else."

I turned off my cell phone and threw it down on the bed with a sigh while I tried to come up with a new plan. I paced as I thought through my options—maybe I should go into jewelry making—when our high-as-a-kite videographer whispered, mostly to himself, "Like, cool, man."

Although I had forgotten all about him, he was so stoned he forgot to turn off the camera and kept filming while I talked with Peter.

"Skeeter, ya gotta look at this," he said.

McClintock had continued to conduct business while holding a clean washcloth to his nose. The Land o' Lakes mayor came into the room and handed McClintock a wad of cash. We couldn't tell what they were saying, but we had a clear shot of their faces. I was sure our lip reader would be able to decipher what was said.

Oh my God, I thought. This is it—the story I've been chasing. Video of the mayor paying for sex with a youngster. Stories don't get better than this. I felt a smile growing on my face. This was why I went into journalism.

McClintock left the room and the mayor and the girl were left alone. The same girl who sounded so confident when I overheard her talking in the restroom suddenly took on the body language of a beaten dog. She didn't look Hizzoner in the eye. Her sparkle was gone, replaced with the body language of deep fear. Her head hung on her neck and her shoulders were slumped. I couldn't see any words coming from her mouth, but her eyes had the vacant stare of someone who had mentally moved to a different locale.

I was surprised to see that the mayor, for all the spring in his step when he first entered the room, didn't look much happier. He took off his tie, jacket, and shirt almost mechanically and folded them neatly on a chair. He said something to her and she slipped out of her dress, hanging it in the closet like a good girl. In just her bra and panties, she began to loosen his belt, pulling down his pants and briefs. His body was hairy, and sagging.

He sat on the edge of the bed and slipped off his shoes and socks, which she balled up and placed in the wingtips she had set neatly on the floor. Neither of them looked at the other's face. He said something else and she began to unhook the clasp on the front of her bra, still avoiding his gaze.

As I watched the video I couldn't help but think that Bambi wasn't much older than my Rebecca. It made me sick to think about how McClintock had approached her. I understood why Peter had slugged him.

Rebecca long ago stopped letting me see her naked, so it had been quite a while since I'd seen all of a young woman's skin. Even though it was tinged with green by our camera's night scope, I couldn't get over the beauty of this brand-new woman body. Strong breasts. Long, graceful limbs. Firm tummy yet to know the bulge of a baby. Hips eased wide just below a narrow waist.

When he began to stroke her hair she flinched, then squeezed her eyes shut tight as he pulled her down on the bed beside him. In moments, he was on top of her. The sex, if you want to call it that, couldn't have lasted more than ten minutes. After he was done he rose, sat on the side of the bed, and lit a cigarette. When she got up on the other side her face was totally without expression, as though she were a zombie. Someone whose life had left her body. She dressed and left the room. They didn't exchange a word.

Chapter 34

The still-high shooter handed me the videotape, packed up his gear, and left. It was early morning when I stuffed it in my cloth book bag and headed for the car, after leaving a big tip, courtesy of the newspaper, for the maid, who would find the bed hadn't been touched and the room smelled faintly of marijuana.

I held the tape in my hand, feeling a little sick and elated at the same time. Clearly, we had the goods on McClintock and the mayor. I was about to write a story that would tell the world about the creep who had done serious damage to many young women. Even better, the story would be a serious contender for some big-time journalism awards and go a long way toward moving me a notch higher on the newspaper's food chain. It might even send a message to Billie that she could return to her family and go back to high school.

Yet the tape I held in my hand was nothing but images of depravity. Of the worst kind of abuse of power. Of man's inhumanity to woman. The joy I had felt about this juicy story tinged with regret. Was this really the way I wanted to make a living, thinking about something I didn't wanted to think about?

Nonetheless, I knew the story wouldn't get in the paper if I didn't write it. After a few hours of sleep, I headed into the newsroom and called Thom at home. When I described the evening, we agreed that even though Peter had turned out to be a failure as a plant, we had plenty of supporting material from the videotape to go ahead with the story.

"Start writing, Skeeter," he said. "The lawyers will look at it Monday."

Sunday is my favorite day in the newsroom. Banks of muted televisions tuned to sports events and CNN give the room a comforting movement encased in silence. A ringing phone is unusual and the number of e-mails is significantly reduced. Except for the sports writers and the weekend police reporters, the place is empty. Editors or other "old folks" over forty are seldom around. People who work on Sundays are usually low on seniority. It feels like "the kids" are running the place, and that's how I like it.

Secure in the knowledge that Helmey and the girls were working on the loft in Rebecca's room, I settled down at my desk. The hot sludge that passes for coffee steamed to my right, and my notes spread to my left. I threw my byline up on the screen, then stared at it until my screen saver began running a scroll of the First Amendment: "Congress shall make no law . . . abridging the freedom of speech, or of the press. . . ."

Getting started is always the toughest part of writing for me. What can I write that will make the reader want to keep going to the next paragraph? And the one after that? The easiest action for a reader is to stop. How could I prevent that?

I had so much to say, yet the words somehow weren't making the trip to my fingers, so I harkened back to the advice of an editor I had in college. She told me that when I was stuck I should read my notes, put them away, and then pretend I was writing a letter about the story to my mother.

"If your mother can understand what you're writing, most readers will understand, too," she said.

It worked, thank God. I was happily typing away, looking like I was playing the piano while gazing out the window, when it dawned on me that the story needed a comment from McClintock and the mayor of Land o' Lakes. I didn't have a home or cell phone number for McClintock, so I figured that could wait until Monday when I would call him at his school. I did have a home phone number for the mayor. He answered on the first ring.

"Mayor, this is Skeeter Hughes from the *Citizen*," I said. "I have some questions for you."

"How nice to hear from you, Skeeter," he said. "You know, I never told you how much I enjoyed the profile you wrote about me a few weeks ago. I had several nice comments about it. I did get to praise you to your publisher, however. You know, we went to college together. I told her you're a fine reporter. Accurate, honest, hard-working."

He wouldn't be thinking that way when our conversation was over, I mused to myself.

"What can I do for you on this bright, cold Sunday?" he asked. I could hear the Vikings game on the television in the background. I looked up at the TV monitor overhead and realized they were beating the Packers, twelve to six. I figured what I was about to say to the mayor would ruin his day even if the Vikes won.

"I'm not quite sure how to tell you this, Mayor, so I guess I'll jump in. I was at the Crown Jewel last night working on a story about Matthew McClintock. A videographer and I taped a hotel room where McClintock was … conducting business. We got some tape of you having sex with a girl who appeared to be high school age. We plan to put this story in the newspaper this week. I'm calling to give you an opportunity to comment."

I glanced up at the newsroom clock and noted the location of the second hand as I finished my speech, then watched it make a full revolution as I listened to dead silence on the other end.

"Jesus," the mayor whispered before hanging up.

I typed, "The mayor declined to comment," then went on writing the story hoping the publisher would remember that the mayor said my work was accurate.

I was deep into describing McClintock's divorce and money problems when my phone rang.

"Skeeter, this is Sergeant Victoria Olson," said the husky voice on the end of the line. "I'm surprised I caught you at work on a Sunday. You must be a busy lady."

"These are busy times, Sergeant. What can I do for you?"

"I'm concerned about Billie," she said. "A security camera in the parking lot of the Crown Jewel captured footage of her being forced into a car about four o'clock this morning by a man who looks like McClintock. I've called both her parents and neither of them has seen her. I was wondering if you had heard from her. I'm worried McClintock may hurt her."

"What do you mean, 'hurt her'?" I asked.

"The surveillance camera showed he had her by the upper arm and she was struggling to get away as he forced her into a silver Audi," she said. "The guy runs drugs and prostitution. His kind can get violent."

"I cannot believe you cops," I exploded. "You enlist this girl to do your work, then put her in danger. What were you thinking?"

"No need to get huffy with me, Missy," came the Sergeant's reply. "I repeat: Have you heard from her?"

I decided I couldn't hide what I knew from Olson, so I spilled the whole story about our brief meeting in the coffee shop. Unfortunately, my mouth kept running after my brain had told it to stop. I told her about the article I was writing, about the videotape of the mayor, about McClintock at the Crown Jewel.

I'll spare you the four-letter words, but her reply was swift and sharp and the message was clear: Don't print the story.

"If that girl dies, it will be your fault," she said.

About once a week people try to stop the newspaper from running a story. Often they argue that a tragedy will occur if a certain article appears. Sometimes they have good reasons, sometimes they don't. But their arguments are usually heard. I told her I would talk about her concerns with my editors, then quickly hung up the phone as she was shouting phrases we can't put in a family newspaper.

I needed to keep writing, but I couldn't get her warning out of my head. Less than a week ago I started working on a story about a girl who was missing. Now the girl was still missing and in serious danger. In my head I knew that I had not caused the mess Billie and Sgt. Olson had made. But in my heart I wasn't so sure. I had a nagging feeling that I was somehow responsible. If she were hurt because of me, I would never forgive myself. How was I going to get both of us out of this mess?

Writing a story for the newspaper wasn't going to do it, I decided. I needed to take more direct action. But how? I shut down my computer and headed for the coffee shop where Billie and I had met days ago. I was hoping Billie was a regular there. Luckily, the girl who had made our coffee was working this Sunday afternoon, and she remembered Billie.

"She was in here a second time on Friday. I'm pretty sure it was her because she was sitting alone in that corner for a long time," she said with a nod of her head in the direction opposite the cash register. "Then this good-looking blond old guy came in and sat down with her. They were, like, fighting or something. She was crying, then she ran out. Next time I looked up, he was gone too."

"Could you hear what they were talking about?"

"I don't listen in on customers' conversations," she sniffed.

"Do you remember anything else about either of them?"

"He left a five-dollar tip and told me I was pretty," she said with a smile.

I was walking back to the newsroom, pondering this piece of information, when my cell phone rang.

"Skeeter, this is Joey Pignatello—you know, the guy who worked with Billie?"

"Hi, Joey. What's up?"

"I'm a little worried about Billie," he said. "About two o'clock this morning I got a call on my cell phone. I'm pretty sure it was Billie, or at least it sounded like her."

"What did she say?"

"All she said was 'Joey,' and then the phone went dead. At first I thought that her phone lost the connection. Then I got to thinking about it. She sounded like she was crying. I didn't know who else to contact, so I called you."

I thanked Joey and asked him to let me know if he heard any more from Billie. I briefly considered ringing Sergeant Olson back, then discarded the idea. She was supposed to be protecting Billie and she hadn't done a good job so far. I didn't trust her to do it now.

Now I was even more scared for Billie. It was time to stop nibbling around the edges of the story and find her. Did McClintock have her trapped? Where? Why? As I sat down at my desk, my eyes fell upon the folder with the copies of his divorce settlement. I opened it and leafed through until I found a list of his assets. He still owned a quarter of an acre in Land o' Lakes. I checked the address against our online list of property taxes, then checked it on Google maps, satellite view. It looked like the closest building was more than a mile away. Could be a shack in the woods, and a perfect place to stash Billie. I pushed my feet into my boots, grabbed my coat, and headed for the door, so engrossed in where I was headed that I forgot I hadn't charged my phone. Another mistake.

Chapter 35

It wasn't easy finding McClintock's place, even with a good map. After turning around in private drives a few times, I finally found it just as the sun slipped behind what passed for a ridge in flat Minnesota. The moon hadn't risen yet. The only light came from the darkening sky's reflection on the snow. I pulled the car behind an evergreen off to the side of the road and about twenty feet away from the cabin. The heavy snow still on the branches from the storm Wednesday night gave added cover, but there was a hole through the tree big enough to provide a window, of sorts.

McClintock's place was a fallen down, wood-framed dump on a concrete slab. One step up to the entrance had rotted through and a single decorative shutter swung from a nail over one of two front windows. I couldn't tell if there was a rear exit. A light burning through a dirty bed sheet hung on one of the small windows. Firewood was stacked against the side of one wall, but I couldn't see any smoke rising from the chimney. Six bald tires were piled up about a foot away from the left side of the front door.

Apparently McClintock had a lot of visitors. Many tires had dug deep ruts leading up to the shanty, around it and back again, forming a cul-de-sac that no doubt made for easy pickup and delivery. It was an ideal setup for a meth lab. The silver Audi parked to the side of the place indicated McClintock was inside.

Journalism school had not prepared me for this moment. Neither had the newspaper. All I knew about the situation were fleeting memories of scenes from television. Not exactly text book training. My gut was going to have to be my guide.

I turned off the engine and slipped down in the driver's seat until I could see the shack through the steering wheel and watched for a long time, trying to measure my breath. I didn't want anyone to wonder why the windows were steamed up.

I was about to tiptoe up to the cabin when the trill of my cell phone pierced the silence. I jumped, then dove for the floor where the phone vibrated deep in my purse, then let out a second ring. I prayed the noise had not escaped the soundproofing of the car as I flipped it open. "Hello."

"Why are you whispering?"

"Good God, Michael, you scared me to death. Can you talk more quietly?"

"Why? What's going on?"

He couldn't see me roll my eyes. I had been trying to talk with him all week, and he chose this moment to get back to me. But it was not the time to have that discussion.

"I'm working on a story."

"You sound like you're undercover or on a stakeout or something. What could be happening in Land o' Lakes that requires such subterfuge?"

"Don't patronize me, Michael." My head was mostly under the dash so no one but Michael could hear me. "When are you coming home?"

"I am home," he said. "And so are the kids ... who have been with Helmey a hell of a long time. What's going on there?"

I got about three sentences into what I planned to be a sanitized synopsis of what had been going on when I realized the line was silent.

"Michael?" I said after awhile. "Hello?"

No answer. Then I could hear his voice breaking up and I got only every other word. I heard a couple of clicks on my phone, then looked down. "Recharge" was flashing and then the little battery icon came on and the phone went dead.

Calling for help was no longer an option. Now what? As far as

I could tell, I had reached the site without being detected. I didn't want to push my luck by driving away. I was afraid McClintock would hear the car and take Billie somewhere else, if, as I suspected, he was holding her in the shack. I had no choice but to creep up and get a better look.

I opened the car door just a bit, praying it wouldn't squeak, then slid out and closed the door quickly and quietly, before the warning bell chimed. I crouched by the side of the car for about thirty seconds and listened. Apparently, no one in the shack heard anything worth investigating because no one ventured out.

The snow, deeper than my Sorels were tall, muffled the sound of my steps, but also poured over the top of my boots. I crept from tree to tree until I got close enough to dash behind the pile of tires by the front door.

I have been scared in the past but those times were nothing like tonight. This was a different, deeper kind of fear. I knew Billie and I could be killed.

With my heart in my throat, I peeked in the window. There was one room, about twenty feet by twenty feet. A big pot perched on a stove against one wall and bags of stuff littered the floor. What I guessed was a jug of battery acid and plastic bottles labeled lantern fuel were stacked on the floor next to a case of Sudafed. Even through the closed window there was an odor that smelled like a cross between nail polish remover and cat urine. All the signs were there. This was a meth lab.

I watched a little longer, then realized that what I thought was a pile of blankets or rags on a bed was moving. The light was dim in the room, but as I stared longer I could make out a form. Billie.

My adrenaline was pumping and all my senses were on high alert when I heard the sound of a car moving slowly down the road. I crouched down as far as I could behind the tires and covered my mouth with my mittens so the vapor from my breath wouldn't be seen in the cold air.

Within moments a rusty Buick LeSabre left over from the Reagan administration pulled into the drive, then stopped a dozen feet from the shack. The defroster must have quit long ago, because all

I could make out through the windows were the forms of four very big guys.

When the driver opened his door to get out, I recognized the heavy thumping of a band I had once heard vibrating in Rebecca's room. As he stretched himself out of the car, I got a good look at him: about six-foot-five, with dark straight long hair and brown eyes. He had the body of a basketball player—all muscle, long and lean. He wore jeans, a white T-shirt, and a purple jacket with a Minnesota Vikings logo on the back. His movements were jerky and he kept looking over his shoulder, like he had the feeling someone was watching him. I've read that paranoia is a symptom of meth addiction. In this case, the guy's paranoia was justified.

It took him only three strides to reach the door of the shack, where he pounded with his fist, shouting, "Yo, McClintock!"

After two more poundings, three latches clicked on the door and McClintock stuck his head out. "Whitehorse."

The last time I heard the driver's voice he was talking on his cell phone and someone in the background was yelling at him to get back to work washing cars.

Billie's former boyfriend stuck his head inside the shack. "Yo, Billie?"

"She's got herself in a mess this time," McClintock replied. "Billie is a snitch, but I've got her nice and quiet where she can't cause more trouble."

Billie's mouth was covered with duct tape, but her eyes spoke of fear, sadness and pleading as she looked at her former boyfriend. Nate shrugged. I thought I saw remorse in his eyes.

"I got guys in the car who need some ice," Whitehorse said to McClintock after a few moments.

McClintock said nothing, shut the door, then returned with a sandwich-sized plastic bag. Whitehorse took a couple more looks over both his shoulders, wiped his nose with the back of his hand, jammed a fist into the pocket of his jeans, and came out with a wad of bills, which he stuffed in McClintock's hand. Moments later he was in the LeSabre, spinning his tires in the icy ruts as he pulled around the shack and out of the drive. Hairs on the back of my neck stood on end at the whine like a buzz saw cutting through metal.

My squatting legs were beginning to cramp and the snow in my boots was turning my feet to ice. I had to either head back to my car and get out of there, or do something to save Billie. My choice was clear. If I left without Billie and something happened to her, I would never forgive myself.

I was forming a plan when McClintock turned back inside. I pressed my ear to the flimsy siding. "That was your boyfriend," he told Billie sarcastically. "He told me to stay away from you."

For no apparent reason, McClintock slapped her across the face, then ripped the duct tape off her mouth.

"Why did you do that?" she shouted at McClintock, rubbing her cheek. Now she was crying.

"Because you're a bitch that got in the way," he sneered. "What did you tell the reporter?"

"I didn't tell her anything," she replied.

"Do you expect me to believe that?" He stabbed a finger at her. "You lied about everything else. You know too much. Too much, too much, too much."

"Know what it feels like to die from a meth overdose?" he went on. "Your heart starts to beat very fast, and then you begin to twitch and sweat like a pregnant pig in August. Your blood pressure gets so high you think you're going to burst. But that's not the best part, because then you get a heart attack. Have you ever heard how much pain there is with a heart attack? It's like an elephant is sitting on your chest. Then it's bye, bye, Billie.

"I've never killed anybody before, but I suppose it's time I tried that. Just add another experience to my long resume. Think the school board would like that? 'Principal with experience in murder.' Maybe I could even get a bump in my merit pay. But first it's time for one last good fuck."

I poked my head up over the windowsill enough to see him yank away the oily blanket he had used to cover Billie. Her spiked hair was matted down on one side and she wore the same red sweatshirt and jeans from Friday. Her face was as white as her mother's couch. When he slapped a new hunk of duct tape over her mouth, her eyes went huge, wild with fear.

Chapter 36

No more time to consider my options. Grabbing a piece of firewood to use as a club, I stepped up to the door and pounded with my fist.

Bam! Bam! Bam! I beat on the door, then jumped back behind the pile of tires. I could hear McClintock working his way through the three latches. I wouldn't have much power over his six-foot frame. My best ally would be surprise.

He opened the door tentatively with his right hand, sticking his nose out a couple of inches. Even though I was standing to the left of the door where he couldn't see me, I held my breath, worried that the vapor from my breathing would collide with icy cold, creating smoke that would give me away.

He squinted those beautiful blue eyes, sniffed the air like a ground hog coming out of his hole, and peered out to the turn-around. I could feel his brain wondering why there wasn't a car within sight, even though he had clearly heard pounding on the door.

He stepped out in his stocking feet on the space in the porch that had been cleaned of snow by many boots. As he was about to peek around the door, I yelled something I can't remember anymore and brought the log down at an angle on his forehead with both hands, landing a gash above his right eyebrow. He reeled back and landed on the floor with a thud. He seemed to be knocked unconscious, but I knew it wouldn't last long.

I dropped the log, raced to Billie, and pulled the duct tape off her mouth, apologizing the whole time for the ripping pain.

"Oh my God, I can't believe you're here," she said, as I set to work untying her hands and feet.

"You're going to be fine, Billie," I said, mostly trying to convince myself.

I was so focused on freeing her that I didn't notice movement behind me. Until I heard a click.

"Turn around slowly," McClintock said.

He was waving a gun at me. I know nothing about guns except that they scare me. Especially when they're pointed at my head.

"You don't want to do anything stupid," I said.

"Looks to me like you're the one who's stupid," he said.

"Excuse me?"

"I heard about your silly little videotape," he said.

"If you put down the gun, we can talk about it." Silently I cursed myself for giving the mayor so much detail when I called him for a response.

"In your dreams, sweetheart," he said, tipping a little to the left.

All my senses fired at once. Even though the room was cold as a meat locker my armpits had gone wet. I heard wind blow through each crack. The smell was an overpowering mix of damp, rotting wood, sweat and meth that made my eyes water as though I had peeled an onion.

I watched him closely, my mind spinning, trying to figure out how I was going to get out of this. From the corner of my eye I saw Billie inching her way toward his left, giving me the sense that she was thinking the same thing I was thinking. If we managed to get far enough apart, we could rush him from both sides. I had to keep him talking.

"You want to put that gun down before you hurt somebody," I said to him.

"What's the matter, MS. Hughes?" he said sarcastically. "Scared?"

"Frankly, yes."

"You should have thought of that before you got yourself into this. What's with you reporters, anyway? Always sticking your nose where you don't belong."

Arguing that this was exactly where a reporter's nose did belong would have been suicide. I struggled to keep my tone neutral, my voice quiet.

"If you put the gun down and let Billie go, I'll forget all about the story."

"You're lying, Hughes, and we both know it," he said.

Mentioning Billie was a mistake. It prompted McClintock to steal a quick glance in her direction, at a time when I was trying to divert his attention away from her. I had to get him thinking about something else. My mind reeled. As a reporter I've often kept people talking well beyond what they had planned. But I'd never had an interviewee who was holding a gun on me before. Take it from me, it's much harder to think of questions when your life is in danger.

"Is this where you want to be right now, Mr. McClintock?" I asked. I kept my voice soft and high-pitched, trying to play to him as an inferior on the bet that he might relax a bit in a situation where he had the dominant position.

"No."

"You know, you could be on your way out of the country," I said moving one step to his right. From the corner of my eye I could see Billie creeping toward the club I had dropped. "I bet you've got some serious cash stashed away. You don't need to be dealing with a girl like Billie. You've got better things to do with your time. Why don't you leave and we'll pretend none of this happened."

"That's not going to work, Skeeter," he said. "You bitches know too much."

"So, how are we going to resolve this?" I asked.

"I'm going to shoot you," he replied, and cocked the trigger.

"No!" Billie shouted as she leaped for the club, then swung it low against the backs of his knees while I tried to yank the gun from his hand. We struggled and the gun went off, shattering the pot on the stove with a stray bullet. The meth that had been bubbling spewed into the low flame on the stove and ignited. McClintock jumped up, threw us both off, and bolted for the back door.

"Outta here!" I shouted to Billie.

We ran out the door and got about twelve feet away before an explosion rocked the shack. We dove into the snow, face down, arms thrown over our heads as fiery debris sprayed the air. The smell of burning hair from the embers hitting our heads was everywhere. Little flames danced and sizzled around us. I felt pinpricks on my legs as sparks landed on my jeans.

We lay there for a couple of minutes. Relief washed over me like a soothing balm. "Are you ok?"

"I think so," Billie said. Slowly she began to wiggle her toes, move her legs and arms. Then she sat up. "Nothing broken."

I rolled over and gazed at the stars bright against the night sky and thanked God I was alive as I tried to get my muscles to relax. But the adrenaline was still pumping, which was fortunate, because I heard the crunch of snow tires as a rusty pickup truck charged down the rutted road toward us, then skidded to a stop. After he threw the truck in park the driver reached for a shotgun.

Billie's breath caught as a man in a brown jacket, jeans and boots stepped out of the cab. I went into defense mode again, fearing that we were in for a second round.

"I been watching this old shack for months, seein' folks comin' and goin' at all times of the day and night," the farmer said as he looked down at us. "Mother and I figured there was some of that meth goin' on. But ya know, out here we mind our own business. No need calling the cops, 'cause it was just a matter of time before the whole thing caught fire. We were hoping some of those druggies would get blown up by their own mess. Would serve them right. Are you girls druggies?"

"No, sir," I said.

"You all right?" he asked Billie.

"Yeah, that was fun," she replied with a weak smile. "Let's do it again."

"Please call the cops," I said to the farmer.

He went back to the pickup and exchanged his shotgun for a cell phone. A minute later the flashers of a state patrol car came our way. Out stepped State Trooper Trevor Johnson, the new love of my life.

"You again," he said, looking down at me.

"Hello, Trooper," I said. "Good to see you again."

"What kind of trouble are you in this time, Skeeter?"

Chapter 37

McClintock and his Audi were long gone when Trooper Johnson hustled Billie and me into the back of his patrol car and gave us blankets and coffee from his Thermos. Billie and I shivered side by side for about five minutes, and then she began to cry. The "fun" had worn off for her. I put my arm around her and she put her head on my shoulder and cried more.

"I'm so sorry," she sobbed.

I said nothing. Just let her cry for a while longer.

"I heard Nate talking about me," she said. "Sounds like he knew all about McClintock, doesn't it?"

"Yeah, it does," I said, softly, wanting to be comforting but not willing to lie to her. "I'm sorry."

She cried more. "I tried to help Nate—with his drugs, his life. Look how he turned on me. Men are bastards."

"Yeah, some are," I replied. "Some. Not all. Not even most. How did you get involved with Nate?"

"He was a nice guy when I first met him," Billie said. "He's had a tough life but he was doing the best he could. I wanted to help him. Then he got into meth, and there was nothing I could do."

After the Land o' Lakes fire department put out the fire and Trooper Trevor had taken us back to the station to take our statements, I drove Billie home. The short trip seemed to take forever. Silence draped inside the car. I don't know what Billie was thinking, but I was wondering how I would react were she my daughter.

We pulled into her mother's driveway and I turned off the engine while we sat for a moment.

"Do I have to go in?" Billie asked.

"Yes, you need to go in," I replied.

She heaved a big sigh and pushed the car door open at the same time. I followed a couple of paces behind as she moved up the path, then stopped dead in front of the door, apparently unable to move. I reached around her to ring the bell. Even though it was early in the morning, Cathy Berry opened the door almost instantly.

"Billie!" she shouted, throwing her arms around her daughter and bursting into tears at the same time.

"Hi, Mom," Billie said, and then she started to cry too.

Seconds later, Peter Berry came up behind Cathy.

"DAD!" Billie shouted, and dived into his arms. "What are you doing here?"

"Your mother and I agreed to worry at the same place," he said.

Billie hugged Peter, then Cathy. When Billie pulled away, holding her mom's forearms in exactly the spots where I had noticed the bruises, it occurred to me that maybe Cathy did bruise easily. The marks I had seen earlier in the week were acquired innocently.

Cathy hung our coats in the hall closet then ushered us into the living room. Billie looked her in the eye defiantly, then pushed past her and plopped down on her mother's white couch, oblivious to the damage her filthy, smelly T-shirt and pants would cause.

Her hands on her hips, Cathy looked at Billie sitting on her couch and shook her head. "It needs cleaning, anyway," she said to herself, delicately lowering to sit beside Billie. Without makeup, she faded into the white upholstery. Her eyes held more emotion than I had thought possible. Joy, sadness, anger, relief—and exhaustion.

"Can we get you something to drink, Skeeter?" Peter asked.

"No, thanks," I said. "It's great to see you all together."

"Thank you for bringing Billie back," Cathy Berry said to me softly.

"I'm a full-service newspaper reporter. While I have you all here, I'd like to ask a few questions for the article I'm writing."

"It's a bit late, but we owe you that much," said Peter Berry.

I almost hated to break the moment by continuing with my questions, but I knew that this was my best opportunity to talk to them all together. "Billie, where have you been for the past week?"

She had told me earlier that she was sleeping on the couch of a friend she had met at the Mall of America, borrowing his car after he worked, but that explanation set off my phony-baloney detector. It didn't feel right. I hoped I'd get a straight answer out of her in a setting where she felt freer to talk.

Billie took a sudden interest in her dirty fingernails. "I told you. I was with a friend."

"That just doesn't fit, Billie," I replied. "Are you sure that's where you were?"

"Yeah, it's true."

"Who was your friend?"

She looked me in the eye. "Vicky."

"You mean Sergeant Olson?"

"Yep. We're a team. We're working the case together." She lifted her chin with a proud air.

"You what?" Cathy shouted. "All this time we've been in a panic looking for you and you were living with a cop? The police were supposed to be looking for you, not hiding you." The tender mother-daughter moment was over.

"Chill, mom," Billie said. "I was on a case. We were working to bust McClintock."

"Who picked you up from the SuperAmerica last Friday night?" I asked.

"Vicky," Billie replied. "McClintock called my cell and wanted me to meet him at the Crown Jewel. When I called Victoria to tell her we finally had a bite, she wanted to take me there, so I let her give me a ride. I figured nailing the creep was more important than watching a stupid movie. I thought Mom would understand."

"No, I do not understand," said Cathy. "And I never will."

"You were the one who sent me the e-mail warning me about another firebombing, weren't you?" I asked Billie.

"Yeah, I didn't want you to spoil the investigation."

I could feel my blood pressure start to rise. This child had scared me to death. I tried to take a moment to get my emotions under control before I continued with my questions.

"And if it weren't for me you'd be dead now," she added.

"What are you talking about?"

"Who do you think called the state patrol after you took that stupid dive off the ramp into Land o' Lakes?" she asked defiantly.

"That was you?"

"Yeah, it was me. I was tailing you to make sure you didn't stick your nose any further in my business. I almost didn't call the cops, but then I decided you didn't need to die, even if you are a pain in the ass."

"Where did you get a car to follow me?"

"I had McClintock's Audi," she replied. "I had him convinced that we could be partners. I was going to get more girls for him. He thought it was getting too dangerous for him to keep hanging out at the mall. I told him I could do it better. I was going to turn him in after I got more dirt on him. Then you screwed it up when you opened your yap to the mayor."

Her parents looked at her dumbfounded as all this unfolded. There was a long silence, then Peter spoke: "Why did you do all this?"

"I did it for Nancy, and other girls like her," she replied. "When she told me what he had done to her I had to get involved."

"What did McClintock do to her?" Peter asked.

"He sold her," Billie replied angrily.

"Oh my god." Cathy put her hand over her eyes, then pulled it away and picked a piece of burned wood from the couch. "How?"

"She was at the mall one day when he found her crying on a bench," Billie said. "He told she was pretty and then he bought her some clothes. Next thing she knew, he convinced her to go on a date with some guy."

"How do you know all this, Billie?" Peter asked.

"Because she told me about it," Billie replied. "She couldn't stop crying when she talked."

"What did she tell you?" Cathy wanted to know.

"He told her he'd call her 'Jade'. He said the guys loved Asian girls. Then he took her to the Crown Jewel to meet him."

"Who was he?" I asked.

"She didn't know his real name. He said he was some kind of finance guy and he wanted her to go to a fancy business dinner with him."

"Didn't the people at the dinner figure out she was a high school girl?" I asked.

"He told her to pretend she didn't speak English," Billie replied. "I've seen her do a great imitation of her mother trying to speak English. She's very believable."

"Why did she let McClintock get her into this?" Peter wanted to know.

"I think it was because she had been trying to be grown up," Billie said. "Last fall she bought a push-up bra and always wore skimpy T-shirts and jeans cut low with a two-button fly. Even though she tried hard, she looked twelve, not fifteen."

"And being some finance guy's date made her feel grown up?" Cathy asked.

Billie nodded. "McClintock gave her a long, backless dress and strappy black high-heel sandals. She told me that at first she felt sexy and she liked it, a lot."

"And then it all went wrong," I said.

"She told him she was a virgin and she didn't want to have sex," Billie said. "McClintock told her all she had to do was smile, be beautiful and have a nice dinner."

"He lied?"

"Yeah, he lied," Billie said. "When the banquet was over she went back to his room with him. She thought McClintock would be there to take her home."

"He wasn't there," Cathy said, with a shudder.

"No. She said she sat on the bed while the guy went into the bathroom. She heard him brushing his teeth and she thought he was just going to kiss her. When he came out of the bathroom he was naked. She'd never seen a naked man before. She told me it was gross," Billie said with half a laugh.

"What did she do then?" Cathy wanted to know.

"She told him it was time for her to go home."

"But he wouldn't take her home?" Peter asked.

Billie shook her head, remembering the scene as Nancy had described it between sobs. "'Sorry, sweetheart,' he said. 'You're mine until 8:00 a.m. I paid good money for you, Jade, or whatever your name is.'

"Nancy said she tried to run, but before she could reach the door he grabbed her hair then tore off her dress," Billie said, in tears herself. "Nancy said no one had ever told her sex hurts."

Cathy and Peter were in tears by the end of Billie's story.

"Billie, why did you take down the flyers that were posted about you?" I asked after awhile.

"How did you know that?"

"I saw them in your purse the day we met for coffee," I replied evenly. "Why did you take them down?"

"I saw the note from Mom that she loved me and I took them all so I could read them over and over."

"Of course I love you," Cathy said. The harsh tone I had heard her use before she heard Nancy's story was gone as though she had a new-found respect for Billie. This time she sounded like a mother in love.

"Do you, Mom?" Billie said through a sniff.

"What would make you think I don't love you?"

"Sometimes when I'm trying to tell you about something important, like the time I had that big fight with Nate, you don't listen. If the phone rings while I'm trying to talk to you, you always answer it. It's like selling a house is more important than me."

Cathy put her hands on either side of Billie's face and looked her straight in the eye. "Nothing is more important to me than you, Billie."

Pure relief painted Billie's face like aloe on wind-burned cheeks, but she said nothing more. "I'm not sure what to do with you," Cathy said to Billie. "You've been in incredible danger. And you've certainly put me through hell."

"I didn't mean to worry you, Mom," Billie said.

"Well, you did," Cathy said.

Peter Berry nestled on the couch, putting Billie between him and Cathy. He took Billie's hand in his, gently stroking the top. "You gave us a huge scare."

"I'm sorry," she said.

"I even punched McClintock in the nose."

"Why did you do that?" she wanted to know.

Peter filled her in. "I hit him because I thought he was hurting you."

"Wow, Dad, I'm impressed," she replied. "I didn't know you had it in you."

"What made you think you could trick somebody like McClintock?" Peter asked. "Didn't you know how dangerous that was?"

"I figured it was good training to be a cop," she said. "And danger is part of the job."

Her parents could only look at their daughter in silent disbelief.

"Sergeant Olson didn't tell me she picked you up Friday night," I pushed on. "You two need to get your stories straight."

"Sergeant Victoria Olson has been known to lie." Then, with a sassy sigh, "I never would have guessed a reporter was gullible."

I didn't want to debate my analytical skills with her, so I kept the focus on her behavior.

"What happened when you got there, Billie?" I asked.

"Something must have spooked McClintock, because he was gone," she said. "Vicky said I could bunk with her until he called again. Her place is much cooler than this dump, so I stayed."

"Wait a minute," I said. "Sergeant Olson told me she was worried that you had shown up, with McClintock, on the Crown Jewel security camera a few hours ago. She sounded pretty sincere about not knowing where you were."

Billie bit off a piece of fingernail then spit it across the room. I watched the expression on Cathy's face move from appalled to forgiving, making me think she had mellowed a bit.

"I was afraid that McClintock had spotted her when she drove me to the Crown Jewel Friday night and that was why he disappeared," Billie said. "Then I decided I'd be better off working alone. So I ditched her."

Chapter 38

After leaving Billie with her parents, and checking up on the girls, I grabbed a couple of hours of fitful sleep, then headed back into the newsroom. I still had a story to write, and Thom was leaning on me to get it done so the newspaper's lawyers could go over it carefully enough to prevent a libel suit.

With a Venti cup of coffee steaming on my desk, I was back at my computer writing away when my cell phone rang. I was tempted to let the call roll over to voice mail because I didn't want the interruption, then thought better of it. The caller ID said it was from a cell phone. Good thing I answered.

"Hughes, this is McClintock," he said. "You don't know the whole story, but I'm willing to fill you in."

The sound of his voice made all my muscles tense. This man would have killed me. And Billie. Yesterday. I wanted to slam the phone down. But I have two built-in antennae. One is for danger. The other is for news. Unfortunately, both were vibrating at the same time. The antenna for news was moving a tad faster.

"So talk."

"Not on the phone," he hissed. "Meet me at the Crown Jewel parking lot."

"Surely you're kidding," I replied. "There's no way I'm going to risk my life by meeting you there."

"You want to talk to me." It was a statement, not a question.

"Why?"

"Because I can tell you a much better story about names far bigger than mine. Here's a hint. What mayor is raking in big bucks from a drug operation?"

I figured my safest bet was to meet him in a public place. "I'll be in the park at the Mall of America in two hours." OK, it was stupid. I recognize that now. Sometimes I act first and think later.

I hung up to focus on what I had written so far, which wasn't much. Sometimes writing for me is a way to leave. I stick my head in the computer and don't see or hear anything. Only the story. Sometimes I only notice the time when I get hungry. More than once colleagues sitting next to me have had loud conversations and I haven't heard a word. Call it escape.

Nonetheless, I'm a very slow writer, mostly because I'm care-ful—no, make that paranoid—about getting not only the facts right, but also the nuances. I spend a lot of time shifting between my notes and my screen. I was on my zillionth trip when my phone rang again.

"Hughes," I said, this time grabbing the phone absent-mind-edly.

"Olson," said the sergeant, with a deep, raspy chuckle. "I hear you found our girl."

"I had planned to call you about that, Sergeant," I said. "You didn't tell me she was living with you."

"You didn't ask," she replied. "Besides, I'm under no obligation to tell you anything."

Guess what? I thought. I'm under no obligation to tell you any-thing either, including that I'm about to meet with McClintock.

"Is that why you were so insistent that I sit on the story?" I asked.

"I'm not going to explain my reasoning to you," she said. "Lis-ten, Hughes, you're going to have to wait a few more weeks before putting this information in the newspaper."

"Sorry, Sergeant," I replied. "No can do. Billie's home and we've got the goods on McClintock. Readers deserve to know what I know, as soon as possible."

"If that appears in the newspaper, it will hamper an ongoing investigation," she said emphatically. "We had an agreement that you would withhold the story until I approved running it. I do not approve publication yet."

This is why I hate making promises about stories. It always bites me in the butt.

"Does your chief know you were housing Billie Berry and then lost her?" I asked.

"That's none of your concern," she said.

"Actually, that's a pretty good story," I replied. "Land o' Lakes police sergeant enlists help of teen in prostitution investigation, then keeps the girl in her home while her parents pull their hair out wondering where she is. I'd heard you have a reputation as a rogue cop. Sounds like this is a good example."

"What's your point, Skeeter?" she said.

"My point, Victoria, is that I'm giving you a choice here," I replied. "We have no agreement about keeping the second story out of the paper. I'm willing to offer you a deal. I can print the story about McClintock, or I can print the story about you. What's your pleasure?"

"That's blackmail," she said.

"I prefer to think of it as negotiation," I said. "Your choice, Sergeant."

"We'll have McClintock in custody by this evening anyway," Olson said. "I'm sure your readers would prefer that story."

I had to agree with her.

I probably should have told her I was going to meet McClintock, but if she knew I was on to more, she'd find a way to stop me. I didn't work for her. I worked for the newspaper. Hell, I worked for its readers. I wasn't going to let her get in my way.

Chapter 39

I went back to the story when Thom strolled by. I kept staring at my screen, pretending not to see him when I was really watching him out of the corner of my eye. I just didn't want to talk to him at that point. After another half hour the coffee took its toll and I headed for the lady's room. When I got back, Thom was sitting in the chair I keep to the side of my desk.

"Make it fast," I pleaded. "I'm trying to get this done."

He cleared his throat, then squirmed a bit in his chair, using the heel of his shoe to play with a piece of duct tape covering a rip in the carpeting.

"I've been to the mountain, talked with the boss, and it's not good." He couldn't bring himself to look me in the eye.

"Is there a problem with the story?"

"No. The bean counters won't pay for your car."

"This is a joke, right?"

"Afraid not," he said. "Like I told you, the problem is the company pays reporters 46½ cents a mile, and that's supposed to include your car insurance as well as wear and tear on your car. If they broke that rule for you, they'd have to do it for everyone."

"Exactly how often do shareholders have to cough up the money to pay for a reporter's firebombed car?" I asked.

He shrugged.

"I don't believe this." I shouted, smashing my hand so hard on my desk that it spilled the last of the coffee in my cup. Thom jumped up in time to avoid getting coffee spots on his clean, white shirt. "You're kidding me, right?"

"I wish I were," he replied.

"You know ad revenues are down. I do have a bit of good news, however," he continued, while I mopped the coffee off my notes. "The company is willing to give you an interest-free loan to replace your car."

"My, that's generous," I said sarcastically and loud enough for anyone sitting within twenty feet of me to hear.

"The paper has never had a car firebombed before, so they're not sure how to handle it. They thought this was fair."

"Do you think that's fair?"

"This isn't about fair," he said. "Face it: This is a business, Hughes. The days of the benevolent owner who publishes newspapers primarily for the good of the readers have died. They went away when all the small, medium, and even big papers were bought up by chains whose first allegiance is to their shareholders."

And there it was. Thom, my one-time hero of journalism, had been completely sucked into the corporate machine. It made me want to cry. My eyes felt like sandpaper, my arm was sore from slugging McClintock, and my hair still smelled from the explosion. I figured I had two options: I could tell Thom what the paper could do with its loan and quit, right then and there, or I could take what Thom had said and mentally put it in a neat little box up on a shelf until I could handle it a little more gracefully.

"Go away," I whispered to him through clenched teeth, "and let me finish my story."

He rose from the chair without making a sound and lumbered away.

Chapter 40

I probably should have told Thom that I was meeting Mc-
Clintock in less than an hour. I should have told him McClintock
promised to share a much bigger story with me. But Thom and I
weren't on the same page anymore, metaphorically or otherwise.
His goal was to keep the newspaper in business. My goal was to
produce the best journalism I could. One didn't necessarily negate
the other, yet here we were. I went back to my work.

Half an hour later I looked up from my screen and realized it
was time to go. I carefully put my notes in a manila folder marked
"Wolf, B. B," tucked it in my drawer, and logged off the computer.
Didn't want the demons that can live in there to get to my work
while I was gone.

As I pulled into the Mall of America parking ramp, the reality
of what I was about to do hit me. Meeting McClintock without telling anyone was stupid. In my head, I heard Helmey's warning that
I have daughters of my own who still need me. I pulled out my cell
phone and called Sergeant Olson. She said she was in Woodbury,
a suburb of St. Paul about twenty miles north and east of the mall
—about half an hour's drive, in light traffic.

"I'll be there as soon as I can," she said. I was glad she didn't
hold a grudge.

It's hard to imagine anything sinister could happen at an
amusement park where it is always summer, even in the middle of a
Minnesota January. The fragrance of freshly spun cotton candy and

tropical greenhouse plants mix to form an aroma that is nothing like a shopping center. It smells like wholesome middle-America, which is exactly what the developers had in mind.

There I was, watching moms and dads, grandmas and grandpas stroll while holding hands with their tykes who had cartoon characters painted on their faces. Not a scrap of litter, not even a straw lost from a slushy or a leaf from a small tree littered the winding walkways. As I sat waiting for McClintock to show, I made a mental note to find out how the managers of the amusement park kept it so clean with an apparently invisible workforce.

What was I thinking? I admonished myself. My next story for the newspaper was at the top of my mind when I should have been planning my get-away from McClintock. That realization made my hands start to shake as I came back to the here and now. Good God, how did I get into this mess, and what was I going to do?

I was watching an eight-year-old inching his way up a pegged climbing wall on my left when I felt a warm body slide on to the park bench immediately to my right. Even though I knew he was coming, I jumped a bit. As a roller-coaster car made a deafening racket crossing the tracks above my head, I felt something stick into my side—something that felt a lot like a gun. The fine hairs on the back of my neck jerked to attention as the deep timbre of McClintock's TV-anchor voice tickled my right ear.

"Pretend we're friends, sitting on this bench."

"OK," I replied, my heart beating so hard I could feel it hitting my ribs.

"Good. Now get up slowly."

"Why should I?"

"You don't want any of the shoppers to get hurt. If you go quietly, none of them will."

"Where are we going?"

"We're going to go for a ride on the Ferris wheel."

"That's ridiculous," I whispered, barely able to get the words out because I was literally scared spitless. "Why the Ferris wheel?"

"We've got to talk and I don't want anyone to overhear what I've got to say."

"Why the gun?"

"That's insurance that we can have a civil conversation."

"You don't need any insurance. I came to hear what you have to say. You're a smart man. Why do something stupid?"

"And you're a smart girl," came the reply. "So shut up and do what I say."

His right hand quivered as he grabbed my elbow, making him look like a gallant gentleman helping me to my feet. As we slowly walked along the path to the Ferris wheel, a mental focus from the gun stuck in my ribs encroached upon my fear. He was smart, but also frightened, and a desperate coward, the scariest of combinations. He had size and at least one weapon on me. I prayed that Sergeant Olson would get to the mall soon.

Every car on the Ferris wheel was full, but the line was short, so we got on right away, just as the attendant was letting riders off. Our car ticked up one notch, letting the riders below us get off and another set get on. I did a quick calculation and saw that there were twelve cars on the wheel, making it a third the size of the original. Damn you, George Ferris, I thought. A memory flashed in my brain where I'm about five years old and my second oldest brother is taking me on a Ferris wheel at a carnival that has set up on an abandoned lot near our house. When we get to the top, he starts to rock the car and I scream at him to stop, afraid he'll rock me right out. He laughs at me.

"I've tried repeatedly to warn you to stay away from this story," McClintock said. "You won't listen. Now I'm telling you for the last time: drop it."

I couldn't drop the story now even if I wanted to. I hoped McClintock didn't know that.

"OK," I said, hoping he'd believe me.

He said nothing as our car on the Ferris wheel rocked like a fishing boat in rough seas and rose into the seven o'clock position on the wheel. The car in the twelve o'clock spot was at the top.

When he set the gun down on our bench I thought about knocking it out of the car with one swift sweep of my arm. But I was afraid that it would fire when it hit the ground, possibly hurting some innocent kid. It wasn't worth the risk.

"Who else knows about this?" he asked, raising the gun to my ribs. I gripped the metal bar holding me in the car so tightly I thought my fingers would leave indentations.

Our car went up another notch, to eight o'clock. For a minute I thought I was going to throw up. Then it occurred to me, throwing up was a good idea. If I barfed on his lap, it might distract him enough to get the gun away. I tried to think about Suzy puking her guts out.

"Only me," I lied.

Another mistake.

"So if I get rid of you, I get rid of the story, right?" he asked.

"Look," I said, "why don't we finish the ride and get off this thing? I'm not good at conversation when my feet can't touch the ground."

"Sorry, that won't work either," he said. "I guess we're trapped. It's going to be you or me."

The Ferris wheel nudged up to nine o'clock and the car rocked harder. I thought more about throwing up. It was getting more likely because I was beginning to feel dizzy. The Ferris wheel tops out on the third floor of the mall, about a hundred feet above a concrete floor. I imagined a fall from the top, through steel beams. Sudden death.

"I thought you were going to fill me in on the bigger fish, such as the mayor," I replied. "Think. If you shoot me, how are you going to get out of here?"

"Ironic, isn't it?" he replied, ignoring my question. "I guess I've been trapped my whole life. I'm very handsome, you know. Always have been. Even when I was a little boy. People don't realize it, but being good looking is its own kind of pain, just like being ugly. When you fit the model profile, people expect your life to look as good as you do. Sometimes I look at ugly people and wish I could be more like them. Then society wouldn't expect so much of me."

He was handing me such a load of crap I thought it was going to fill up our already too full Ferris wheel car. Maybe I would throw up. I could see it now: the handsome defense. "Your honor, my client has been burdened his whole life with that Ralph Lauren look," I could hear his attorney arguing. "His perfect nose, his bird's egg blue eyes, his square jaw all made him do it."

I wanted to keep him talking, hoping desperately that he would get lost in his own twisted thinking enough to give me at least a small opening. "And your life didn't fit your face?"

"No. Not because I didn't try. I worked my way through college, you know," he said. "Thought I'd be a teacher and make the world a better place. But teachers aren't paid as much as I wanted, actually needed. Some of my Land o' Lakes students lived in homes twice the size of mine."

The car jerked into the ten o'clock position, swinging precariously. Two more stops and we would be at the top.

"So you went looking for ways to get more money."

"Yes. I was promoted to principal, but that still didn't pay enough. Then I married my wife, who was making lots of money. I figured I could provide the face, and she could provide the bucks."

"Even that didn't work, so you headed for the casino."

"You are the nosey little reporter, aren't you?" he said. "Yes. I figured I had already won the good-looks lottery; why not try my hand at Black Jack? And I was good, really good."

"Good enough to buy a fancy place on Potato Lake. Good enough to buy a big fancy boat. Then what happened?"

"After a while, my luck ran out," he said sadly. "I lost my touch. Then one day I was sitting at the table with the Land o' Lakes mayor, who spotted me a couple of hundred dollars. I was riding high again most of the night. By the time the sun came up, I owed him $36,000."

"And Mayor Baldwin's not one to let a debt slip?"

"No. He knew I got along well with kids, especially teenage girls. He had some friends who ran an operation in Chicago where they got girls to, shall we say, 'service' wealthy men in the community. It was all up and up. The best kind of clientele."

"So you signed on?"

"What else could I do?"

"Tell me about the bigger fish. How deeply is the mayor involved?"

"Pretty deep. Junior high school principals don't know the heavy hitters that he knows. My job was to acquire the girls. He handled the rest of the business."

Acquire the girls. Hearing him talk about them—girls who just as easily could have included Rebecca—as though they were just hunks of flesh made me so angry I gritted my teeth and clenched my fists. I was trying to contain my anger, knowing that if I let it loose I'd kick him in the balls and scratch his eyes out. But as the car moved into the eleven o'clock position, the time wasn't quite right.

"Give me some names," I said.

"The president of the bank of Land o' Lakes was probably our best customer."

"Did you take him up to Potato Lake?"

"Yes. Along with some of his cronies. How do you know about Potato Lake?"

"I read about it in your divorce file. Did your ex-wife know what was going on when you took them to your lake place?"

"No. Well, maybe. If she had thought about it for more than a few minutes, she would have known something was up. I suspect she didn't want to think about it."

"Who else is part of your clientele?"

"A couple of very old judges were the best. You'd think those old coots had never seen a naked girl."

"Where did the meth come in?"

"That was a side business," he replied. "It brought in pretty good money too. At least until the cabin blew up."

I let that thought hang there for a couple of beats. "You know, you've got nothing to lose by turning yourself in and telling the cops who the real bad guys are. No offense, but locking up the mayor and a bunch of bank presidents is a much bigger deal than convicting a junior high school principal. You could plead guilty and probably get off with a light sentence."

Now I'm handing out free, probably wrong, legal advice, I thought as I heard myself give that little speech. No matter. My goal was to save my life, not clear up his problems.

"And what?" he asked. "Get in some witness protection program? You don't know these guys I've been working with. They don't fool around. If you put that article in the paper I'm as good as dead. Sweetheart, this is the end of the ride."

So far I had managed to keep my eyes on him, instead of looking down. But I started to sense movement below us, so, terrified, I peeked over the edge of the car. Sweet Jesus.

He began to laugh. At first it was one of those deep-from-the-gut kinds of laugh, and then it went on and his voice got higher as the wheel moved to twelve o'clock, the apex. The guy had clearly lost his mind. I had one of those rare moments of clarity. I saw him as a threat, to my daughters, to Billie Berry, to every mother's daughter. The fact that he was nuts was secondary. He was a predator.

"It's over, McClintock," I said, pointing down to where Sergeant Olson stood, looking up at our car. A cadre of other police officers surrounded her. "The cops have got you now."

He looked over the edge of the car, then raised his hand to point the gun at me. At the same time his weight shifted and the Ferris wheel, apparently at the urging of Sergeant Olson, gave the car a sharp jerk. In a flash I decided it was going to be him, not me, who was going to die. With reflexes I honed during those years of karate with Rebecca, I blocked his hand with my forearm and shouted "KEEEEEYIIIIIIIII." The movement was so fast it caught him off guard and he lost his grip on the gun. He lunged for it as it bounced off the top of the guardrail that kept us seated in the Ferris wheel car. I reached out to steady myself on the front of the car and the combination of my weight and his forward momentum sent him over the edge.

Like a big, floppy rag doll, he slid over the side of the car, hanging for a few seconds with one hand caught on the side. Then his grip slipped. One leg caught on one of the beams, changing his trajectory until his head swung into another beam, smashing it like a pumpkin thrown against a brick wall. I watched his body land in a bed of ferns.

Chapter 41

The world went silent. High above all the activity below, I could watch with a detachment that felt strangely soothing. Everything below moved in a surreal slow motion.

I've watched TV reporters in situations like this stick microphones in the faces of witnesses and ask, How do you feel? Actually, they don't care how those people feel. The asking of the question is usually edited. What remains is footage of those people saying just about anything. What they say isn't the point. It's how they say it that conveys the emotion. How did I feel? I wondered.

My first reaction was relief. Relief that it was McClintock down there and not me. This man, who had threatened me moments before, would never hurt me. Not Billie. Not Rebecca, or anyone else. Ever.

My next thought was horror. I'd never seen anyone die violently before. It's not something I'd like to see again. Blood and brain matter spattered everywhere. I knew that the vision of his body, broken like a pile of matchsticks crunched under a heavy boot, would be with me the rest of my life. Moments ago we had been involved in verbal thrust and parry. Now he was dead. I heard myself think —maybe I even said it out loud—that it would take a long time to process what that meant and my role in his death.

When sound returned to my consciousness, I realized passengers were screaming from the Ferris wheel cars on either side of me. Security personnel responded to the shrieks, and from my perch at the top I saw people rushing to McClintock's body. My old pal public relations lady Melanie Foxx appeared with a blanket to cover him, making the scene less gruesome.

Security officers froze the Ferris wheel while they waited for police and emergency crews to arrive. I guess they didn't want to have any more people walking around the area than they had to.

Sergeant Victoria Olson seemed to sense I was looking down at her, because she glanced up at me over her shoulder. She gave me a half-smile and a tiny salute, then ambled over to the guy who was running the ride and said something. He gave a nod and started the wheel moving.

Anyone who has ever waited to get off a Ferris wheel knows that it feels like an eternity as the thing moves around, stopping as each car unloads. This time it felt like two eternities. I collapsed into Sergeant Olson's arms as I tried to exit the car. My rubbery legs wouldn't hold me.

"Hold on there, Skeeter," she said, as she shielded me from the sight of McClintock and took me away. "You'll be all right." She hustled me out of the mall and into her squad car, where I sank into the front seat, resting my head on the back.

"Just take some deep breaths. Close your eyes and concentrate on your breathing." I did what she said. Pretty soon my heartbeat was slowing down and I began to feel like I had some control over my extremities.

"What the hell did you think you were doing?" she shouted at me after I had regained my senses.

"It seemed like a good idea at the time." Even I knew that sounded lame.

"You're in no position to be flip with me," she said slowly in a deep, scary voice. "How did you end up at the mall with him?"

"He said he wanted to tell me more about the story," I said. "I thought I'd be safe in such a public place."

"Reporters have got to be the most gullible people on Earth," she replied.

After taking my statement, Sergeant Olson drove me back to the newsroom, which was abuzz with activity. Ramon, the cops reporter, had heard a call on the police scanner asking for backup after a man took a header over the side of the Ferris wheel. When he heard the name Matthew McClintock, he called Thom over to listen. Thom was dispatching Ramon out to the mall to cover the death just as I walked in the door.

"I've got to hand it to you, Skeeter," Thom said. "You do get yourself into, um, situations. Tell me what happened."

I filled him in, leaving nothing out, for the first time. Unlike other conversations I've had with him, he listened beginning to end, without interrupting with questions of his own. When I was done, he put his thumb and forefinger to the bridge of his nose, looked down, and gently shook his head.

"We'll continue this conversation later," he said. "Now, what about the story on McClintock? Does the competition or the TV stations know you're working on this?"

The competition. He meant Michael. I hadn't thought about him. "You don't need to worry about that."

"Fine," I said. "We'll run it in the morning with the story about McClintock's header."

I finished the story in record time—about an hour. As long as I was thinking about the story, I could keep my mind's eye away from the sight of his broken body. I hit the send key, which zapped the whole thing to Thom's computer, then sent him an e-mail saying he could reach me at home if he had any questions.

Exactly a week ago I had been sitting in Cathy Berry's living room getting the lowdown on Billie, I realized, shaking my head. It had been a long week.

Finally at home, I crawled into bed and slept like a dead woman, if the dead dream. My mind saw weird images of a Ferris wheel full of teenage girls in sexy gowns hanging from the cars. I saw Billie's boyfriend pointing a gun in my face, but just as he was about to pull the trigger, he turned into McClintock, who laughed uproariously. Billie's mom and dad were fighting in one of the cars of the Ferris wheel. Billie was in one, alone, crying. And my daughters were in another car, looking at me curiously. "I don't get it, Mom," Suzy said in my dream. I was trying to ask Michael to explain it to her, but he wasn't listening.

I woke with a start from the feeling that I was falling over the side of the Ferris wheel car. I lay in bed a while longer, breathing hard from the dream, when I heard a key in the door. It was too soon for the girls to be home from school.

I grabbed my red terrycloth robe and wandered into the living room. "Michael, what are you doing home in the middle of the day?"

"What are you doing here?" he asked. The look on his face told me he was as startled as I was.

"I'm catching up on some sleep after the week from hell," I said, then told him all about it. I was almost to the part about Mc-Clintock's shack blowing up when he began to walk away. I followed him into the kitchen, and kept talking while he reached into the fridge and grabbed a beer. He popped the cap and began to leaf through the mail, which I had left on the kitchen table when I came in.

"Michael, you're not listening to me."

"Huh, yeah, well, I suppose."

"You suppose what? I'm trying to tell you about my week and I can't get your attention."

"I didn't expect you to be here," he said slowly.

"So?"

"So, I'm here for a reason." He chugged the entire beer, then belched.

"What's that?" I didn't like the way he refused to look me in the eye.

"I'm here to pack."

"You off on assignment somewhere?"

"You could think of it that way if you want to."

"What does that mean?" I asked.

"It means I'm leaving. You."

Epilogue

That was a month ago. Since then, a grand jury has indicted the mayor, three judges, and a bank president on charges of drug trafficking. The Crown Jewel got a new manager after the owners learned the former manager was part of McClintock's cabal.

Sergeant Victoria Olson was reprimanded by her chief for letting Billie Berry live with her, and then losing her, but it was nothing compared to the scolding she got from Cathy Berry. Billie has gone back to Land o' Lakes High School. Last I heard, she was hoping to get admitted to a criminal justice program at the University of North Dakota after graduation. Peter and Cathy Berry have returned to communicating by voicemail.

The newspaper gave me a week off after the story ran. I spent it sleeping when the girls were in school and hanging out with them when they were home. We bought a used del Sol with the loan from the paper and replaced the girls' soccer equipment.

When I started work on this story I made a lot of assumptions, many of them wrong, about Billie, Sergeant Olson, Peter and Cathy Berry. I vowed not to make that mistake again.

I've given a lot of thought to my mothering, too. Looking back, I wish I had told the girls more about what I was doing. I think they would have been more comfortable with my absence if they knew it was for a good reason. I can't shield them from the knowledge that my work is sometimes dangerous. I can show them that calculated risk is part of doing a good job in any profession.

Thom and I are still at odds, and probably always will be. I sense that he realizes he's crossed over to the dark side of the corporation, and it doesn't make him happy. Occasionally I worry that someday I may join him.

I'll remain a reporter, for now. Working in journalism is like falling in love with a not-so-good man. There are lots of thrills but it's bad for your health.

I'm not ready to end the love affair. At least not yet.

Nor am I ready to end it with Michael. He has moved in with friends for the time being. We're seeing a counselor trying to figure out if we want to stay married. I hope we do, but I'm prepared if we don't.

Journalism awards are generally given for work published during a calendar year, so I've got to wait to find out if my work won any prizes. Meanwhile, I got a tiny raise and a new beat. I'm now the reporter for missing persons.

AN EXERPT FROM THE NEXT SKETTER HUGHES MYSTERY –

Whose Hand?

FEBRUARY

MINNEAPOLIS, MINNESOTA

I studied the crags in the wind-burned, old-man face of B.J. Johnson. His long blond and silver hair was pulled into a ponytail at the nape of his neck, leaving his bald pate open to the elements. The ragged collar of a black cotton t-shirt peeked through the v-neck of a dirty blue-green sweater with a run in the left sleeve. He wore faded camouflage pants -- the green kind from a jungle war, not the sand-colored from a desert war -- and heavy rubber boots. Nicotine had stained the dirty fingernails on his left thumb and forefinger.

He had suggested we meet in Linden Hills, a neighborhood on the west shore of Lake Harriet. The coffee shop was housed in what had been an independent drug store until it fell under the pressure of Walgreens. It was adjacent to a women's boutique in what had once been a used bookstore.

At least a dozen laptop computers connected wirelessly to the Internet as patrons seated at tables and on black leather couches sipped their java and stared at their screens. Original photographs of dramatic winter scenes hung for sale on the walls. A couple of women chatted quietly over a corner table. It was the kind of place where a good conversation was better than a month of therapy, and a lot cheaper, too.

"Is this your usual place?" I asked, unable to imagine him as a regular here.

"Hell, no," he said. "But I've lived in Linden Hills my whole life."

"How's that?"

"I grew up just a couple of blocks from here, then my wife and I bought her parents' house when they passed on. We lived in Linden Hills long before it became so dee-zire-able. Couldn't afford to buy a house here now. But I like to drink coffee and I figured a high-falutin' reporter like you would like a place like this."

I couldn't afford to live in Linden Hills, either. But I had high school friends who had grown up in the neighborhood so I knew what he meant. A generation ago it was filled with people who were interesting, not moneyed. They were potters and painters and folks who made gourmet dog food for a living. For a while it was called the land of 10,000 golden retrievers because of a particularly pro-lific pair whose owner lived in the neighborhood. There were a few very big houses and more small houses and rental duplexes. As the real estate market began to take on almost mythic proportions, the small houses were bought by people who tore them down and built very big houses on their lots, selling them for three or four times what they paid for the small houses. A big part of the attraction to the area was nearby Lake Harriet.

Any runner in the Twin Cities can tell you that Lake Harriet is 2.8 miles around. During the warm months sailboats skim the sur-face like swans. Each summer Sunday morning a different church offers services at the band shell overlooking the lake. People have married on her shores, learned to swim in her waters, fed genera-tions of ducklings.

I reached in my purse and pulled out a pen and my notebook, the long skinny one with the spiral at the top, and flipped it open to the first page.

"Start at the very beginning and tell me this story."

Leaning a little forward in his chair, he looked me straight in the eye. The smell of caffeine mixed with stale cigarette smoke blan-keted his breath.

"Remember those warm sunny days early last October?" he began. "I was out in my fishing boat in the middle of the lake. It can get 80, 90 feet deep in the middle, there, you know. I've even caught musky late in the fall. I just liked sitting in my boat, watch-ing the trees change color along the shoreline. Anyways, I had been lowering my line all day long. My butt was getting numb and I hadn't caught a thing."

"I cast off one more time, and sat a bit longer. Then I felt a slight tug. Finally, I thought, a bite, and began to reel it in. It felt like maybe I'd caught a boot. There was weight but no wiggle, you know what I mean?"

"Yeah, I do." I'd fished some with my girls.

"I began to reel it in with my new Shimano Baitrunner reel my boys gave me for my birthday. But that was no fish that broke the surface of the water."

His crow's feet grew deeper as he broke into a smile and took his hands away from his coffee cup to rub them together. He pushed the ceramic cup aside with the back of his hand, as though he didn't want it to come between us.

"It was someone's hand," he said.

He said it loudly with a combination of shock and mirth. So loudly, in fact, that the guy sitting over in the next table looked up from his computer. Then leaned back in his chair to get a better perch to watch my reaction.

"A hand?" I asked. "Are you sure it was a hand?"

"Yes, ma'am."

"What did it look like?"

"It looked like a human hand, but it had been in the water a long time, I figure. All bloated and kind of mushy looking."

"What did you do?"

"First thing I did was shout a word I wouldn't repeat in front of pretty lady like you. A sight like that can really jack up a guy's ticker, if you know what I mean."

"I can imagine. Then what?"

"I tried to reel the thing in. A big ol' Northwest plane was coming in low over the lake just then, making such a racket I couldn't think straight. I leaned over a little too far, I guess. I was holding the pole with one hand and reaching with the other and the blessed thing slipped through my fingers."

"Meaning the hand, or the pole slipped through your fingers?"

"Both. I lost the reel my sons gave me." He sounded sad.

"How long did it take you to reel the hand in?"

"Quite a while. Must've come from deep water."

"Was there a ring? Tattoo? Anything?"

"All I saw was some some of that milfoil hanging on it."

I let the thought hang there a moment while the cappuccino maker hissed along with the soft jazz playing in the background. I was trying to formulate the next question, but I kept thinking that the owner of the adjacent dress shop wasn't worried about coffee spilling on her merchandise because an open sliding door invited customers to float back and forth between the two establishments. Maybe I was subconsciously avoiding the gruesome image.

"Was it a right hand or a left hand?" I finally asked.

"Ma'am, I was so shook up I didn't take the time to figure that out.

"All five fingers?" I asked, trying to suppress a grimace.

"Looked to me like all the parts were there."

"Did you drop a buoy marker?"

"No," he said, shaking his head.

"Did you try to get a visual marker, like line up where you were with a house along the shore?"

"I was pretty shakin' up, so I just rowed back into shore. On my way I passed a guy who was taking his sailboat out of the water for the season. They have to have all the buoys empty by the end of October. Anyways, I told the guy what I saw and all he said was, 'Is that so, Pop?' Imagine. He called me 'Pop.' Like I'm too old to be believed."

"Did you call the cops?"

"Yeah. They said they'd send somebody out to take my statement, but they haven't yet. I don't think they believe me. Even my boys don't believe me, but I swear on my beloved wife's grave, that's what happened," the old man said.

I wasn't surprised he had trouble getting people to believe him. Sometimes it's hard to separate the story from the rheumy eyes and tremulous hands of the teller. Believing the mental picture of a hand fished from Lake Harriet took some work. Urban myths about sunken treasure and six-foot-long fish have been floating around

Lake Harriet for decades. But they're just that: urban myths. I wondered if this was just one more.

"Mr. Johnson, I hope you won't take any offense at this next question, but I can't help but notice you seem to have a cataract in your right eye. Are you sure you saw a hand, and not something else you mistook for a hand?"

"My right eye may be a bit cloudy, but my left eye is 20/20," he said. Then, with all the earnestness he could muster, "I pulled a hand out of Lake Harriet."

"Who do you think the hand belonged to?" I asked.

"Beats me," he replied.

I gave him my card and suggested that he call me if he thought of anything else. He promised me he would and rose from the table, absentmindedly pulling at the crotch of his pants before reaching for his hat and scarf. Then we shook hands and he gave me a sly wink before ambling out the coffee house door.

People like to tell me stories. Sometimes on the phone. Sometimes in coffee shops. Sometimes in their homes. I always listen, but skeptically. Each time I try to figure out if the storyteller is just another nut looking to get his name in the newspaper, or the real deal. I listen because that's my job. I'm a reporter for the Minneapolis Citizen and my beat is missing persons.

As I watched B.J. trudge down the sidewalk, his heavy rubber boots leaving big prints in the newly fallen snow, I decided that I believed his story. Don't ask me why. Maybe it was intuition. Maybe it was my reporter's DNA. Something told me the story wasn't just some old codger's fish tale.